I0761217

Rebel English Academy

Also by Mohammed Hanif

A Case of Exploding Mangoes

Our Lady of Alice Bhatti

Red Birds

Rebel English Academy

A Novel

MOHAMMED HANIF

Grove Press
New York

First published in 2026 in Great Britain by Grove Press UK
an imprint of Grove Atlantic

First Grove Atlantic US hardcover editon: February 2026

Text designed and typeset by Tetragon, London

Printed in the United States of America

Library of Congress Cataloging-in-Publication data is available for this title.

ISBN 978-0-8021-6598-5
eISBN 978-0-8021-6599-2

Grove Press
an imprint of Grove Atlantic
154 West 14th Street
New York, NY 10011

Distributed by Publishers Group West

groveatlantic.com

26 27 28 10 9 8 7 6 5 4 3 2 1

For Paco

Rebel English Academy

ONE

On the Night of the Hanging

On the night of the hanging, everything is as calm and orderly as it should be in a jail devoted to the safety and care of one very important man. All prisoners but one are asleep in their cells, restless, dreaming of their victims or their loved ones, which in most cases are the same people. The Rawalpindi sky is clear and full of stars; all the talk about omens is rubbish: there are no meteor showers, no storms brewing on the horizon, the sky is not going to shed tears of blood, the earth is not about to split open and swallow its wretched inhabitants and their grief.

The man who is awake has asked for a safety razor, claiming that he doesn't want to look like a mullah in death. After consultations with superiors, the jail superintendent has sent for a barber, who shaves the man gently, making sure to clear the fuzz from his earlobes. The man asks for a cigar and the jail superintendent doesn't need to ask for his superiors' permission. No man who is about to be hanged in three hours and forty-five minutes has ever tried to kill himself with a Montecristo. The jailer makes sure to light it himself; the man chews on his cigar, takes two deep puffs and regrets it, thinking maybe he should have quit when he had the time. The man asks for his Shalimar perfume, sprays himself and lies down on the floor. A mosquito buzzes near his ear. On any other night he might have called in the jailer and given him a dressing-down for infesting his prison cell with poisonous insects, might have accused him of being a tool of the White Elephant, his favourite invective for the United States of America, but tonight he just shoos the mosquito away half-heartedly, listening to the rising and fading whirr of its wings. He is grateful for the company.

Everyone agrees on the above events. Those who wanted to hang him, those who wanted to save him, those who wanted a martyr in the early morning whose blood could help them bring about a revolution, even those who were indifferent, all agree up to this point that the man lay down on the floor, pulled a sheet over himself and stayed still, dress-rehearsing being dead.

Although everything was still and orderly in and around the cell where an about-to-be hanged man practised his death pose, there was activity, quite a lot of activity, around the country in some crucial spots. Many would later say, specially journalists and diplomats who made a living out of exaggeration, that it was the longest night of their lives, that they knew something historic, something catastrophic was about to happen. But only those who had been woken up without warning with a degree of rudeness would remember this night when their own time came. An imam was hauled up from his small room adjacent to his small mosque and ordered to get ready to lead the funeral prayers of a very important man. One of the world's sturdiest planes, a C-130, was on standby at Rawalpindi air base to ferry the body to the man's village. A military truck followed by six machine-gun-mounted jeeps made its way towards the airport, with some sleepy, some alert soldiers, their commander wondering why a dead man needed so much protection. Elites stay elite even in their death, he thought. Some soldiers sang a tea jingle: 'Chai chahyie, kaunsi janab.'

'Shut up,' barked the commander. 'We are on VIP duty.'

A caretaker at the village graveyard was asked to start digging a grave, and when he asked what size, he was slapped. 'Your own size,' he was told.

Above are the facts that everyone agrees upon. As with every hanging, there are differing accounts about the man's walk to the gallows. How did he walk? Some say he never actually walked. That he collapsed on the shoulders of his jail guards and had to be carried. His jiyalas say that he walked on steady feet, head held high, climbed onto the podium as if addressing the nation one last time, kissed the noose and put it around his neck. Others say he was carried on a stretcher and two policemen, themselves shaking at the gravity of the moment, had to prop him up by his armpits before fitting the rope around his neck. You can't hang a man when he is horizontal on a stretcher.

There was one oversight by the jail superintendent, but that was taken care of by the ingenuity of a captain who happened to be on the scene on a top-secret mission. After discovering that the jail administration had forgotten to order a coffin, the captain barged into the jail armoury, looked around, saw a body-sized wooden crate that was used to store the jail guards' rusting guns, shouted at them for not having any respect for their weapons and handed the crate over to the jailer who, in gratitude, leapt forward to kiss his hands. The captain put his hands behind his back and reminded him that he was on post-hanging photo-shoot duty and would like a few private moments with the body after the man was hanged. The jailer agreed, knowing he had no choice in the matter, and asked the captain if he would like to witness the hanging. The captain declined the offer, saying he wasn't on hanging duty.

He was here on a different mission.

Before being taken to the waiting cargo plane, the hanged man was left alone in the jail superintendent's office for a few minutes with the captain, who had brought a professional photographer with him. In those few minutes, the photographer had to perform the most shameless, and as these things go hand in hand, the most high-powered, assignment of his otherwise mediocre career. He pulled down the hanged man's soiled shalwar and, with the flash on, took half a dozen photos of his genitalia. It was done in the forlorn hope of confirming the persistent rumour that the hanged man was not circumcised and hence a Hindu. The very fact that photos were never processed or released was proof enough that the man was indeed circumcised and hence a Muslim. The man himself might have argued forcefully that the one didn't prove the other, that many Muslims in his hometown never bothered to circumcise their children. But this little episode ended when the captain made a phone call and reported that the bastard was dead *and* circumcised. There was a sigh on the other end of the phone. The director of Field Intelligence Unit's internal security said that the bastard was lying and cheating even in his death. 'And you, Captain, you had one job. What are we going to do with you?' said the director and put the phone back on its cradle with historic disappointment.

The nation was thus spared the indignity of waking up to newspapers with pictures of a hanged man's genitalia on the front pages.

The captain was punished with a transfer to a town where car number plates started with the letters OK and where people from far-off districts came to get their vehicles registered. The captain had done a brief stint in OK town cantonment after getting his commission three and a half years ago and knew that the vehicle registration plates were the only exciting thing about the city. He knew he would need to create his own entertainment and come up with a mission to shine on this punishment posting.

Three nights after the hanging, when our captain, let's call him Captain Gul, is inspecting his room in the Bachelor Officers' Quarters and testing the strength of his bed, all the while looking at himself in the dressing table's smudged mirror, admiring a hint of a cleft in his chin, his wild side-burns and lush black moustache, a few miles away there is a knock on the door of the Rebel English Academy which, despite its misleading name, is a law-abiding and affordable tuition centre for basic English. Its founder and sole teacher, Sir Baghi, is about to receive a young lady guest he is not expecting at all.

TWO

Allah's Will

MOLLY RAFIQUE MUST HAVE PLANNED IT THIS WAY, although he would insist forever that it was all Allah's will. When Molly sneaks his young lady friend into the academy, Sir Baghi is finally enjoying an afternoon of solitude. He had sent his students home the moment they heard a newspaper hawker shouting in the street about the hanging. Baghi knows that it will be a very long weekend. He wants to use this unexpected holiday to mark papers, review his syllabus and read the fourth chapter of *To the Lighthouse*. He also plans a visit to Venus cinema for a matinee in the hope of finding some random afternoon love. It's not in his nature to be optimistic but he is hoping that the cinema won't be shut down.

Molly's lady friend carries a faded sea-green sports bag, with the logo of a panther in the middle of a leap, 'Pride of OK Town' inscribed under the panther in fading gold letters. She is wearing baggy tracksuit bottoms, a white dupatta embroidered with white and yellow nargis flowers loosely draped around her neck, a girl old enough to know that she needs a dupatta but young enough not to know what to do with it. She has the air of somebody about to take a leap and start running, somebody who is being chased by their own past or, at least, what they hope is their past.

Molly is sweating, his forehead a network of the entire world's troubles. A sheen of sweat covers his shaved upper lip, his famous beard quivering. 'Can you look after my guest while I do the funeral prayers?'

Funeral prayers? Baghi groans, the veins in his neck bulge because of the unspoken words. He always buttons up his always-black shirt's collar, less a sartorial choice and more an attempt to hide a crimson hammer and sickle tattoo on his upper chest. Baghi is past his shouting days but he still gets the occasional urge. He knows the mosque is Molly's business but why does Molly want to have a funeral in absentia for a man hanged two hundred miles away and buried in his village in the dead of the night three days ago? A man who was clearly a feudal despot in the clothes of an awami pseudo socialist, bald and squeaky and certain of his own immortality, the type of man who, from his death cell, writes a threatening pamphlet titled 'If I Am Assassinated' … and is assassinated anyway, someone who says you can kill a man but you can't kill an idea. Baghi wants to tell Molly you can't have a funeral in absentia for an idea. But the mosque is Molly's business. On another day he might have said, Molly, surely you don't want to start a socialist revolution in your mosque? Better not to start it anywhere – look at me.

'What can I do? The bazaar is full of jiyalas and they want a funeral. I know he wasn't very nice to you but he is gone to Allah now, where we all must go one day, and we must honour the dead,' says Molly, moving towards the door.

Yes, we must honour the dead, Baghi wants to say, even if the dead once had a chilli-powder-laced rod rammed up my ass for writing a letter.

Baghi also wants to say that this is a teaching institution and not a resting place for girls with hurriedly packed sports bags but, before he can say it, Molly is gone, leaving behind the smell of his favourite ittar, a confused mixture of rose and jasmine, and his guest with large, searching eyes, scanning the place for something familiar.

She puts down her bag, moves towards Baghi and holds out her hand. Baghi observes her hand, hesitates before taking it. When was the last time he had shaken hands with a woman? This was not the kind of town where people shook hands with women, not the kind of neighbourhood where people left single women in bachelors' quarters to be entertained. Her handshake is determined and it forces him to look her in the face.

Ruin, he thinks, she is going to ruin us.

In five years of teaching English to sons and daughters of peasants and shopkeepers, Baghi has developed a revolutionary technique: single words spring up to describe a moment in life. In order to teach these students, you didn't need proper sentences. Verbs and nouns and adjectives and qualifying adverbs could wait. Usually, a word was enough to describe a given situation, an intention or, in this case, a sense of impending doom.

Baghi rarely gets to say that he was right because it has been proven, often enough, from matters of politics to affairs of the heart, that he was almost always wrong. Later it would turn out that he was right in this moment when he forgets all the flourishes of a successful English tutor and a closet revolutionary, looks at her and comes up with the perfect word: ruin.

Baghi doesn't much care for the native language tradition which has evolved many ways of describing a face, specially a woman's face – in fact, most of classical poetry was devoted to capturing a woman's features. Snakes and wine goblets featured prominently. You looked for wine goblets in the eyes, poisonous vipers in the hair, and the face was always book-like. To Baghi's enduring irritation, nobody ever said which book, a slim T.S. Eliot volume or a copy of the Original and the Biggest *Heer*. The English language, Baghi believed, was more accommodating, more precise, yet more expansive. You could do away with wine goblets and coiling, hissing snakes; you could just say her nose was sharp and quivered gently when she breathed, a little dimple on the left cheek, which still had baby fat, set off a mole on the right cheek.

If he was into women, he would say she could probably set anybody's bed on fire and turn their life to ashes by loving them and then abandoning them to waste away their life writing below-average poetry, invoking as many snakes and broken goblets as they pleased.

Baghi had wanted to do many things in life: bring a violent revolution, make the rich suffer, give all the peasants' children a world-class education. But right now he was content doing small courtesies; he was going to ask his lady guest to have a seat and politely inquire if they had met in a past life. But before he can say it, she plonks her bag on the floor and takes a seat. He offers her tea, he offers her water. She refuses with a wave of her hand and sits on the chair; she looks towards the ceiling, the bookshelf, the blackboard, then speaks suddenly, and while native poets may have heard a koel cooing, Baghi only hears a dry-throated, husky voice which some men with unresolved sexual urges might find desirable, a voice defeated but refusing to surrender, the voice of someone ready to get up and go looking for a fight again.

'Do you often entertain his friends?' The question sounds like an accusation to Baghi.

'No,' Baghi says. 'Not like this.' He fingers his buttoned-up collar, stutters and finds himself defending his friend and landlord Maulvi Rafique's character, not that his character needs defending: he is a man of God, a rising star of the spiritual marketplace; people offer him mutton qorma and cash in advance to listen to him telling them how to live their lives and how to prepare for the afterlife. She is waiting, still looking at him, as if urging him to explain his life as the entertainer of stray women. 'I mean, sometimes we have friends over, common friends, and we talk, but if you are asking if he has brought a woman to my academy, I would have to say no. This is an institution of learning and not a…' She is not listening to him any more. She is the kind of woman who tunes out when a man starts to bullshit. That's one of the many reasons on Baghi's list for staying away from women.

'I didn't know he was the Bhutto type,' she says.

'Not a good day to be his jiyala,' Baghi says.

'There never was a good day to be a jiyala,' she says, looking up at him, expecting him to say more.

'He's a maulvi, offering prayers for the dead is his job.' Baghi shrugs.

Baghi doesn't like to talk politics with women. Once a female comrade caught him stroking the penis of a young budding Stalinist during their study circle and had him expelled from the party. He has learnt his lesson and likes to keep his affairs away from female comrades.

'Can I get you something cold or maybe a hot drink?' Repeating oneself is the essence of life. When he tells this to his students, he attributes it to Virginia Woolf but he is not sure if she ever said it. That is under the category of Things Virginia Woolf Might Have Said, an evolving list in his teaching career. The bourgeois comrade who caught him in the study circle also accused him of never having read a word written by a woman. Baghi is trying to prove her wrong.

'Water,' his guest says.

Baghi takes out one of the two glasses he keeps aside for guests. Students drink from plastic tumblers – no casteism in this academy, no hierarchies, but they are young and careless and Baghi has no patience for glass shards in the feet and blood on the floor. She accepts it without a word, gulps it down in one go. 'And how do you know Maulvi sahib?' He is deferential and doesn't call him Molly in his absence as he has called him to his face since they were children. Stay away from me, Molly, he used to say when a young Molly hugged him at some pretext and tried to rub himself against his belly. Molly used to bristle when he started calling him Molly but Baghi could tell that he secretly enjoyed it. He was his Molly boy before he became a serious scholar of religion who accepted cash only for his sermons and refused to eat farm-bred chicken and knew people who could spring you from a police dungeon.

She looks at Baghi as if trying to decide if she should lie to him or just slap him. 'I pray behind him. This is the only mosque where women can pray but you wouldn't know because you don't believe in God.' Baghi is startled. He doesn't believe in God but over the years he has learnt to keep his non-faith to himself and his academy students. She has probably heard it from Molly. 'He's a friend, more like an elder brother to me. There was a fire at my house so he offered to put me up, temporarily,' she says and watches him for a reaction.

Molly has friends? Baghi knows that he has followers, many, many followers, worshippers who prostrate behind him feverishly, broken people trying to put themselves back together, repentant paedophiles, proud murderers, lovers, addicts, heartless traders, all flock to him for salvation. Baghi believes he is the only friend Molly has, the only one who refuses to pray behind him or anyone else. But no, Molly has another friend-sister who is here sitting in his chair, a friend with hazel eyes and roasted-wheat skin who has landed in the academy with an oversized sports bag because, obviously, Molly has no other place to take her.

Does Mrs Molly know that her much-respected husband – my god on this earth, my companion, my protector, mera sohna – has a lady friend-sister who is sitting in the same compound a few metres away?

The mosque loudspeaker turns on and Molly's friend-sister seems surprised at the proximity of the electric crackle and the piercing sound of prayers that follows. She takes her dupatta and covers her head, probably realizing for the first time that she's sitting in a mosque, in Allah's own house.

Baghi rents from God and he likes to believe that, like most slumlords, Allah is a bit stingy with space and always moaning about people not paying rent. The ochre mosque is round in structure, and since the people of this city lack imagination, it is called the Gol Mosque. Its inner sanctum forms the prayer hall, rows and rows of neon-green plastic prayer mats that are rolled up every night, its exterior a circle of shops, first-floor offices that wrap around the mosque. It sits at the centre of four very crowded bazaars. This is a perfect mixture of worldly trade and afterlife bargains and, by the grace of Molly, Baghi has added to it an institution of secular learning.

Baghi is on the second floor, the last office. It's supposed to be an office space but his special connection with Molly has ensured that nobody objects to the fact that he has turned an office space into a tuition centre and his residence. Cloth merchants around the mosque suspect that he corrupts young minds by teaching them that Allah doesn't exist under the cover of teaching them English.

'You don't remember me?'

Baghi is blank for a moment. 'Were you a student? I would have remembered.'

'Not to worry. I was here only for two weeks. I failed. Are you still a good English teacher?' Nobody has ever asked him that. Nobody. Because they all know that he is the best there is. They might also say that teaching English is the only thing he is good at. The revolutions he had hatched lay in dust. The Mazdoor Militia he had started folded after one industrial action with two dead and even the defunct militia expelled him after his open letter to Ummah. Brief visits to police lock-ups and picnics in shabby rehabs were all in the past. But yes, he is good at something. Something useful. Send a peasant's son to Baghi's Rebel English Academy, a young boy who can't even call his own cow 'cow' in English, and within three months he would write a perfectly composed essay called 'Our Cow' that would get him passing grades in high school. Send him for another three months and he might get a job as a clerk, six months and he might pass the police recruitment exam and become an official torturer.

'I try. This is the most I can do, I just help them.' He doesn't tell her that some of them go on to become police officers and diplomats. He is trying to be humble like you should be with a young woman you have just met. You are supposed to rub your own nose in the dust in the hope she will pick you up by the scruff of your neck and say, oh come on, don't be humble. She has no such plans. She sits there waiting for him to pick himself up. 'Some of my students have become UN diplomats – one almost became a foreign secretary. But they were hard-working children, no credit to me.'

She has no interest in his glorious career where he grooms future UN diplomats. 'I failed my English in FA,' she says as if he was personally responsible for her failure. 'Second division for every subject and F for English. Zero, anda.' She makes an egg with the forefinger and thumb of her right hand. 'I went to college for a year on sports quota. District gold medal in 400 yard hurdles.'

'I am sorry to hear that,' he says. He doesn't remember her name but it seems rude to ask her now so he continues. 'I wish you had stayed longer than two weeks because the system I have devised—'

He gets an appreciative smile out of her but then she cuts him off mid-sentence. 'I used to come with my friend. My friend became a doctor and she says you gave her a new life, English life. Now she lives in Norway. Maybe you should try teaching me again.'

Baghi blushes. And also panics. 'Are you planning to stay?'

'I can leave, if you say. Or should I wait for your friend to come back?' she says. 'He spends a lot of time with his Allah. How come he is your friend when you teach students that there is no Allah, that it's just the ultimate human invention?'

Baghi is sweating now. The ceiling fan changes a gear and starts spitting hot air. 'I didn't mean that. Of course you are…' He wants to say welcome but he remembers the tall, scrawny girl with big eyes and a boy's croaky voice, fine little fuzz on her upper lip, chin covered in fiery pimples, worn-out Bata running shoes on her feet, asking him things no student dared ask him.

Sabiha Bano. Comrade Abid Ali Abid's only daughter. Last seen leading a protest for her father's release more than a year ago.

*

'Why is your name Baghi? What are you rebelling against?'

At first Baghi tried to ignore the raised hand, wide eyes and feet tapping nervously on the floor. This was the first time he had allowed girls in his class and found a girl-boy with rippling shoulders and a neck that throbbed with pent-up energy. 'It's not my name, it's my pen name, I used to write poetry. Sometimes poets take pen names. Ghalib's real name was Asadullah but he wrote as Ghalib and everyone calls him Ghalib.' Baghi was patient and telling only half the truth.

'They say you call yourself Baghi because you say there is no Allah. You are a rebel against God.'

Baghi only believes in what he read in a pamphlet about dialectical materialism but his students are too young to grasp the concept so he tells them leave your Allah at the doorstep along with your shoes. 'What do you think?'

'This is His house, no?'

'Why don't you go ask Him if He exists? I am here to teach you the Queen's English. I hate her but at least I know that she exists.'

The fuzz from her upper lip is gone, cheeks and chin filled out and smooth; she seems well fed and well scrubbed now, a pinkish hue trying to burst out of her toasted-wheat complexion, a fiery teenager camouflaged by life to look like a woman.

Baghi had just about managed to shut her up once. Here she is again: girl with a tongue has become a woman with a tongue.

'I'm sorry about your parents.' Baghi doesn't know if he is consoling her or telling her that the subject is closed.

'Told you there was never a good time to be Chairman Bhutto's jiyala.' Sabiha Bano grimaces.

'I gave up politics a long time ago,' says Baghi.

'Your friend said that you are a good man, and you have a nice safe place. I told him yes, I was his student. He was a good person and famous English teacher and taught me some difficult English words but I still failed my English.'

Baghi can't remember if anybody has ever called him a good person. Is that what he has become? A good person? Not the ghunda number one, not a rabble-rouser, not the first one to break through the police barricades, not the loudest drunk, not the borrower of small forgettable sums, not the prince of the cultural underground, not someone who can find a place to live without paying rent, not even a reformed revolutionary, but a good person?

Maybe if we live long enough we can all become good persons, he thinks, and when we die we can become really, really good persons.

Like that feudal fucker of peasants and workers, and sham leader of a sham Ummah, Bhutto.

'So did you figure out if Allah exists or not?' Baghi asks jokingly, trying to form a bond.

'He does. More than before. He speaks to me. Who do you think sent me here?'

THREE

Snow Leopards without Winter

CAPTAIN GUL HAD OPTED FOR INTELLIGENCE SERvices after a brief and eventful stint in the Armoured Corps in this very cantonment. He had joined the Field Intelligence Unit for the excitement and adventure it promised but here he is, awake at six in the morning, in the dullest of cities, to a ruckus of birds he'll never learn the names of. Bed tea already on the side table, a wake-up call from his pregnant girl in Pindi asking him what he did last night, him trying to remember where he was and indeed *what* had he done last night. He had seen ghosts while driving into OK town, silhouettes of men behind curtains of dust, moving slowly, then he had realized they were sweepers sweeping the dusty roads. His car had been stuck behind a tractor trolley, the trolley carrying a bloated load of sugar cane and greedy children clamouring over it to pull out a few. Green fields he had seen, full of mustard flowers, and then these fields had given way to hillocks of rubbish where donkeys roamed and munched on garbage bags. The gate at the cantonment had opened to reveal a familiar world, white lines in the middle of the road, whitewashed flowerpots and tree trunks. He had smiled and remembered the military motto that if anything moves, salute it, if anything is still, paint it white.

He also remembered that this is where he was given the nickname Lieutenant Piston after a late-morning raid on his bachelor officer's quarters when he failed to turn up for duty. His commanding officer was repulsed and impressed when he found him passed out and counted five used condoms on the floor of his room. What are you? A man or a piston? The commanding officer didn't quite know what punishment to give him, so he was shamed into celibacy for a few days. After a few weeks of bumbling games of tennis and Friday prayers, he slipped back into his routine of picking up the local phone directory and dialling random numbers. If a female picked up, he told her his rank and how he was bored in the trenches, ready for martyrdom but still bored, and waited for the magic to work.

When life changes, you change your life code. So what if the Pindi girl claiming to carry his child, his superiors, even his parents hadn't noticed? He still believes he is a changed man since the night of the hanging.

In his mind Captain Gul is on the path to reform. No long-term relationships, no promises of marriage and children, get in and get out, commando style. No poetry of his youth. Before embarking on his journey to OK town, he had burnt his personal code book where he meticulously noted his exploits and gave his lovers code names. Jaws was the nurse who liked her nipples bitten till there was blood. Indian Bullshit a religious-studies school teacher who liked to play dead during intercourse. Fire Brigade a married beauty and mother of two who had set his room's curtain on fire when she found Indian Bullshit's earring on his bedside table. It was all behind him. He was going to do things differently from now on.

He thinks about what to tell his pregnant girl who is two hundred miles away asking searching questions about what he had done on the first night of being back in OK town.

Searching for an answer, he reaches for the quarter of Murree gin lying under his bed. Two swigs and then with the clarity and confidence of an intelligence officer who has just taken his first field command he says he had read *Reader's Digest* and did she know how long snow leopards can survive without food? Without waiting for her to reply, he tells her that he had bad dreams about their unborn child and was now sure that he didn't want to name her Shabnam any more. He was bad at naming things anyway so she should go ahead and choose.

'Did you miss me in your dream?'

'Like a snow leopard misses winter,' he says and gives her a long smoochy phone kiss, which he believes to be his speciality. 'Duty calls.' He sends her another I-am-off-to-work kiss, intending to put the phone down. He doesn't want to start his day with unsolvable problems. He can hear her heavy pregnant breathing, her anticipation, her silence asking him to say something more. Captain Gul wants to say he wasn't sure he was ready to be a father and maybe they should explore other options. But he isn't ready to say that yet. It doesn't sound manly. Maybe tomorrow.

His assistant, the only other member of this Field Intelligence Unit, walks in. A man with scraggy red hair and a grey rectangle of a moustache, slight but strong build, severe face, the face of a professional torturer, someone immune to pain. Subedar Laal Khan is carrying car number plates. OK 786 or OK 302. He holds them up one by one. Captain Gul is still trying to remember what had happened last night. He looks at his assistant, confused. 'What's that?'

'What number would you like to go with, sir?' he says. 'These are car number plates.' Captain Gul can tell a car number plate when he sees one. 'Last one took OK 007 with him. But I think it brought bad luck. Now he is organizing the tree-plantation drive in Abbotabad. It's too flashy, not really suitable for an intelligence field commander.' The captain knows immediately that Subedar Laal Khan is trying to assert his authority, like old faithful hand-me-down servants do when they meet their new master and want to make them dependent on their judgement. Gul chooses to ignore him and coos into the phone. 'Promise me one thing,' he says. 'You'll whisper my name to her after every prayer.'

'But we don't know if it's a girl,' his girl says.

'I am a spy, trust me I know these things.' Captain Gul is not sure that the impending baby is his but he is too much of a man to admit this. He doesn't want to contemplate the question: if not me then who? 'Call of duty,' he says and disconnects the phone.

Captain Gul is at the beginning of his career. One day he hopes to be on the world stage. He hopes his name will be whispered in Westminster and Langley, in the ruined palaces of Afghanistan and solitary cells in high-security Indian prisons, and he hopes it will be whispered with fear and awe, but right now he is here, hungover and being asked to choose between two flashy car number plates.

He takes another sip and looks into the bottom of his quarter, realizing, with sadness, that he has ashed his cigarette in it. Legends at a young age don't have easy mornings. 'No fancy number plates, who do we need to show off to? This is an intelligence unit, not Lucky Irani Circus.' He spits out his last sip of gin laced with ash.

He wants some more time in bed.

Captain Gul is thinking of getting up and taking a tour of the city when the phone rings again and someone shouts even before the receiver reaches his ear. 'What the hell have you done, you brainless piston?' Gul tries to make out which one of his bosses he has made angry. His nickname had travelled with him all the way to the intelligence headquarters. 'Bhutto is coming back? How the hell can he be coming back? Weren't you on duty that night? Didn't we give you a professional photographer? How the hell can you fuck up a photo session at a hanging?'

Captain Gul realizes that his officer is being paranoid and has probably seen one of those pamphlets claiming 'Bhutto Lives'. 'I put him in the coffin myself, sir. Well, not myself, but I was there, I put the lock on the coffin with my own hands. Bloody hell, sir,' he lowers his voice to a whisper to pass on a confidential nugget, 'they didn't even have a coffin. I had to arrange it.' His explanation doesn't go down well with his officer.

'Why don't you just claim that you arrested the bugger, tried and sentenced and hanged him with your own hands? You were on duty, not on hanging duty – you were on the photography detail and look at the results you got us.'

Gul mumbles something about just doing what he was told and humbly tries to suggest that maybe the person on burial duty should be getting this early morning bollocking. Yes, I am calling the colonel who supervised the burial, he is told. 'But the word in the bazaar is that behenchod B is headed this way. Bhutto is coming to your town. Yes, I know you put him in the coffin but try telling that to those jiyalas in your city. Either they are all insane or you've royally fucked up. Now wake up and make him go away. You are already in OK town so I can't even think of another punishment for you.'

FOUR

Iron Syrup & Other Herbs

MAYBE LIVING RENT-FREE IN THE GOL MOSQUE compound has turned Baghi into a good person and that's why Molly has brought and parked his lady friend-sister here. Maybe, given time, Baghi's private residence will turn into a refuge for women fleeing arson scenes.

The funeral prayer is coming to an end. On the loudspeaker, Baghi can hear him murmuring his wish for eternal peace for the soul of the hanged martyr – as Allah says, human eyes can't see them but martyrs live amongst us. Bhutto Lives, Molly whispers and his congregation repeats after him, louder and louder. Molly brings his prayer in absentia to an abrupt end. He sounds impatient. He wants to get it over with Allah and his Bhutto business and get back to his lady friend-sister. There is always a clutch of people who want to engage him, tell him their personal problems, share political gossip, ask questions like what it means when it says in the book that women are your fields and you can enter them from any direction you wish to.

Footsteps in the corridor, a knock, and even before he can get the door, Molly comes in, shuts the door behind him and stands there looking at Baghi, then looking at her. 'I was leading the prayers,' he says. Baghi wants to say, you are an imam what else would you be doing in the mosque? Selling guavas? Molly has made a flourishing career out of stating the obvious with the right emphasis. Baghi has been analysing the secret of his recent stardom and concluded that it's all about rhyme and repetition. If you can use seven adjectives to describe the love that Allah has for his creation why use one word? If death can be described as your reunion with your creator, your one and only rendezvous with your beloved, your carousel into an eternal life, your chance at sharing a heavenly abode with seventy-two beautiful ladies who never fart or menstruate and whose orgasms last for eight hundred years, why should you just call it death?

'By the grace of Allah, quite a crowd,' Molly says. 'And some didn't come because they think he is not really dead.' Baghi tells him that it was on the radio, in all the papers. 'They don't believe it because it was in the papers,' Molly says. He is curt with Baghi, not wasting any words. 'Can you go to the bazaar and buy us a few things?'

Who is us? Baghi wants to ask. I am not your errand boy, he wants to say.

'What things?' he asks.

'The usual things normal people need. Some Coca-Cola, Seven Up, something to eat.

'Our professor here is a socialist at heart, stays away from small pleasures that Allah has created for our enjoyments.' Molly puts his hand in his pocket and takes out a few notes. 'And you have only one towel in your bathroom so maybe another one, a soft one.'

Molly has lots of minions. Many of his worshippers would be more than happy to run errands for him all day because they believe that he could lighten their burdens on this earth and secure them a small comfortable place in the afterlife. But he is asking Baghi to go do his shopping. Baghi understands:

Molly wants him out of here for a while. He also doesn't want anyone else to know that he has a lady visitor.

He ignores Molly's hand with two ten-rupee notes and pats his pocket – I've got money. It's a defiant attempt at salvaging scraps of his socialist dignity.

'Don't listen to what they are saying in the bazaar,' says Molly. 'All gossip.'

The corridor is deserted except for two women in black burqas who are sitting on the visitors' bench under the sign of Noor Nabi Advocate & Palmist Associates. The wall along the narrow staircase is splattered with posters for the upcoming birthday celebrations of the Prophet, where Molly is one of the main speakers. There is a long list of titles before his name: the defender of faith, the prince of orators, the naked sword of truth, the dagger in the heart of blasphemers. The last one is the only one that Baghi didn't come up with. Baghi makes a mental shopping list. He can understand the need for fizzy drinks, but exposing the contents of his bathroom to a lady, even a friend-sister, is worrying, not to mention that a new towel means that the visiting friend would be here for longer than an afternoon visit. The visiting lady friend would need a bath, the visiting lady friend is probably on the run, the visiting lady friend is what they call desirable. Of course he wants me out of here, to keep her for himself. They have never talked about it, but like everyone in the bazaar, Molly knows that Baghi doesn't sleep with women, not even friend-sisters.

Baghi has never liked the expression ghost town. Trust the English to call people ghosts when they decide to stay in for their personal safety. The bazaar is deserted. Royal Fancy Jewellers is shut, all glass and iron grilles with half a dozen steel locks and two sleepy guards holding twelve-bore rifles. G.M. Wine Shop is boarded up because the man who was hanged tried to save his neck by banning alcohol, conveniently forgetting his own speech where he had declared 'Thank god I drink Scotch and not the blood of the poor'. And then rows and rows of fabric shops, all shut; even the juice stalls are shut as if people were going to stop drinking orange carrot juice in grief.

Further down the road a man who claims he brings aphrodisiacs from the Himalayas is giving a passionate lecture about his travels. Baghi walks slow, lurking behind the audience, almost certain that he wouldn't be recognized as most of the crowd are day labourers waiting for prospective employers who are not likely to arrive today. They are carrying their spades and paintbrushes, hammers and plastic buckets, and are listening to the man describe the properties of Himalayan gifts. A child is trying to listen by sneaking in between their legs. Baghi wonders about a nation where even on a day like this, when death hangs in the air, people are still interested in finding aids for their libido.

The Himalayan quack brings his voice down to a dramatic whisper: 'A man, a true man, can never be hopeless, you can't hang hope, hope springs eternal. In the foothills of Nanga Parbat, I saw a man who had been standing on one leg for seven years. He told me to go back to this city because the hanged shall be unhanged. And he shall return. He lives. And while we wait for him to return, let's give our wives the enjoyment they deserve. With me I bring the cure for your nightly shame. You there with the spade, how sharp is your tool...?'

By the time Baghi reaches Iron Syrup & Other Herbs, the fire has been put out. In place of the landmark herb store stands a burnt-down structure, exposed beams and scores of twisted green glass bottles. 'What happened?' Baghi asks no one in particular. Above the store a charred billboard, the famous logo for the Iron Syrup, a blond man flexing his bicep and two female, admiring eyes fixated on it. Only one eye has survived the fire, and the muscle man's blond hair is covered in soot. Everyone wants to be the first to break it to Baghi.

'Electric fault. Hakim Wasif Ali Wasif is dead, family not showing the body, too much burnt, eyes melted in sockets they are saying and second wife has disappeared. Two dead, only one body.'

'What happened?' Baghi asks again. There is a collective shrug and then whispers. 'Probably drank too much of his own syrup,' says a man with stubble and smelling of hash, his shirt buttons open and showing off his man breasts. 'And second wife was an athlete so she ran away. There is a reason Islam has forbidden women from outdoor sports.'

'Set himself on fire to protest the hanging,' a young boy whispers in his ear. 'Family is not telling anyone.' The boy waits for him to appreciate his access to confidential information. 'And nobody is talking about the second wife.'

Baghi turns away to leave this little pharmacy of hope which has now turned into a crime scene. The boy shouts after him: 'Tell your Maulvi sahib to announce the passing away on the mosque loudspeaker and tell him not to mention that he burnt himself. The family probably doesn't even want to give him a funeral.' Baghi turns to lecture the boy about not spreading gossip about the recently deceased when he notices a police jeep coming towards the burnt shop, a hand wielding a baton hanging outside the jeep window, striking rhythmically. Baghi knows that policeman in the jeep, he is a former student. He is not scared of him but he is in no mood to socialize with the police. He walks away from Iron Syrup & Other Herbs. This unnecessary death is not his business. But the second wife, the athlete wife, didn't run very far. No wonder Molly doesn't want him to believe the rumours in the bazaar. He is probably fucking that rumour in his academy.

Baghi abandons his food shopping and rushes back carrying a bottle each of Coke and Seven Up. The women in black outside the Noor Nabi Advocate & Palmist Associates office are gone. A handsome middle-aged man with two toddlers is sitting on the waiting bench. He has folded a newspaper and is fanning the boys. Baghi always wonders what kind of people come here in the middle of the afternoon. Are they afraid of missing out on their destiny if they wait till sunset? He turns the handle on the academy's door. It's locked on the inside. He decides to wait for a few moments and starts to pace outside the door. Noor Nabi, advocate and astrologist, peers out of her office to usher in the man with the two boys, notices Baghi with his drinks and shouts at him. 'I see Coca-Cola, I see Seven Up. You are having a party?' You never know with Noor Nabi. Is she serious or in her usual business of jinxing your fate? Her lawyer's shiny black coat is speckled with dandruff around her shoulders which, in the bright afternoon light, looks like silver dust. 'A burning in the bazaar to protest the hanging, entire nation mourning the hanging, but I can see you have something to celebrate. Remember, celebrations on such inauspicious days bring bad luck. You should let me see your hand sometime, it might save you from pain.'

Baghi is relieved that Noor Nabi has clients and can't go on. As soon as she disappears into her fortune-teller's den, Baghi approaches his door with determination.

He's going to confront Molly. A man burns, his shop burns, half his house is in ashes, and the girl who runs away from the inferno is now hiding in his home. Living rent-free in the mosque doesn't mean that Molly can start fornicating with fugitives in Baghi's place of learning.

A gentle knock. Wait, says Molly from a distance. He is probably in the kitchen. Then Baghi hears a chair being dragged, a muffled commotion, something being thrown, loud urgent whispers, all signs of a civil war. Baghi can only make out Molly's feverish whisper, Allah's will, Allah's will. The Molly that opens the door is not the Molly he left behind forty-five minutes ago. His eyes are red, his beard dishevelled, his shirt scrunched up, big patches of sweat on his left shoulder. Baghi sees beyond him and there is the lady visitor, bundled up in the chair, her arms tightly wound around her knees, like a forfeited castle. There is a ruckus in the room, his bookshelf is in disarray, Frantz Fanon and Virginia Woolf are on the floor, the blackboard is askew, one chair has fallen on its side. It's quite obvious there has been a struggle here, some sort of chase. It's not obvious who has won, though. She turns to look at Baghi, her eyes are naked daggers, and she seems to be saying: *Why did you leave me with this monster? He is your friend, isn't he? Is this how you entertain his guests? Is this what you do with your students?*

Not that he needs a sign but Baghi is sure that Allah doesn't exist because if He did exist, did He really need the likes of Molly to say nice things about Him five times a day?

For a man of Allah, Molly seems to have a slightly frisky relationship with his maker. Within the premises of the House of Allah and barely fifty metres away from his loving and waiting wife, his hanged hero still warm in his grave, Molly is busy testing his faith with a runaway woman. But then Molly is not always about heaven and hell and rings of fire or eternal salvation. He is more of a storyteller – that's why he gets the crowds. No different from that man on the corner and his sassy Himalayan stories. He sells dreams of perpetual erections. Molly sells eternal salvation.

He launches into his sermon now. Having wrecked his living space, he is ready to absolve Baghi. 'You don't know how lucky you are. Allah loves you more than He loves people like me,' he says. Baghi appreciates that extra godly love but he is not sure if he wants to know what he has done to earn it. Molly's face moves towards his ear as if he is about to share a deeply personal secret. 'He loves sinners. Adores them. He is consumed by them. He thinks of them day and night.'

This place is owned by the mosque, which is owned by the Gol Mosque Trust, and the trust is run by Molly so there is no room for argument. Molly goes towards his guest, holding out both hands towards her, Coca-Cola in one, Seven Up in the other, as a peace offering after a brief but unexpected skirmish that has definitely taken place in the room. She chooses Seven Up and drinks it in one long gulp. Molly offers Baghi the other drink but he declines. He wants to ask him what in God's name happened here while he was gone. Instead he shows his defiance by pushing the drink away. Why would they choose his academy to have a scuffle? If Molly wanted to spend time with a lady friend, he could have found another place. If she has come to seek spiritual solace, why are they having a wrestling match? Baghi hasn't been in a carnal relationship for a very long time but he has read enough newspapers to know that what happened here had nothing to do with love.

Molly continues in his saviour mode. 'Allah has created this beautiful universe for us and there are signs…' and here he goes on a long list of signs. The sun and the moon coordinating their rise and fall, buffaloes licking the slime of their newborns, the symmetry of eyes, ears and nose – imagine if our nose was on our belly. The beauty of a woman giving birth – imagine the pain, now think of the wrinkly baby in your hands. Molly puts both his hands on Baghi's shoulders and says, 'Thank you, my friend. There is something that tells me that we'll be together on the day of Qayamat, and when we are presented in front of Allah, He'll forgive a sinner like me because of you. You, Baghi, you. Because you have given protection to someone weaker than you and never tried to take advantage of their weakness. That's what Allah wants because He is most powerful and He never takes advantage of the vulnerable. That's the test and that's the life and you have just passed – what do you call it in English, with flying colours? Do colours fly? I don't know, but see, I have learnt from you.'

God doesn't take care of the vulnerable, Baghi wants to say. He has made them vulnerable. He practically thrives on their suffering.

'The Iron Syrup shop burnt down,' Baghi announces. 'People are saying Hakim Wasif Ali Wasif set himself on fire to protest the hanging and someone from the household has gone missing.' Baghi doesn't look at the lady visitor.

Molly, instead of reacting to this news, goes towards his lady friend and stares at her. 'Life is Allah's gift,' he says in a tired voice. 'It's not ours to take. He loves us so much that He is calling us all back. Every single one of us. Let's wait for our turn to return to Him.'

Sabiha Bano pulls her dupatta on her head and listens to him with her head bowed.

When the door shuts behind Molly, Baghi's vulnerable protectee doesn't look at him. She picks up her bag and starts taking out her things. And he feels like an outsider in his own home. Baghi doesn't want to believe that he is the kind of person who is protective of their private property. How can he have anything against people, specially vulnerable people, coming into his space? After all, who started Mazdoor Militia (Baghi Faction)? Who was the businessman who came up with the idea of People's Publishers? Who introduced this nation to the finest literary works of forgotten Soviet people's writers? He has always lived amongst the people and hopes to die amongst them. *But this is my room here.* And she is unpacking. He sees her things creeping into his life. Her woman's clothes. Her shoes, jogging shoes, women's jogging shoes. And the smell from those things. Slightly perfumed. Smell of marriage. Smell of doom.

The last time she stood in front of this bookshelf, she was a lanky boy-girl with an athlete's muscular shoulders and smelled of warm, dusty orchards. Now she is a well-groomed girl-woman, her chest fuller and her skin glowing, a living advertisement for her late husband's herbal products. Baghi feels a mild guilt and, like a true fallen revolutionary, steps up to make up for his past failures.

He moves towards his bookshelf and starts taking books out to make space for her things. He wonders if he should leave some books on the shelf to assert his claim of ownership. Should *Wretched of the Earth* stay or make place for her tracksuits? He decides to let *To the Lighthouse* stay.

She seems at home now, now that she has found a shelf. She plonks her things on his shelf without arranging them. Definitely not what Baghi expects a woman to do in this town. Then she pulls a pistol out of her sports bag, slightly rusted, almost a toy pistol. She points it at Baghi's head, then lowers it to his chest, then to his groin, then back to his head. Baghi stands there, stunned at first, then amused and then nostalgic. He half raises his hands in mock surrender but she offers the pistol to him with her ruinous smile. 'Your friend is a sister-fucker.' Baghi's ears burn. Even his staunch woman comrades never used this kind of language. 'Are you a sister-fucker too? Take this from me before I kill someone.'

'If you shoot and kill someone, you kill a little part of yourself, but if you shoot them here,' he puts the muzzle on his kneecap, 'they remember you for all their life.'

Baghi stops himself from bragging about his steady hand with a pistol. He picks up a sheaf of papers and a ballpoint pen and plonks them in front of her. 'This is no place for guns. I used to give you essays to write. You can write more, about what you know. Choose your own topic. Anything from your life. Just write what's on your mind.'

'Why should I tell anybody what's on my mind?'

'I won't read them while you are here. Write what other students write. But remember you are not an ordinary student: you are a witness to history. I may not agree with your parents' politics but they stood on the right side of history. Our Father, Our Mother, Our Cow if you have one. Feel free to make one up.' Baghi brings his voice down to a whisper. 'Just don't put anything on the paper that can be used against you in the courts.' And then he says in his stern teacher's voice. 'This is a place of learning and I can't have you here if you are not learning something. Or at least trying.'

'Molly sahib was right,' she says. 'You have become a good person or you are at least trying.'

Sabiha chews on the pen, stares at the blank page and smiles. 'Can I write about my English teacher too?'

HOMEWORK 1

Our Cow

I humbly begin this treatise in the name of the most merciful and the most vengeful, creator of all things minor and major. Our English tutor Salim Ahmed Salim alias Sir Baghi has tasked me to write an essay about our cow. I can't write that the cow is Allah's splendorous creation because Sir doesn't believe in the existence of Almighty and His numerous manifestations. Although he knows and has taught us very many muscular words of English lingua franca he doesn't know zilch about cow. He is a man with his abode in the city who gets his milk from a milkman who gets it from a village milkman who gets it from the owner of the cow. He wants us to write about cow without being cognizant of our cow but I plan to write this treatise as well as the others about essay topics as they manifest to my humble self. Because when I have tried to bear witness to things as they manifest to men, they turn out to be not very propitious. I am also in an advantageous position to write this because Sir Baghi has promised not to read them. It has to be expounded here and now that, for a man who doesn't believe in God's word, Sir Baghi is a man of his word.

It can be affirmed without an iota of doubt that our cow is a splendorous beast. It has very curvaceous horns and its udders are a piece de resistance. The story of our cow begins on the night when I wake up from a plethora of dreams to a very heart-piercingly painful moo of our cow. There are eight men huddled like ancient warriors around and on top of the cow. They are no warriors because I recognize them to be the fellow comrades of my very esteemed father, Comrade Abid Al Abid, labour union leader at Satlaj Cotton Mills. There is a little fire exuding light in an otherwise very dark and pitch-black night. First I am gobsmacked to see what are these men, all making honest living from their sweat and blood at the cotton mills, doing wrestling with a cow. Our cow is very restless under the collective gaze of these men. She knows that something inauspicious is going to manifest itself. Our cow is wise. People presume that water buffaloes with their sage-like visage are also wise but they only have the intellect for fodder and cudding. When the ominous clouds cover the sky our cow makes a moo sound. When her wonderous udders are full with her mother's milk she also makes a moo cry but this is not heavens are going to open and the moment has come to clear the washing line moo but can somebody come and milk me moo. Our cow's progeny, a four-month-old calf full of youthful vigour and innocence of the angels, is standing in a corner over a pile of nutritious green fodder. He is trying to partake from this pile but alas little does he know that they have put a plastic wire mesh muzzle on his mouth so that he cannot partake of his mother's milk every hour of the day as youthful calves are desirous to do.

A man adorned in a brown shawl, who I assume to be Comrade Sadiq Ali Sadiq, wields an iron machete and is putting it in the fire to make it red-hot. My heart sinks, shudder after shudder runs through my spinal cord, my eyes well up with tears at having to witness the impending woes of the cow. The cow's moos are splitting my heart but Mother

Bano is sleeping beside me like a baby, clutching to one side of the bed. I shake her shoulder and wake her up. Coming out of her nightly dreams of falling off a cliff, she witnesses the scene with her famously beauteous but groggy eyes and misunderstands the situation like sleepy people do. They can't differentiate between the real-life paradigm and the paradigm in their dreams. She comes to believe that her esteemed husband and his comrades are trying to commit proverbial slaughter of the cow. She rushes to our wood-burning stove like an avenging angel, pulls out a log still burning and runs to the men. Now there are two fires in this darkest night of our soul. One near the cow, Comrade Sadiq Ali Sadiq dipping a machete's iron face into it. The other one in Mother Bano's hand. Everyone is mortified of mother's furious foray into the cabal of men. Even the night sky.

Can Mother Bano take on the collective might of eight comrades, vanguard warriors from the Satlaj Cotton Mills Labour Union, singlehandedly? Only time will tell.

FIVE

Stop Playing with My Heart

THIS MORNING CAPTAIN GUL FEELS LIKE A VICTIM of his own success on the amorous front. On occasion his love-starved fellow officers have offered to share the burdens of his love life, asked him to introduce them to his ex-lovers to-be, but Captain Gul is of the firm conviction that love is not a team sport. This morning he had a rendezvous, which, like any other rendezvous, started with a phone call the night before. After cabling his head office that he had penetrated a network of jiyalas who were spreading Bhutto Not Dead rumours, and that he was lying low and winning their trust before catching them all in one swoop, he thought of calling his Pindi girl but then remembered that he hadn't yet prepared his speech about the impending baby, which was to include the argument that overpopulation was the real curse for Ummah. But he wanted human interaction, he needed to communicate, he had things to say, he wanted to hear a female voice speaking in his ear, so he picked up the OK town phone directory and started dialling numbers starting with the letter S. It was probably his fourth or fifth call when a girl answered. He told her he was calling from the northern front, he couldn't give the precise location for operational reasons, but he was alone in the trenches, up in the frozen mountains, that he could be a martyr by the morning as enemy forces were on the move tonight, it was a cold and harsh night, he didn't care if he lived or died, he was sure to inflict heavy damage on the enemy before laying down his life for his motherland. While he was waiting for them, and he was ready for them, he was lonely and bored. He sipped his gin slowly and recited her some poetry, some patriotic poetry first:

We give our life for the land we love,
imagine
what we can do for someone
who loves us.

And then some generic poetry:

Is there a fellow traveller,
in this treacherous night.

She recited back some poetry:

Will there be a fellow traveller
when dawn breaks this treacherous night.

He said the next day he was visiting the OK town cantonment and he would be staying at Bachelor Officers' Quarters No. 4 and maybe they should meet, but maybe they shouldn't meet because he wasn't sure if he would want to go back to the trenches after meeting her because he had never heard a melodious voice like hers, *have you been taking classical music lessons by any chance*, he wasn't sure if he could live without her and what that would mean for the country's defence. Maybe they shouldn't meet after all. The next day he forgets the promises he made last night. He even forgets her name. It was something starting with S. She turns up in the morning while he is still asleep, dreaming of rusting tanks and wild pigs grazing on torn books. He is woken up by a cold hand on his chest. He reaches for his revolver under the pillow, hoping it is one of his fellow officers playing a prank. The hand is soft and moves up to his neck. 'How dare you?'

Through half-closed eyes he sees her face. A nice, acceptable face, not the kind of face where he'll have to invoke the Armoured Corps motto of hide the face, hit the base. Then he sees his revolver in her hand. 'What time is it?' he asks, feigning a yawn, ignoring the revolver.

'It's time for you to stop playing with my heart,' she says, brushing the tip of his revolver against his nose gently.

He shivers and stiffens. He might have no control over his own desire but he can spot desire in a woman and that he believes is God's ultimate gift to mankind. There were reluctant girls, girls wanting to get married before the night ended, some even wanting to decide future children's names before going anywhere near a bed, women hoping to get paid by miming desire, girls doing it just so they could tell you about their broken lives afterwards, but there was something divine about a woman and her militant desire, like a Napoleonic army on the march, walking into a man's room, retrieving his revolver from under the pillow and asking him why he was such a liar. His field intelligence training makes him think for a moment about how she got easy access to his bachelor officer's quarters, why he didn't get a call from the guard room about a lady visitor.

He rummages under the bed and is relieved to find a quarter bottle of Murree vodka, happy to hear a bit of slosh. He opens the quarter and takes a swig and extends the bottle towards her. 'Russians might have fucked up their Lenin but they definitely knew how to make vodka.'

In Captain Gul's experience men are wrong when they assume that women only like to talk about feelings, specially their own feelings. It's his firm belief that general knowledge about the world turns women on. Even some bits from *The Guinness Book of World Records* can help. This insight, he believes, was one of the secrets of his success with women. Many men assumed that women were not interested in international security or world history and only wanted to crib about their sisters or best friends or sleazy uncles. Captain Gul had lectured women about malnutrition stats amongst children in the developed world. He had given them the inside story about the role of French commandos during the siege of Mecca, described the mysteries of the Bermuda Triangle, and by the end of the conversation found their lips hungry and arms yielding. As he is telling her about the private life of Lenin, she takes the bottle from him, sniffs it, puts the cap back on and places it on the side table. 'Russians? They still can't make it smell good. It smells of stale piss. God only knows what it tastes like.' She slithers into his bed, creeps under the duvet and finds him ready and quivering, the suddenness of this other presence turning him on instantly.

Captain Gul does a hip-hip hurray in his heart and tries to slow things down. But it seems she is ready to take him in, cutting short his expert moves at practised, cunning foreplay – an attempted massage on the small of her back is swiftly terminated, gentle caresses under her armpits are accepted with some giggly impatience – and when he realizes that she wants to fast-forward to the moment of consummation, he realizes that he doesn't have any condoms. There is a moment of hesitation in which Captain Gul thinks of all the places he could find protection. The officers' canteen would be closed, the cantonment pharmacy is a fifteen-minute walk away, and he wants to keep Laal Khan out of his love life.

He hates the word condom or rubber, which makes it sound less like lovemaking and more like a butcher's business. Although he takes secret pride in being called a piston by his fellow officers, he takes even more pride in his personal resolve to be a responsible piston. Besides a singular historic lapse in Pindi, he has always used protection and has navigated nimbly through tricky situations, sometimes by lecturing women about the bliss of non-penetrative lovemaking, sometimes by saying that he was not emotionally ready. He was on a mission not to enter a woman without a reasonably strong shield. He has read in Clausewitz's *On War* that sometimes a retreat is the only victory. But this morning he has the optimism of someone who has taken a new command in a dull town and turned it red-hot. He is ready to yield because he believes, he'll never know if wrongly or rightly, that he is reasonably safe. Also when he squirms and hesitates at the last moment, offering to go down on her, she says surely a man of his experience knows when to withdraw. The cautious and responsible man that he is, Captain Gul has withdrawn many times, adding to the push and pull of desire, and this morning he is certain that he can't throw away his seed, that he'll withdraw before that moment arrives. When in the middle of this responsible lovemaking he is interrupted by the ringing of the hotline in his room, he considers it divine intervention. He pauses for a moment, pushes one last time before he pulls, and reaches for the phone. His commanding officer is inviting him to tea. A fleeting suspicion crosses his mind. Coincidences trouble him: in his line of work serendipity is usually a trap set by the enemy. But when he bids her farewell with the promise of meeting her the same time next morning, he doesn't know that he has made non-safe love to his commanding officer's daughter. He finds out only when Laal Khan comes in with his Order of the Day cable from headquarters and, without looking at him, murmurs, 'Sir, the lady is CO sahib's daughter. We fear her more than we fear CO sahib. And we fear CO sahib a lot. She was friendly with your predecessor and he left without saying farewell to anyone. He also took the OK 007 number plate with him.'

OK town may not be big on security threats, thinks Captain Gul, but it does seem full of dangerous love.

SIX

Leaders of the Muslim Ummah, You're Welcome

BAGHI WANTS TO TELL HER THAT HE HAS BEEN accused of many things in his life but nobody has ever called him a peacenik. He doesn't go around turning the other cheek. There is no such thing as peaceful resistance, he believes. Our oppressors are armed and so should we be, he used to say. He also doesn't believe in the English teacher's favourite cliché that if you show a gun in the first act it'll have to go off in the third act. This world is not a Chekhov story – Chekhov would've felt lost in these times, in this city. No rustic glamour here, no panting horses, no enigmatic woman carrying a small dog; all there is is a painful birth, a miserable life and even death comes long after it's due. But before that always the struggle, and a pistol that may or may not work.

The last time Baghi handled a gun it didn't end well. Somebody got a shattered knee and he had to go underground for three years. The gun didn't misfire, nor did he miss his target. He didn't believe in peaceful resistance but he was not a happy murderer either. He was a chronic petition writer who got very angry with his boy lover and started believing that when you kill someone you kill a bit of yourself, but when you take out someone's knee they remember you for life. Now out of Bhutto's dungeons and rehabbed, Baghi believes that some revolutionaries were basically gleeful murderers. To think that it was the year 1979 and some of his fellow travellers still had Stalin's statue on their shelves.

Baghi had launched himself on the world stage five years ago and, as a result, had got a chilli-powder-laced rod rammed up his rectum. Days before the heads of thirty-eight Muslim countries were about to arrive in Lahore for the 2nd Organization of Islamic Countries summit hosted by Bhutto as his bid to become the boy prince of Ummah, Baghi wrote a welcome letter and mailed it to all the embassies of Muslim countries who were attending.

Baghi had blurted out a revolution on a piece of paper and he had paid the price.

Mazdoor Militia (Baghi Faction): A Welcome Letter to the Leaders of Muslim Ummah

Kings and Princes and Crown Princes and Presidents and Prime Ministers, Your Excellencies, Your Highnesses, Exalted Murderers, Extremist Exploiters, Slaves of Capitalist Empires, Cronies of Corporate Killers, read this and read it now because it's your death warrant!!!

Will you not read your own black warrants?

This open letter is a clarion call to tell you that we see you, we see you behind your silk robes, your turbans, your uniforms and medals, and your Savile Row suits, we the Baghi Faction of Mazdoor Militia, we see you for what you are: you eat the flesh of your people and you devour it with a healthy dose of our blood.

You Qaddafi, you Shah Faisal, you Shah of Shahs, you sold-out son of Palestine, you hunter of your own people, you

Idi Amin, you Anwar Sadat and all the other minions who call themselves the leaders of Islamic countries and who have gathered here to learn from each other more brutal ways of oppressing their own people.

We welcome you to the land of the pure.

Remember the red palaces you inhabit were built on the tired bones of our workers. The soft beds you sleep in are woven by our toiling masses who struggle to feed their children. Now that you have all come together in our land, the so-called land of the pure, we want to tell you that we have enough filth in this land, we don't need the sins of your fathers and your forefathers to pollute this unfortunate realm further. You drink from crystal goblets and shit in gold bowls. I welcome you to the historic city of Lahore, to the historic Royal Mosque which was built by the labour of toiling masses for the pleasure and legacy of a king. As you dine in the Royal Fort, luxuriate in your foam baths and sample the hard-working concubines of our country, remember this: your end is nigh!!!

Pakistan is red.

Asia is red and soon the whole world will be red with your vulture blood.

Your allegiance to Allah doesn't deceive us. By gathering in the name of Islam, by invoking a union of the Ummah in which all blacks, browns and the pale ones stand shoulder to shoulder, you are using the tried and tested tool of class exploitation. What unity in the name of Allah? He doesn't exist. If He does why did He choose the likes of you to be His intermediaries between Himself and His creation?

Look at yourself in the mirror, Shah Faisal: you are the custodian of the House of Allah and you can't even count how many wives, how many children you have?

Idi Amin, how many people have you killed with your own hands?

Yasser Arafat, you carry a pistol – tell us that you don't use it against your own people?

Mujib ur Rahman, you call yourself father of the nation – how many people's intellectuals have you put in your dungeons?

And oye Shah of Shahs, you and your forefathers have been oppressing your people for two thousand years now.

By pledging to get together in the name of Allah, you are covering your crimes by the fig leaf that you have created for yourself in the name of Allah.

Mazdoor Militia (Baghi Faction) warn you not to come.

Our liberation armies are ready for you.

We don't need Ummah, we the people are the real Ummah.

Here in this land of the pure, you'll die a miserable death. We'll get you when you are sipping your fine wines, when you are prostrating for your pretend prayers, when you are pulling your cocks and showing off to your concubines. We'll ambush you when you are listening to each other's lies, when you are making a fool of more than one billion people.

And if we don't get you here, in this very land of the pure where you have come together to strengthen the twin yokes of capitalism and religion, the two biggest scourges of humanity, we shall get you when you return to your palaces built upon the tired bones of your own working classes. Your wife will poison your dinner, your nephew will come to pay his respect and shoot you in the gut, your loyal soldiers will pretend to salute you but fire tank guns from close range. Those of you who are lucky will die a swift death; others will be strung from electrical poles in public squares.

Your royal testicles will be chopped off and stuffed in your mouths.

Your coming generations will change their last names, your graves will be desecrated, your statues will be pulled

> *down, people will make bonfires of your official portraits, your exalted names will be found in the rubbish bins of history. Let this letter be a solemn promise from our Mazdoor Militia (Baghi Faction), let it be a historical document that you were warned about your ignominious end.*
>
> *Yours Brutally,*
> *and Historically,*
> *Rebels of Tomorrow*

Afterwards, Molly found him crumpled in a police dungeon, blood still dripping from his shalwar, hugging a wall, scratching on stones with his broken nails, whimpering and convulsing. Molly held him and gave him water and Baghi, for the first and last time in his life, shed tears of gratitude, hugged Molly, clung to him, refused to let him go even when Molly said that he needed to sort out some paperwork to secure his release. Molly had already prepared a confession that read 'I am a drug addict. I was under the influence of strong medication for my schizophrenia. I did write the letter but I wrote it in a state of delusion. I pledge and swear that I'll never again in my life indulge in any political activity of any kind.'

Molly had brought him fresh clothes, but as soon as he put them on Baghi, another patch of blood appeared on his shalwar. Molly draped a shawl around him, another one on his head, pulled down to hide his rearranged face, and walked him out of the dungeon and his life of a global revolutionary. Baghi would never be able to eat chilli powder again.

'Let's please not forget that this place is a school. Young people come here for learning and I don't think I can have this gun here. It's also not legal to live here or have guests. But since your friend brought you here…'

She has no patience for Baghi's lecture. 'Everyone says you like revolution, you almost changed the world order. You don't believe in God and now you don't believe in guns either? You? Are you sure you are the same person?'

'No, no, please don't get me wrong. You are most welcome to stay here till you find a better option. Please consider this your home. It's just that I have principles and I can't have a gun in the vicinity of young people. They already say that I am corrupting young minds.'

'Are you?' she says, relaxed now, a smile trying to curl around her lips. 'Why didn't you try to corrupt me, or did you? I did it for myself on sports quota. I want money back for my two-weeks' fees.'

'I gave up politics,' he says. 'Now I teach English. That's all.'

She is one of those people who ask a question when they have no interest in your answer.

'Go and dump it in the gutter. Lots of them around you.' She waves it in Baghi's face.

He flinches, recovers. 'You are carrying it, you must think you need it? You don't look like someone who will carry a gun for the sake of it.'

She is exasperated. 'What do I look like, sir? A bank robber? Maybe I should have done it. I can still run faster than your fat police.'

An idea is forming in Baghi's head. Not a pleasant one. But some unpleasant ideas are essential. 'I think I'll keep it at our friend's house.' His days of doing rash things are over but he is not sure if he trusts himself or her with a gun.

'It's a present from my grandfather. I'll want it back. You will go yourself or should I come with you? Say salam to his wife too.'

And with that sneer on Sabiha's face, it sinks in. It's not the gun that scares him. Nor the pile of flowery shirts and bras parked on his bookshelf. Nor the fact that she is on the run and if she is on the run someone must be chasing her. No, he's not afraid of whosoever is coming after her; what scares him is that she reminds Baghi of himself. A very young, very angry and very much in love Baghi.

HOMEWORK 2

Our Mother

By the grace of Almighty Mother Bano is a famously beauteous creature. When she was young and walked to the well to fetch water in her earthen pitcher, boys from seven villages scrambled up the trees to get a minor glimpse of her sashaying visage. She was always a virtuous lass who never looked up in the trees but such are the ways of the cruel world that she attained the repute of a wandering beauty. It can be said with absolute authenticity that she didn't roam the streets in an endeavour to find admiring lovers: she walked the streets because she liked walking and exploring nature. When I became a middle school competition runner the village folks, who are erroneously presumed to have wisdom of the ages, started saying Mother was a walking beauty, now her daughter is a running beauty. Mother Bano always advised me not to run because she opined that when a woman walks, how far can she go, but if a woman runs, first she runs from home, then she runs away from her husband and beautiful children and sometimes she can run so far that she forgets how to navigate her back home. But on this night of our cow's tragedy, mother is running with a log of fire towards the men who in her dreamy paradigm are committing the slaughter of our cow. The cabal of men crowding our cow don't see her charging with her infernal fury. The first target of her arsenal attack is Comrade Sadiq Ali Sadiq, known to everyone from his past endeavours as the ringleader and honourable secretary general of the Satlaj Cotton Mills Union. His brown shawl is alighted and the fire licks his walrus-like moustache. He slaps himself to extinguish the fire licking his face, and his comrades forget to torment the cow and try to control my mother who, relieved of her burning log, is lashing with her tongue and shouting, You rascals, good for nothing species of mankind, stop the slaughter of my cow. My esteemed father Comrade Abid Ali Abid shouts back at her that, you ignorant woman, our cow's tail has maggots, we are trying to cut her tail before the maggots reach her brain. Mother shouts at them, questioning their qualifications for diagnosing and then trying a brutal tactic to cure our cow, employing such barbaric methods like a hot machete, glowing red in the night. Comrade Sadiq Ali Sadiq throws off his brown shawl in a dramatic gesture and expounds in a grave voice suitable to his stature as the secretary general of the labour union: a woman who attacks and insults the working classes is a traitor to the proletariat and no better than the maggots we are trying to control. My esteemed father Comrade Abid Ali Abid first raises his hand, admonishes his secretary general in a pleading tone for 'being disrespectful to the mother of my children'. Esteemed father has only one child, that's my humble self, but he habitually declares my mother as the mother of his children, alluding to a past traumatic event too traumatic to discuss at this stage. While men are fighting and arguing over who has been insulted more, I stand with the youthful calf, his eyes misty at the plight of his mother. I put my arms around his neck and with his youthful enthusiasm he tries to lick my face but because of the muzzle his tongue barely touches me and I feel his hungry breath on my face. Comrade Sadiq Ali is addressing the men now and saying that any man who has acquired a wandering beauty as a spouse should either re-evaluate his life choice of being a brother in struggle or learn to control her.

I deploy the nimbleness of my hands to remove the calf's muzzle so that he can lick my hands and face and become less anxious about the plight of his poor mother. Oblivious of the arguments raging around her, our cow gets up with some effort and takes a step towards her calf but stumbles at the second step and falls again. The cabal of men had put fat chains around her ankles. Mother Bano shouts uncivilized curses at the men, alluding to the red-hot machete and their male reproductive organs, and my father pledges to cure her of the maggots in her brain by cutting her into pieces. Comrade Sadiq Ali Sadiq leads his comrades out of our humble abode. I hug the youthful calf's neck with my supple yet firm arms.

SEVEN

Tell Me the Story of Your City

IF CAPTAIN GUL WAS AN ORDINARY POMPOUS INTELligence officer, and not someone destined for glory, he would have summoned the local administration, made them wait outside his office for three hours and then given them a fifteen-minute audience to get a measure of this place, figured out who had started these bloody Bhutto Lives rumours, thrown some people in the lock-up, filed a report and kept his tea appointment with his CO. If you sleep with your superior's daughter in the morning, you should have the courtesy to pay your respects to her boss father in the afternoon.

But Captain Gul is fired up, ready to go play the old game of fuck-you with civilians. He knows you can't get a measure of the place unless you get out of your comfort zone.

So here he is, hangover now ebbing, his brain cleared of his early morning encounter. He has left his bachelor officer's quarters and made it to the district police headquarters, where he already feels at home.

He has again rejected Subedar Laal Khan's offer to choose between OK 302 and OK 786 and said surely the unit's white Toyota Corolla already has a number, the real number. 'What are we? Highway bandits? Just let it be.' Subedar Laal Khan told him that actually the car wasn't registered for security reasons. 'Then drive it without a bloody number plate.' Captain Gul asserts his authority without being rude. 'I know you are the backbone of this unit, but new rules, more transparency.' Laal has driven him here in sulky silence and now Captain Gul is thumbing through police files and finding it difficult to tell between cases that involve murders, attempts to murder, honour murders and not-intended-but-still-murdered murders. He pushes the stack of files towards A.D. Malang. 'You are an officer of the state. I hear you are a local. A.D. Malang. Allah Ditta, I assume?' Malang nods. 'You would know what goes on here. Just give it to me. Keep it brief, focused, just like your name – Mr A and D. Don't tell me the whole story. Leave the boring bits out. Didn't someone once write a poem about this city? I want to listen to that poem but this is not the time for poetry. Me and you, we are at the epicentre of a national fuck-up.'

Assistant Sub-Inspector A.D. Malang doesn't like people to guess his name from his initials. He has been briefed about the arrival of the new chief of Field Intelligence Unit. He hasn't really dealt with them directly but has learnt enough in his job to know that this was his chance to prove his credentials as a crack officer. 'They like crack officers,' his boss had told him. 'They don't like office clerks, people who go by the book.'

A.D. Malang doesn't trust army people with civilian haircuts who don't wear uniform. This captain with his floppy hair and unruly sideburns looks like an aspiring matinee idol.

Malang decides to play the office clerk. 'We have a peaceful district. We have not had a major incident for a while.'

Captain Gul stares at him approvingly, as if encouraging him to go on with we-are-a-peace-loving-people bullshit. He knows this much about civilians: they bullshit before they get to the point. You need to be patient.

'We have got the All South Asian Wrestling Championship going on. Lots of crowds to see the visiting Indian wrestler, some out-of-towners, gambling types, but they are generally peaceful.'

'Fat men fucking around in mud,' says Captain Gul. 'They look nice in pictures but nobody cares about them in my line of work, even if some of them are Indians.'

'There is an odd case, this boy, sir.' Malang clears his throat as if about to share the city's most shameful secret. 'He first slit his sister's throat, because she was standing on the rooftop doing what girls do on rooftops, probably talking to a boy, then he went underground, then cut his penis off right in front of the police station before surrendering. He is in ICU and we have recorded his statement, but if you want to catch up with him, we can arrange a visit.'

Save your best for last, Malang was told. Give them nothing and then make it seem they have stumbled upon something. Make them feel intelligent. After all, they call themselves the Field Intelligence Unit, his boss had told him.

Captain Gul thumbs through a file buried in the heap and comes up with 'Eight members of a family locked up in a tube-well engine room and burnt to death'. Captain Gul picks up the paper from under the pile and, without looking up, says, 'Very peaceful.'

A.D. Malang is relieved that Captain Gul has picked up the First Information Report. He finds it hard to explain generational family disputes to outsiders – a dispute running between two families, who were actually one family for three generations, and now all the grown-ups have killed each other. You can expect peace for a few years until their children grow up and it starts again. All they need is some encouragement and a jerrycan of Regular.

'It was a family dispute, sir. You know these junglees, they have feuds going back generations, sometimes over a stolen water buffalo, sometimes an eloped woman. In this case both a woman and a buffalo. This is how they settle – they don't bother people outside their families.'

'And there was another burning in the bazaar? Some herb seller went up in flames?'

'That was an electrical fault, sir. Very old building.'

'What about this?' Gul throws a crumpled page in front of him. A cyclostyled copy of *The Daily Struggle* has a headline in block letters.

Bhutto Escaped. Will Address the Nation from Gol Mosque

A.D. Malang pretends to be puzzled, pulls at a hair in his neatly trimmed moustache. 'Sir, there were a few protests before the hanging. A couple of attempted burnings. But since the hanging—'

Captain Gul throws more pamphlets in front of him.

Burn yourself.
Set yourself on fire.

He has seen someone screaming the exact same headline in the bazaar. He knows that he has to let the loonies have their fun. These rags provide an outlet. 'Sir, some jiyalas believe that he is not really dead. That the military government is hiding him somewhere and if they continue their protest he'll return. Better to ignore this bazaar gossip.'

'Why should we believe that these eight people didn't set themselves on fire to bring that bloody Bhutto back? Your city seems to be missing him a lot.' Gul pulls out posters, front pages of local rags, cyclostyled pamphlets dripping blood and tears, barely glanced at and filed away as a matter of routine.

He will return.
He slipped through the noose.
He dug a tunnel and made his escape good and sailed to Tripoli.

'Make photocopies and send them to me. Find the publisher, the printer, the typesetter, everybody. Before lunch.'

Malang sits at attention and tries to tell him about the local hacks and artists who provided some comic relief in troubled times. 'Every city needs a few jokers. His supporters are in shock and when in shock people say crazy things. I wouldn't worry too much about it, sir.'

This makes Captain Gul furious. 'Eight people burn themselves to death, your local rags are full of "Burn yourself and he'll return" and you are sitting here telling me about some sister-fucker who chopped off his own penis? Take me to the crime scene.'

Malang stands up to salute. 'Which one, sir?'

'Every single one of them,' Captain Gul says.

EIGHT

We Are Nothing. Be Everything

WHEN BAGHI TOOK THE GUN FROM SABIHA BANO, their hands touched for a moment, and his hand trembled, like it did the first time he held his first true love Mehboob's hand. Young Reds were playing a literal but musical Urdu translation of 'The International' with gusto. Mehboob with his thin pink lips and the eyes of a dove left behind by the flight had a permanent smile on his face as if there was an inner joke playing in his mind. 'My father is dead, my mother is a pimp. Nice to meet you,' he had introduced himself. Mehboob had stumbled into the youth camp after running away from his mother, a single woman and a minor army contractor, who had occasionally contributed to the evening entertainment of the bored army generals since Mehboob was a child. He had seen girls come in and go out of his house for a long time, seen them dress, undress, share make-up tips and discuss the shapes of their clients' organs. He had run away from home when his mother started asking him to choose one of her girls and give her grandchildren. Baghi didn't feel the need to introduce himself; instead he guided him to the Young Reds concert. As the anthem reached 'eruption of hunger', Mehboob's hand touched the back of Baghi's hand, accidentally, then intentionally, one finger, then the other; by the time they reached 'we are nothing, be everything', their hands were in a tight embrace. Balls heavy with desire, they realized for the first time in their young lives what it was like for two human beings to be united for a cause; they were so much in love that they often confused their hormones with their cause.

They spent the next few months holding hands and listening to soaring revolutionary anthems and later jumping over walls, thumping chests in front of police barricades, spitting in poor policemen's faces, smashing empty vodka bottles on footpaths, taking naps on railway tracks, jumping on seats in smoke-filled cinemas, stealing from orange orchards, dancing at strangers' weddings, jumping into canals and pretending to drown by holding their breath under water, walking barefoot on burning streets in June, staying awake by keeping their eyes wide open and reciting the Manifesto, praying to wake up in the communist republic of Prague, kissing behind corners while a May Day procession with candles approached, doing karate chops over road construction workers' night fires, rubbing against a shared quilt in winter nights, reading *Das Kapital* loudly in front of mosques as worshippers came out after Jumma prayers, punching walls, calling their teacher a son of a whore to his face and then pretending they didn't know what the word whore meant, picking up stray kittens and putting them on their shoulders, picking up dead dogs from the middle of the road and giving them elaborate burials, emptying their pockets to give every last penny to a fake leper, waiting for the traffic light to turn red before crossing the road running.

The end was sudden. Mehboob got bored and disappeared, and Baghi borrowed a pistol from the one-man militant wing of Mazdoor Militia, went looking for him, from one smoke-filled college hostel room to another, and found him in the arms of a very big, very hairy Trotskyite comrade. The explosion of jealousy that Baghi felt was stronger than his passion for a new world order. Baghi pointed the pistol at Mehboob's naked knee. Then he took a screaming, cursing, fainting then coming to and screaming again, Mehboob in his arms, hauled him down the stairs to the main road, stopped a rikshaw, pressed a hundred-rupee note into the driver's hand and asked him to take Mehboob to Civil Hospital emergency. He dumped the gun in an open sewer and took the next train out of OK town.

Now he weighs the gun in his hand, contemplates it and thinks maybe this pistol, the girl who has brought the pistol, has a purpose after all. She reminds him of Mehboob, his permanent urge to run away from what they had and, ultimately, his treachery. She had run away from his academy once. Maybe he had offended her young mind with his lecture on Allah. Maybe she didn't like his teaching method. Maybe she had heard those Baghi takes it up the ass rumours in the bazaar. He never liked Bhutto fanatics, but he wants to make it right: he will keep her safe. Even if she has taken a life, even if she is ready to take her own life. She is sitting in the chair now, bent over her sheaf of papers, doodling, pretending to do her homework.

'You don't eat in the academy? I am grieving. Meat is good for grief. How'll I ever do my homework if I don't eat? Do you want me to write an essay called "My Hunger"?' she says without looking up and with an impish smile. 'Sir, since you don't believe in Allah, food will not bring itself.'

HOMEWORK 3

Our Father

On the night of my father's shamefacedness in front of his cabal of comrades, he declares that he'll cut my mother. Mother Bano ignores these ominous threats; she is busy cleaning the cow's tail, tearing off strips from her white cotton dupatta, dousing them into kerosene oil, fashioning them into bandages and then applying them to the above-mentioned tail. Then she lets the youthful calf suckle its mother for longer than he is used to, and the cow closes her eyes while standing, her pain fading and ebbing away like the ghastly night. My esteemed father looks at his machete which is not red-hot now and decides it's too rusty to cut anything. He orders me to go out and find a sharpening stone. I try to plead with his humanity, he counter-pleads with his fatherly love. I go to the big canal which has only a puddle of water this time of the year and mark time with little urchins who are chasing baby fish in the water. To a cursory observer my urchins might appear half clothed but it would be because of the fact that they are using their shirts as nets to catch fish. One gives me his half-torn shirt; I catch a yellow one with protruding green eyes and let her slip out of my hands. Comrade father has made hollow threats in the past to inflict harm on my mother, but now that he feels shamefaced in front of his comrades, I don't know how his rage will manifest itself. I take a sandy stone, clearly not suitable for sharpening metallic objects, walk home at a leisurely pace and present him with it. His outrage is a sight to behold: foam on his mouth, proverbial smoke coming out of his ears, he stops well short of hitting me and dubs me a loyalist puppy of a bitch of a mother. He storms out of the house swearing on a deity that he neither believes in nor prostrates to, pledging to bring back a stone and sharpen his machete and show his comrades who is the leader of his own household. With esteemed father's departure the night is sad but full of calm, no crying cow, no angry mother – she doesn't even cling to the side of the bed and gives me a soothing hug. Next morning he stumbles through the doorway, in a state of inebriation probably, certainly in a state of physical disarray, bruised and bumbling, swearing again upon a deity that he doesn't believe in that he'll avenge his honour and inflict harsh punishment on my mother for shame-facing him in front of his comrade workers. Mother Bano goes through his pockets and declares that he is ever the degenerate gambler who has lost the little money he had in a place of ill repute, imbibing moonshine and playing cards. He protests that he had stood watch at the picket line at the mills and that labour struggle was entering its final phase and he'll never back down. Mother gives him a bowl full of our cow's warm and nutritious milk and expounds to him that from tomorrow little Bano will go with him to the mills, strike or no strike. 'I have failed in my endeavours to make you a good man. Now it's little Bano's turn to strive for the same.'

I am happy that I don't have to attend school in pursuit of my education, because school has already turned into a place of fallacious promise. My dreams of district championship are in peril because my PT master and mentor and I don't see eye to eye on my breathing technique while running. I'll be happy to be in the company of men who proclaim to be fighting a final battle royale for the rights of the workers.

NINE

Welcome to the Family

THE GUARDS OUTSIDE THE COMMANDING OFFICER'S house are expecting Captain Gul. He accepts four salutes before he is escorted into a corner of the tennis-court-sized drawing room. Swords and trophies displayed in a big glass case at one end, a life-size portrait of the commanding officer in the middle, touched-up pink cheeks and a chest full of shiny medals and ribbons. The real CO lacks the pink hues and serenity of his portrait, has a paunch suitable to his rank and a certain nervousness really unsuitable to his status. Captain Gul salutes. In return he gets a big hug and is asked to sit on the same sofa, their knees almost touching. A waiter in a white safari suit appears, hovers for a bit as if expecting orders and then disappears, shutting the doors behind him.

How are you liking our city? he is asked.

Captain Gul can't say that he has been here less than a week and the only thing he has properly seen is CO's daughter. 'It seems very promising. A bit quiet but promising.' CO stares ahead and Captain Gul realizes that he has made him sit beside him because he doesn't want to look him in the eye. Captain Gul feels a surge of power. When a two-star general's knee is touching yours, you can suck some of the power from it.

'May Allah forgive me for saying this but, young man, don't you think Arabs living in Jahiliyya had at least one great idea before the arrival of Islam?'

It sounds vaguely blasphemous to Captain Gul but then you don't move up in the world by questioning a two-star general's faith. He nods and mutters something about great poetry and trade routes, not forgetting to add that, given how things were at the time, they weren't so bad.

'No, boy.' CO has no interest in pre-Islamic poetry or the Bedouin road-taxation regime. 'They used to bury their newborn girls. Islam put an end to this horrible custom.'

Captain Gul had assumed this was going to be a Welcome to the Home of Braves and let-me-know-if you-need-a-bootlegger type conversation. He is not expecting a discussion about filicide in ancient times. 'Yes, sir, Islam was a very modern religion. That's why we call the pre-Islamic period Jahiliyya.' Captain Gul is relieved that he paid attention in his Islamic history class.

CO looks sideways at him, studies his face. 'But now I feel that maybe burying them at birth or at least burying some of them was the right solution, probably the only bloody solution.'

Captain Gul is not sure if he should respond to this provocation. He stays silent and nods. CO gets up, Captain Gul tries to stand up but finds a hand on his shoulder pressing him down into the sofa. CO begins to pace, four steps in each direction. Nervous but purposeful walk. 'When I found out, my first reaction was to take out my service revolver, one bullet to her head, one to mine and be done with it.' Captain Gul hopes CO has mistaken him for someone else – maybe his staff mixed up his meeting schedule. 'But then I told myself she is carrying my blood. And now yours.'

Captain Gul gets up in confusion, brings his heels together. 'Sir, but I got—' Life has prepared Captain Gul for many things but it hasn't prepared Captain Gul for the full-handed slap that stings him in the face. The trophies and swords are a silvery blur in his vision.

'Don't sir me, you little piece of shit. Sit down and listen to me and listen with your ears and not your spy ass.'

Captain Gul has been hit before but not since he became an officer. Suddenly he is the four-year-old being slapped by an older brother, a seventeen-year-old trainee on whom senior cadets are betting to see if he can take fifty-one slaps without crying.

'She is my only daughter and I wouldn't have thought of marrying her off in such circumstances. But what's got to be done has got to be done.'

Captain Gul realizes that he is being served a marriage proposal with the proposal part missing. Before he can come up with a cover story, he gets a bear hug and hears the cursed words: 'Welcome to the family'. When a two-star general wipes a single tear from his eye, you know your life is about to become a shit show. He had escaped from Pindi, a lucky break. He could have strung the mother of his alleged child along for a bit, had thought of arranging an abortion at a safe house, but how could he even begin to have that kind of conversation here in this drawing room, with its walls covered with swords and paintings of polo players. He had not yet managed to get rid of the child from the Pindi girl and now an OK baby was on its way from CO's daughter. He still doesn't know her name. A part of him might have felt proud at his top-class fertility rate but the rest of him feels disoriented. He feels like his own spermatozoon, sad and lonely, racing against his other spermatozoa.

CO's voice sounds distant. Gul registers phrases like your parents should have been here, that they were middle-class people, civilians but God-fearing people, the kind of people who were the moral centre of the nation. Both teachers, your background check says. I am looking forward to meeting them.

Captain Gul doesn't want to tell him that both his parents were terrors in neatly pressed clothes, perennially disappointed in his academic underachievement. Captain Gul had been a solid third division in high school, barely scraping through his exams and never even aspiring to the first position in his class that his parents always wanted for him. There was something about books that made a young Gul sad.

'Sir, since I joined the forces, my battalion is my father and my unit is my mother.'

'I have seen your file. You were a real shooter – what did they call you when you were posted here in Armoured Corps, a piston?' CO punches him in the gut, playful now but it still hurts. Captain Gul again doesn't anticipate this coming. Another picture of CO on the wall, slimmer, younger, in a tracksuit, raising a gloved hand, a medal around his neck. Gul himself has stayed away from the ring and gyms, preferring wildlife documentaries and *Reader's Digest* articles about intelligence failures and code crackers of the Second World War. He thought he was going to make a career in the ultimate battle that is waged for hearts and minds.

'I am honoured, of course.' Captain Gul puts his hand on his heart, hoping to ward off another punch. He knows that he needs to speak and he needs to speak fast before his fate as a new family member is sealed.

He is preparing to give a little speech to raise some doubts about whether he can spawn a baby within a day after a brief, furtive encounter, to suggest they see a doctor and discuss a pregnancy test, and of course tell them he is on a top-secret mission to thwart the hanged man's return, to stop his jiyalas from setting themselves on fire. While he is still trying to get his story right, the double doors open and the girl whose name starts with S walks in pushing a tray trolley laden with fine snacks and with a mysterious smile on her face, threatening a lifetime together with happy, healthy children.

TEN

The Widow Maker

BAGHI WRAPS THE REVOLVER IN A KITCHEN TOWEL and tells Sabiha that he'll be back after handing the gun to Molly. He wonders if guns are allowed in the mosque. If Allah tells us what to do in the marital bed and in the toilet and what verse to recite before getting on and off a camel, does He say anything about bringing unlicensed guns into His house? Molly has two guards who accompany him when he travels to address rallies, mainly to keep him away from his zealous followers who want to kiss his hands. His guards usually stay at the mosque door – he has this bizarre faith that whosoever wants to harm him wouldn't do it in the mosque. Molly obviously hasn't read Islamic history. Or newspapers, God bless him.

There is a small queue outside the Noor Nabi Advocate & Palmist Associates, people probably wondering why the day has ended and their promised destiny has still not arrived to give them a warm embrace.

Baghi goes down the stairs and finds Molly in a huddle with two worshippers outside his house. He sees Baghi approaching, raises his voice. 'May Allah forgive him, my brother knows too many words but has too little faith.' The worshippers are haggling over dates for a speech Molly is going to give. Molly has double-booked himself and is very generously offering to return the advance fees but they have already made the announcement and they aren't backing off. The word honour is repeated several times, and appeals are made to Molly's ego – 'There isn't a single speaker like you, not just in this district but in the entire province' and 'We can't even think of replacing you with any other maulvi. People will wait, people can wait.'

'But I will not arrive before midnight. You know these people they won't let me go without feeding me. I won't be able to arrive before midnight.'

In the end they decide to change the time of the speech. There are double handshakes, hugs, they promise to have an excellent gathering and depart.

Baghi hands the towel-wrapped gun to Molly without saying anything. Molly looks at him with complaining eyes as if Baghi is trying to lead him away from the righteous path by handing him worldly goods. 'This is hers. Your guest's,' Baghi says, expecting answers.

Molly removes the towel, looks at the pistol and says: 'What am I going to do with this?' Then he shouts for one of his guards, a portly middle-aged man, a serving policeman who moonlights as a private guard. He hands the pistol to him. 'Here, keep this,' Molly says. 'You have been asking for one.' The part-time guard grins and marches off. Molly gives Baghi a look which says I have solved your problem just like I solved all previous problems, what do you want now? Baghi keeps staring at him, waiting for an explanation. 'Those who have Quran in their chests, they don't need guns,' Molly says. 'We live in the House of Allah, the giver and taker of lives, why do we need a gun?'

'Your friend is carrying it, and her husband is dead.' Baghi chews the words friend and husband in order to underline his disapproval.

Molly puts his hand in his pocket and takes out a miniature copy of the Quran, smaller than his palm. He grins and launches into a speech about Allah's love scale. 'If Allah loves you a little, He gives you a big house, a beautiful wife, healthy children. When He loves you a little more, He gives you a name, some fame, you walk out and people bow their heads in respect, but when Allah is completely in love with you, He gives you this.' He taps his temple with his forefinger. 'And that's what Allah has given you, intellect.'

Baghi knows that when someone is praising you with a set of lies it shouldn't feel good but it still does. 'You are always very generous with your words,' says Baghi. 'But is dead Hakim's second wife hiding in my academy?'

Molly shifts into his man-of-the-world mode but doesn't forget to bring God to the party. He extends his hand holding the miniature Quran. 'I want you to swear upon this that what I tell you will stay in your heart.'

Baghi has seen him do this a lot lately. He has set up his own little court. Traders with loan disputes come to him and he settles them over his pocket Quran. Sometimes cheating husbands come and swear on the holy book to mend their ways. Wayward sons, drug addicts or lovers are brought here to put their hand on the Quran and made to promise and are forgiven one last time. Baghi has done no such thing. What is he being asked to denounce?

Baghi puts his hand on the miniature Quran. He respects books, even the holy ones, but sometimes it's better to put the book away and get on with life.

Molly puts the Quran back in his pocket and puts his arms around Baghi. His beard brushes against his shoulder. 'The fire at the Iron Syrup & Other Herbs,' he says. 'There are no accidents in Allah's world. Her husband set himself on fire. One of those. He wanted them to do it together. But she is a very pious lady and she came to me to ask what Islam says about it. She listened to me and left her house. We need to keep an eye on her. You need to keep an eye on her. Do you know why Allah made women weaker? Allah made them weak to test us, test if we men can be strong enough to protect them and protect ourselves from them. For once, put your politics aside and save a life. If you save one life, Allah will reward you as if you have saved all of humanity. And you have already promised that you won't say a word to anyone. The police probably want to record her statement. Can you talk to your friends in the police and ask them to stay away from her, or at least respect the sanctity of the mosque?'

'I don't have friends in the police. Only a former student. And I don't ask for favours.' What Baghi really wants to ask Molly is how does he plan to save humanity? By fornicating with her in his academy? 'What happened between you two when I went to the bazaar?'

Molly looks at him at him as if he has accused him of attempted rape. 'She attacked me. But I forgave her. You know she is upset. Let's not forget that she is a widow. And do you know what special place our deen has for widows? On Judgement Day, we'll be asked about the women in our lives. We'll be asked what we did for our mothers, our wives, our sisters, but more than anything else we'll be asked about that one time when a widow turned up for help at our door, what did we do for her?'

Baghi is not sure if Molly is quoting the holy book or his personal on-the-move theology. She attacked Molly? Her own saviour?

'I'm not sure she is convinced. She still wants to self-immolate. Her parents were die-hard jiyalas. Remember Comrade Abid Ali Abid? Satlaj Cotton Mills union leader?

His picture with Chairman Bhutto? She was there at the protest when they picked up her mother. She is still traumatized. She has conviction but of the wrong kind,' Molly whispers.

'And will you let her follow in Hakim's footsteps?' Baghi asks.

'I have told her that Islam doesn't allow it. At least for forty days. Because she is in mandatory mourning for her husband. And you might not like it but she believes in Allah and the Day of Judgement. She was one of the first women to turn up when I opened up the mosque to women.'

'She is just a girl who grew up too fast. What happens after her mourning is over?'

Molly looks towards the sky, redirecting Baghi's question to the heavens. 'My wife is waiting. She has made aloo gosht and she won't let the children eat before me.' When a man of God gets scared of the world his God has created, he goes and hides behind his wife.

Baghi decides to leave him to it. 'Students come back as soon as things return to normal. And you know very well I am not allowed to associate with any political types. We can't have some famous jiyala's daughter in the academy.'

Molly nods without showing any signs of understanding the urgency of the situation. 'Remember what Allah says about our responsibility towards a widow,' he reminds Baghi before leaving.

Baghi nods. It does seem like one of Allah's ingenious plans: first make them widows then treat them well and go to paradise.

Molly goes to his wife and Baghi goes into the world to look for food for the hungry widow.

HOMEWORK 4

Our Strike

It can be surmised with reasonable certainty after a cursory glance at the sprawling strike camp outside the Satlaj Cotton Mills that esteemed father Comrade Abid Ali Abid is not the superior labour leader he assumes himself to be. When we enter the cabal of men who are sitting under the red-lettered banners espousing Asia Is Red, and Labour to the Mill, Mill to the Labourers, nobody gets up to greet him. There are three men huddled over a newspaper endeavouring to read the news and simultaneously debate why their strike is not in the news. An octogenarian man with flowing silver locks is walking around with a giant copper kettle selling green tea in doll-house-size cups. Another group of comrades is playing a game of draughts using seashells as pawns. There are others huddled around them, urging each other to bet and giving tactical advice to the players.

Esteemed father is ignored by everyone when he is desirous to join the cabal, even by those sprawled on their shawls on the ground and staring at the sky. A very small group of men is listening to a speech by a man who claims to have descended from the Himalayas to join the struggle. 'I have brought a cure from Nanga Parbat to make your hard labours harder.' I fail to comprehend the salacious nature of his speech's content and can't fathom why men giggle at his utterings. 'Your revolution will last till the cocks start to crow in the morning.'

On a raised platform, Comrade Sadiq Ali Sadiq is perched against a satin pillow under his own portrait with a rose garland around his neck and both fists raised in the air. He beckons esteemed father towards his perch and says in jest that here comes esteemed Comrade Abid Ali, thrown out of home by his wandering beauty, now himself wandering with his little beauty. Esteemed father also laughs gingerly at this jest and asks Comrade Sadiq Ali for a loan of five rupees. Comrade Sadiq Ali wonders aloud why a man fortuitous enough to have a daughter so beauteous would have to borrow money. Esteemed father laughs demurely. Comrade Sadiq Ali produces a note of five rupees denomination and says to father yes, a comrade from her school calls her little princess, also full-speed runner. My face is red with a mixture of humiliation and shame. Esteemed father notices my embarrassment or maybe the five rupees note in his pocket gives him his tongue back because before strutting off to bet on the draughts game he says: Comrade Sadiq, when we strive for a classless society, we also strive for a genderless society. I have raised my daughter as a son, as a prince, but as a prince of the proletariat.

When esteemed father goes to join the huddle around the draughts game, I slink away, cross the picket line, which is only a railing made of bamboos, to the mill's giant iron gate and walk into what is indisputably dubbed as the largest cotton mill in Hindustan Pakistan.

Ergo, the first hall in the mill is so cavernous that I have to bend my neck fully backward to look at the ceiling. Celestial light filters out of the glass slits in it, criss-crossing somewhere in the middle and fading before it reaches the hall's floor. In the middle is a spinner so large that my head spins looking at it. I cross the turbines and spinners and come across humungous piles of yarn, some frayed at the edges, moth food in the making.

A drum of indigo dye lies sideways, its rich liquid seeping out and making a luminous puddle on the floor. I look up and my shadow stretches along the wall of the hall. Then I see another shadow, larger than mine, creeping up and I hear the unmistakable voice of Comrade Sadiq Ali echoing in the cavernous hall, making it difficult to understand what he is uttering, but I can make out the word princess. By now I realize the libidinous undertones in his echoing voice. I slide into a side hall, smaller but full of humungous rolls of thread. I slip through a sliding door and start running. I may not be the district champion yet but I can run faster than any comrade any time of the day.

ELEVEN

Coffins in the Cornfield

ASSISTANT SUB-INSPECTOR A.D. MALANG DOESN'T like to give city tours. He had joined the Rebel English Academy to pass the police entrance exam and he had joined the police force to serve this city, to catch habitual thieves and cage sick-minded killers and root out the perverts who slit their sisters' throats and then take the same knives to their privates. He hadn't signed up to be a tour guide. But during his three years of service he has learnt that when you get a call from the head of Field Intelligence Unit, you stand up and salute and follow orders. Sometimes they have strange requests. One called at 2 a.m. and asked for fourteen Pepsi and three Mirinda bottles, a bucket of ice and then as an afterthought two dozen paans. Another one had a *Spy Who Loved Me* sticker on his official vehicle and kept demanding to be introduced to a saint who had been dead for more than two hundred years. You can argue with your police boss and try to show them the other side of the picture, or a better way of handling a case. With your superintendent's permission you can take a prisoner out of custody at dawn, ask them to run, shoot them in the back and close the case. But with Field Intelligence, you leave whatever you are doing, get into their car and hope to return with a bit of your self-respect intact.

When Captain Gul arrives to pick up A.D. Malang for their field trip, he is in the middle of an interrogation. Before leaving, with a cane, he strikes in quick succession the soles of the under-interrogation prisoner. The prisoner is an old-fashioned thief who takes more pride in never confessing than his actual thievery. 'Where are you going?' the suspected thief smirks after him. 'Your thief is still here.'

A.D. Malang struts out of the police station, tightening his belt, removing his beret so that he doesn't have to salute Captain Gul. A.D. Malang believes in minor, procedural rebellions.

'Come on, let's go. I can't wait to get to the crime scene. Show me what your people are made of. Someone wrote a poem about this city, who was it?'

A.D. Malang likes to underplay his city – it's better to bore outsiders. 'We have lots of poets, sir, but I haven't come across anyone who has written a poem about the city. I don't think the name of our city rhymes with any nice words. Basically it's just a big vegetable market. It's the biggest in the region but still a vegetable market. Who can write poetry about potatoes and corn?'

Captain Gul is the kind of official who doesn't listen to your answer when he asks you a question. He listens to the rhythms of your speech, your accent, whether there is fear in your voice or an urge to impress or a burning desire to confess. 'A.D., then? Let me guess, Allah Ditta?'

A.D. Malang nods. It's not a good idea to remind military officers that they are repeating themselves. A.D. himself is never sure if he shortened his name to fit onto the official nameplate on his chest or with the hope of moving up in life by losing his rustic peasant's name, Allah Ditta. His parents had given him the name because he was conceived seventeen years after their marriage and they believed he was a gift from Allah and not a result of their persistent nightly efforts.

On the narrow road that leads out of the city, they are stuck behind an overloaded donkey cart. Someone has moved their entire household stuff onto the cart and now the donkey, foaming at the mouth, is trying hard to keep his hooves on the road. He moves one step forward then stops, then moves his neck around trying to find some relief from the strangling pull of the loaded cart.

'This is the beauty of this country. One day you are the firstborn of a village potter, he names you after Allah, and then you become the big policeman in your own city and change your name to A.D. It all makes sense. And then you have to hear people complain that this country isn't moving forward,' Captain Gul says. 'I have colleagues, bright military commanders, whose fathers were landless peasants, and you say that this country doesn't give you opportunities. I tell you we can quick march into the future, only if someone will clear this bloody road, do something about these donkey carts standing between us and our crime scenes.'

Now that Captain Gul has thrown A.D. Malang's humble background at him, he can rest easy and just get on with the job, which at this point involves watching a donkey's struggle with his load. The donkey has given up trying to stay grounded and is airborne now, his hooves flailing in the air, the donkey-cart man jumping to get his whip onto the donkey's back as if it isn't the cart load that has lifted the donkey off the ground but the donkey's stubborn temperament. The household items from the cart are beginning to slip: a pair of red gas cylinders roll down, a plastic chair comes rattling down with a set of stainless-steel pots. Captain Gul observes with satisfaction as A.D. grabs the donkey-cart owner's whip, gives him two tight lashes and lowers the donkey down to the road. A.D. orders the donkey to be relieved, his orders are obeyed, and the donkey stands on the roadside panting, licking his chops and showing absolutely no gratitude towards the city police.

They drive past the boarded-up Satlaj Cotton Mills, a tattered red banner proclaiming Mill to the Workers still fluttering on an adjacent electric pole. They drive through a series of garbage dumps with smoke rising out of them, an abandoned ice factory and a series of chicken sheds. An oil-fired rice sheller is making music with its diesel engine in a cleared-up field. The road becomes narrower. They stop at the canal bridge to give way to a herd of lazy buffaloes. The canal is dried up and half-clothed children are trying to catch fish in the little puddles on the canal bed, using their shirts as nets.

They enter fields of ripe corn, dull gold shining in the sunlight and giving off heat. As they approach the village where the crime scene is, a pack of dogs, led by a little yelper, surrounds their car, first threatening them, then escorting them towards the village. A little boy runs towards the car, catapult in hand, targeting the pack of dogs who ignore his hunter's zeal.

The crime scene is a clearing in the middle of the cornfields. There are a few neem trees, so green they appear black, the earth covered in their yellow bitter fruit.

An old man comes forward, his white clothes covered in dust. He is tying and untying a turban on his head, before giving up and joining his hands together as if apologizing to the state officials in advance for what he is about to say. A clutch of villagers appear behind him, looking at the man with folded hands then at Captain Gul's pressed jeans and tucked-in white polo shirt and Malang's starched uniform and gleaming wooden rod. The old man breaks into sobs.

Captain Gul is experienced at consoling crying women. He knows it's a phase that can last from three to thirty-five minutes, but you need to let them complete their cycle, pat their backs, give them a consoling hug even if you are the one who has caused that flood of tears. He moves forward and puts his arm around the old man's shoulder, who at first recoils, then hugs him, holds his hand and starts walking towards the burnt-out shell of the tube-well engine room. Behind the tube well the victims are laid out on eight charpoys, the eighth one the size of a baby cot. They are all covered in white cotton shrouds. Captain Gul has his first glimmer of suspicion. How did they organize eight sparkling white shrouds when the bazaars are shut? He doesn't say anything.

The old man goes to a charpoy and is about to lift the shroud when A.D. Malang shouts at him. 'Stop this drama. Come here and tell us what happened. Captain sahib can smell lies so be careful about what you say. I know your tribe, the killer usually cries the most.'

'What can I say, I wasn't here,' says the old man through his sobs and then goes on to narrate what had happened. 'They brought a drum full of kerosene. They beat them up until they got tired of beating them, then they locked them up in the tube-well shed. My cousins were crying. They were screaming. Then they threw the kerosene all over the shed, cut some maize and covered the shed with it. Dry corn is like gun powder. But they didn't set it on fire immediately. They stood around smoking, listening to their screams, shouting filthy things about their mother, who was also locked up in the shed.'

Captain Gul listens impatiently. And then asks: 'Who were they?'

'Enemies. Enemies. They threw so much kerosene that there were fumes everywhere. Even my dog went crazy.'

He points to a fat bulldog, all drool and yellow teeth. The dog doesn't seem crazy at all.

Captain Gul doesn't have time for these morbidities. 'Were they Bhutto types? Jiyalas? Did they shout "Bhutto Lives"?' Captain Gul asks and watches the man's face for any tell-tale signs of lying.

'Bhutto?' the old man says as if he has heard the name for the first time in his life. 'The one they hanged? No, they were our blood enemies.'

Captain Gul zones out as the old man goes on about a granduncle eloping with his younger brother's wife and seven children, and those seven children growing up to avenge their mother, and the mother's brothers just being released from prison, and something about the horrible smell of burning corn and kerosene and how lucky were the ones who were not in the village that night. Allah was most merciful that the fire didn't spread to the cornfields because what is a dried-up cornfield? Had the cornfield caught fire, there would be no village for the highly respectable officers of the law to visit. The drooling bulldog raises his paw, tries to scratch his fat neck and fails.

Captain Gul makes a gesture to A.D. Malang to wind up this farce and get into the car. He is humbled. This brief visit has brought him face to face with the ground reality of the nation. 'You were right. If these people were protesting, why would they lock themselves up in a tube-well shed in a no-name village and set themselves on fire?' Then looking around he says, 'These simple peasants. They probably wouldn't recognize Bhutto if he came out of these cornfields.'

A.D. Malang knows that you must never appear to be smug in these circumstances, not when you are with an intelligence officer in a ripe cornfield. Malang had seen an opportunity here: use the intelligence man's preconceived notions against him. Who wants to investigate eight murders when you can put them down as Bhutto burners and close the case? He had prepared the ground and knows that their visit is not over. He is waiting for the slogans. Any time now, any time... Malang continues, 'But you were right to take the field trip because—' Before he can complete the sentence he hears a noise, looks back, sees the raised fists of the villagers and hears that godforsaken slogan: Jiye Bhutto. The not-crazy bulldog yawns as if he has heard it too many times and it doesn't do anything for him now.

As they slowly drive out of the village, Captain Gul fixes A.D. Malang with a stare. 'Next time take me before they burn themselves.'

A.D. Malang spots the bulldog in the back-view mirror following them lazily, as if to make sure they don't return. 'There is this photographer, sir, Shahid is his name, quite popular, very political, true jiyala. I might be wrong but my informers tell me he has been planning something.'

TWELVE

That Burning Boy Ran Too Fast

ONE WEEK AFTER THE HANGING, PEOPLE HAVE started to trickle out. Milk shops and bakeries are half shuttered but open and people are scoring bread and eggs like moonshine. The armed guards at Royal Fancy Jewellers have put their guns aside and their legs up and wait to be relieved by the night guards. There is a small crowd outside the Alchemist Pharmacy. There are rumours that, besides selling prescription drugs without prescriptions, the pharmacy sells a variety of flavoured ethanols and horse painkillers cut in halves, spreading joy in a city starved of joy.

There are only a couple of customers at Allah Maalik Restaurant and Hotel, pouring their hot tea into saucers and slurping. It's too early for dinner. Here people have their dinner late as the last act before they pass out. In fact, it seems a plate of bread and lentils is a sleep drug for those who can't afford Alchemist Pharmacy: eat, burp and pass out. Sweet dreams.

The lentils and meat come in a plastic shopping bag, with two flatbreads wrapped in a newspaper. Baghi plans to skip dinner. Men after a certain age don't need dinner. They can just feed on their own ulcers and fear of death and pass out. Baghi thinks he needs to stand vigil tonight anyway. He has a stranger under his roof, a stranger who arrived with a gun, whose husband has killed himself, and although Molly says she wants to kill herself for the same cause, Baghi has his doubts. Baghi has seen militant revolutionaries. She is only a dreamer. He has seen women who attack physically – his sister was one of those. But Sabiha doesn't seem like the type. Unhinged with grief over her parents probably. Part of Bhutto's personality cult, star-crossed socialism. Or someone who just likes to run, an escape artist.

Sleep is a luxury that Baghi can't afford.

The shutters are down on Hussaini Stylish Hair Salon but the usual crowd is sitting on the benches outside, five heads bent over the day's newspaper. One of them yells at him. 'Professor, how is the English business?' That's Hussaini's idea of a joke about Baghi's vocation.

He stops. 'Obviously not as good as the hair-styling business,' Baghi says. 'But I am getting by. God is kind.'

The barber points to the newspaper he has been reading. 'Our media is sold out. Not a single mention of our Hakim's brave protest.'

'They don't cover local news,' Baghi says. 'It's a national newspaper. There are enough disasters in the world to fill their pages.'

But Hussaini is in no mood to let go. 'It's a suicide protest. A suicide by the greatest herbalist of our times, the world-famous inventor of Iron Syrup, to protest the so-called hanging of the world's most famous prime minister. I think the family paid them not to run the news. They probably paid your friends in the police to stay quiet about Hakim's protest. Funeral prayer in absentia for Chairman Bhutto but no mention of his jiyala setting himself on fire. By the way, I didn't see you at the funeral prayer.' Hussaini frowns and raises his voice. 'Oh, why am I asking you? You don't believe in God. I wonder if Maulvi will say your funeral prayers when you die. Your friend in police has been going around telling everyone that it was an electrical fire at Iron Syrup & Other Herbs and not a protest suicide.'

'Not friend,' Baghi says. 'Student. Former student. I do not make friends with my students.'

'You have read so many books, tell us, did they really pull Sir Bhutto out of prison just before the hanging? Was it Arafat or Qaddafi? Has to be Arafat – Qaddafi looks like an old aunt. But then old aunts are full of tricks.'

Baghi shrugs. 'Stop dreaming about Arabs coming to your leader's rescue. He was hanged and buried while you were waiting here for foreign commandos to scale the jail wall and take him away.' This barber should look into his own soul. He has three wives and has made burger-cuts fashionable in the city and he thinks Baghi is spreading western influences.

'Do you teach them English or do you teach them how to become butchers in police uniform?'

There's no point talking to the barber. Nobody ever wins an argument with him. 'Send your boys to the academy next month. A little education never harmed anyone.' Baghi starts walking away, ignoring the barber's attempts to engage him in a debate about the education levels in the subcontinent before the British arrived. Baghi has heard the argument often enough.

'We had people who were literate. They wrote poetry, they built palaces, they cured the sick, they knew how to preserve water and make eighty varieties of biryani, and then the British came and asked: do you know how to speak English?' The barber goes on. 'And we said, no English, and goras said, hey, you are all uneducated. And now they are gone and you are doing their work.' There's a point in there. But only one point. There are lots of other points about history that Hussaini of Hussaini Stylish Salon ignores.

The barber rushes up to him and whispers furiously. 'You live in the House of Allah and teach children that there is no God. Does Maulvi sahib know that you are turning the house of God into a brothel?'

Baghi stops, turns in fury, still thinking of a retort, when he sees a ball of flames rushing down the road. He realizes that it's not a man but a boy who is on fire. Clothes ablaze, he is running towards them, making no attempt to put out the fire. He is running, running, flailing his arms, shouting, 'I saw I saw.' The crowd at the barbershop stands up, but nobody makes an effort to stop him, to douse his fire, to tackle him, to stop his run. It's only when he disappears down a side street that a piercing scream is heard followed by a garbled slogan where you can't make out if he is saying he wishes Bhutto another life or a second death.

Two policemen come running now, panting, stopping to curse the people at the barbershop for not helping the law enforcers, then run again and disappear into the street where the burning boy had vanished. Sub-Inspector A.D. Malang follows leisurely, the commotion in the street, the burning boy who had rushed through here, not seeming to bother him. 'That boy ran too fast.' He points to the street. 'First, he cut his sister's throat, then his own penis, what did he want now? Did he want to bring Bhutto back or his dead sister? Maybe we could have saved him with your help and asked him, but not your fault, he just ran too fast for us.' A.D. Malang is smug with the street justice he has just dished out. A sick sister-fucker dispatched to hell and he can put it down as one more deranged jiyala on his quest to bring Bhutto back.

A.D. Malang notices Baghi and salutes him like he always does. It's done with the kind of decorum he would show the district police chief.

For Baghi, it's a secret joy to see his students do well in life. What teacher hasn't felt that joy? But Baghi is not sure a visit by a policeman is what he needs at this time, even if the policeman happens to be a former student, sharp of mind but given to bouts of deviousness, a perfect combination for a successful policeman anywhere in the world. It was only three years ago that Malang was rote learning one hundred and fifty English words that are used in the law enforcement vocabulary to pass his test, and already there is a slew of habeas corpus petitions against him.

People curse Baghi for creating the perfect monster. Sometimes people come to him for help, to ask if he can have a word with Malang, people in trouble, people with eloped daughters or sons caught in robberies gone wrong. Baghi always refuses. Even when they plead with him to ask his former student to keep his touch light, which is usually a plea to Malang to not pass their loved one onto his subordinates as a midnight snack or not to take them out of the police cell at fajr prayers and ask them to run. Baghi doesn't interfere in the matters of the state even if the state is being run by a boy policeman who was educated by him. And now he is here saluting him, while Baghi is carrying meat and lentils for a fugitive hiding in his academy, a fugitive who has either set her husband on fire or is determined to become a martyr like her husband. A.D. Malang takes the bag from Baghi's hand and says, 'Let's go to the academy and let me serve you food with my own hands. After all, I am what I am because of you.'

HOMEWORK 5

Our Hobby

There is a common fallacy amongst burgeoning athletes, propagated by misguided PT teachers, that while running they must inhale air through nose and exhale air through mouth. It can be granted that these breathing rules hold good in superior-quality stadia with man-made grass and perfectly drawn white circles. The road that leads from the mills back to our village is a track made of dust and potholes; you breathe from where you can and deploy nimble sidesteps to avoid attaining a twisted ankle. Going home at this time would provoke Mother Bano's ire for not sticking with esteemed father, ergo I head to the village graveyard but adjacent to this final abode of our citizenry is a field where my friendly urchins are playing a helter-skelter game of football. Their delight is manifest at my approach because they know I run the fastest and hit the ball hardest. It's my singular privilege that I don't have to choose a team – I just switch sides when a side is losing and an urchin shouts Bano please come to our side.

In the heat of the game I do something that is not expected of me. I take the ball and instead of charging towards the makeshift goalpost, made of stones and urchins' shirts, I kick it skywards. The ball lands somewhere in the graveyard. All the urchins know that only I am entitled to go and retrieve the ball. Although it's a final resting place for hundreds of villagers, there is one grave that has many fables surrounding it. It's a humungous grave, the size of a small mountain, and it's dubbed as the eternal abode of nine martyrs. Village folklore expounds that in prehistoric times these nine men battled a rampaging giant and although they were all slayed by the giant, one by one, they fought so bravely that the giant decreed that they be buried together so they can exchange the tales of their gallant battle for eternity. It's up to the historians to debate the authenticity of this wild tale but while looking for the ball I make my mandatory stop at a puny grave, a little mound of red earth without a headstone, a few shrivelled marigold flowers splattered over it. My junior brother who adorned this world for only eight days is buried here. Mother Bano oftentimes gets teary and reminisces about his luminous eyes, gurgling personality and warm drool, furthermore about his weak heart which took him away from us at an early age. Oftentimes I speculate that if he didn't have a weak heart and lived longer than eight days assigned to him by fate, we could have played football together. Since I am a lonesome sibling I prefer to run and refuse to be part of any team sport.

Urchins wait patiently for me to retrieve the football because they know that I am in the habit of lingering over my junior brother's final resting place, and they have the good manners not to mention it to me. When I hear their excited noise-making, I think maybe they are getting restless and impatient to resume their game of football, but then I hear a whirring sound from the skies. There is a helicopter flying above our heads and it's coming downwards at a perilous speed. The urchins are waving and screaming at the big metal bird. In a village where a motorized vehicle is the type of novelty that excites stray dogs and urchins alike, the arrival of a flying helicopter is an event of historic proportions. I follow the urchins as they run after the helicopter, flailing their spindly arms. The helicopter is coming down further in the fields. Heavens only know who is about to grace this humble village with their presence.

THIRTEEN

The Fire This Time

THE SOLE PROPRIETOR OF SHAHID'S FRIENDLY ART Photo Studio, Comrade Shahid had made up his mind to record his protest the day after the hanging but he was taking his time. People would say that it was Baghi who corrupted his young, innocent artist's mind but Baghi had nothing to do with his planned protest. Shahid did see the image of a burning man in a magazine he found in the academy. Baghi may have given him the magazine, may even have opened the page with the picture of the burning man, when Comrade Shahid came to him crying after the hanging, but in no way did Baghi suggest go kill yourself if you are so hurt. Baghi had given up politics; he was only trying to spawn a sense of an international brotherhood of the suffering.

Now, Comrade Shahid was waiting for the perfect light to do what he had decided to do. It was not going to be an ordinary suicide, no broken heart here or personal grief or what-does-life-mean-anyway kind of suicide. It was going to be a protest, the ultimate protest, so it was only natural that he wanted to get his timing right for maximum impact. He had heard rumours and, being a rational man, he didn't believe the rumours that his leader wasn't really hanged but locked up in a dungeon and would soon resurface triumphant to lead a second and final revolution. He had refused to raise the Bhutto Lives slogan going around the city. He was going to show the world that the only way of keeping Bhutto's mission alive was to turn your own death into a work of art, dedicated to the peasants who were promised the produce of their own labours and mill workers who would grab the mill owners by the throat for fair wages.

His job as a jiyala was to protest but as an artist he needed to get the light right.

The magazine that Baghi had given him carried a picture of a man from a country called Guatemala, a priest who had set himself on fire to protest the price of bread. Flames leapt from his body, as if God himself fixed him with a stare and set him ablaze, and now with his arms spread he was looking towards the sky and saying, look, God, I am coming back to you, bringing back your fire.

The only problem was that, being Baghi's former student, Shahid was a godless man and only believed in class struggle and the power of his Pentax camera. From doing wedding photography and birthday portraits he had become a people's photographer, voluntarily taking pictures of protests, strikes, children with bloated bellies and bare feet, a rural woman walking for eight miles to fetch drinking water. One of his ongoing photography projects was the afterlife of a homeless Baloch saint, a forty-year-old man who looked seventy, chunk of hashish in his hand, the other hand clutching his chest, sleeping on the footpath and shrinking slowly, till one day he disappeared and only a tattered rag was left behind which would be buried with great ceremony and a mid-size prefabricated mausoleum would be erected on it and it would become a centre for small commerce, hope for women who couldn't conceive and a place of solace for after-work drug users. Shahid didn't consider it his best work but he had found fame as the man who photographed Chairman

Bhutto when he paid a surprise visit to OK town, an iconic image, Bhutto standing in the potato fields, hugging a labour leader, Comrade Abid Ali Abid, and raising his fist. The photo had featured in national newspapers and then was used by Bhutto's party in his election campaign posters.

In another life Shahid would have liked to be a wildlife photographer but Baghi had reminded him that he lived in a city. OK town was the biggest city he had ever lived in and Comrade Shahid had come to believe that the real jungle was the one that exists inside a man.

It was one of those artistic ironies of life that he himself wouldn't be able to document his final heroic act. He would rely on one of his two disciples, one of them good at photography, the other at understanding his politics. Shahid had decided to wear white. That would accentuate the palette of yellow and blue flames. He had rehearsed with his apprentice, teaching him to keep his hand steady, to not get overwhelmed by the drama of the moment, capturing the full shot with flames engulfing his entire body but also not forgetting to take a close-up of his face, to capture his face not in agony when he was ablaze but just before, when he raised his last slogan, when he punched the air with his fist and when he finally fell, a shot or two of his melting flesh but not for public release. He was still not sure what to do with the onlookers. They could enhance the composition, scrambling and trying to douse the fire, maybe one of them catching fire himself? But then other people would distract from the central image, from his last message of freedom by fire, his last slogan echoing through OK town, through the country, through history: Jiye Bhutto.

For now, Shahid was thinking of organizing a human chain around himself in order to keep away the police, who were sure to try and disrupt, to try to save his life, to foil his heroic protest and then later paint it as an act of a little-known looney, a frustrated artist in a little-known town.

He had chosen the time of his protest. After Jumma prayers when the sun began to dip, the light would catch him soft in the face and even his rookie assistant would not be able to botch up this historic moment. The sun would be hanging over the minaret of the Gol Mosque, filtering through the afternoon dust, giving him a soft orange glow, his favourite colour. He could see his face on the poster on university hostel walls, murals painted on tall buildings, an image passed around amongst young men and women long after he was gone, a slogan etched around his face: where is your fire?

His comrades had tried to dissuade him. Setting oneself on fire was definitely a powerful symbol. Which newspaper could resist publishing the photo of a local legend on fire? But it would be painful for families to see it, it might scare little children. They suggested a hunger strike. A hunger strike until death. His starving body in the middle of the city, in front of the Gol Mosque, if photographed at regular intervals with him losing weight, his face shrinking, would send a powerful message. It was also suggested that he tie himself to an electric pole or climb the mosque's minaret and then demand to be allowed to address the city on the mosque's public address system. Shahid had heard all these suggestions patiently but, in his artist's mind, nothing came close to the image of flames leaping up to engulf his face, framing the purity of his purpose. He did briefly consider one suggestion. Somebody had come up with the slightly bizarre but original idea that instead of staging his protest here he should travel to Lahore, buy a ticket to the zoo and then throw himself in the lion's cage. The cage, the lion, the lion's jaws around his neck were indeed potentially powerful images to expose the tyranny of the dictator who had hanged his leader. But you couldn't guarantee that the lion would do what it was expected to do. Many years ago, he had photographed the lion in the zoo and he had spent hours waiting for a good shot. The lion had refused to move post lunch, taking a siesta by raising his hind legs in the air and shamelessly exposing his genitals to families visiting the zoo.

Shahid had another look at the photos surrounding him, his life's work, his art, little girls in princess dresses, little boys dressed in bow ties, couples on the day of their marriage gazing into each other's eyes. He reminded himself to dispose of his library of VHS tapes. Some of those made on special request might bring a bad name to his cause. He needed to go through them one by one. He also needed to give the negatives of the pictures to their rightful owners. With every passing day his list of things to do before he set himself on fire was getting longer. This kind of behaviour, Baghi would say, was called purposeful procrastination, to not do something actively. Now he was thinking what to do with his pet poodle and part-time model Mao, who had starred in many photos with children who wanted puppies as a birthday present but their parents wouldn't let them. For a few more rupees children could pose with Mao in their lap for their birthday portraits.

But time doesn't wait for anyone. And the state doesn't wait for you to make up your mind. As Shahid is sorting out the business of his Friendly Art Photo Studio, Field Intelligence Unit's white Toyota Corolla is hurtling towards his studio, a song blaring on the car stereo. The state is coming to help Shahid make up his mind about how to live or die.

Captain Gul likes that 'Chiquitita' song, although he doesn't know who Chiquitita is or what he wants from life, but when the one comes on where those crazy Swedes ask does your mother know, Captain Gul dials up the volume. He had got the intel from Assistant Sub-Inspector A.D. Malang on their way back from the village burnings but he had decided not to bring the inspector along. Instead his aide Subedar Laal Khan sits up alert in the back seat and cradles a jerrycan in his lap. Captain Gul wants to be face to face with a true jiyala and catch him before he sets himself on fire and drags OK town's name into the headlines again. Captain Gul also realizes that photographers can't be trusted with their cameras. He still remembers the nincompoop photographer who botched up his hanging-night assignment. He sings along to Abba: *Does your mother know, does your mother know*, is it him. Is it him...?

FOURTEEN

I Am What I Am Because…

'SIR, I AM YOUR HUMBLE SERVANT, ALWAYS AT YOUR service, but you never allow me to serve you.'

Baghi forces a smile and slows down his walk. 'I do hope I never need your services. I am a law-abiding citizen, the only one there is in this city.' Baghi is desperately hoping to get rid of A.D. Malang before they reach the academy. The place is currently occupied by a fugitive and Baghi will never be able to explain the presence of a woman at his academy.

A.D. Malang's portly sidekick who had failed to catch the burning boy scrambles after them, trying to whisper something in his ear, but Malang ignores him. 'There is no greater joy than to serve your guru.' He turns around and tells his assistant, 'Today whatever I am, I am because of my teacher. I would never have passed the police entrance exam without his guidance and dedication.'

Baghi is dragging his feet, his mind scrambling to come up with a last-minute excuse, any excuse to keep them out of his academy. But Malang carries a mixture of cravenness and authority that is disarming. Baghi can't tell if he is here to pay his respects to an old teacher or to raid his abode. For the police exam, Baghi had taught him how to spell Competent Authority. Now he has become one.

As they approach the door, Baghi stalls. Should he faint, pretend to lose his key? Malang stands aside, waiting for him to open the door and let him in.

The police are not new for Baghi. Baghi has dealt with the police. The police have dealt with him. He spent so much time with them that some of them became closet comrades.

But Baghi was a rebel then with a grudge and revolver, not a tutor peddling English lessons that helped people to move up in life and join the ranks of their tormentors.

Baghi opens the door, trying to stop his hands from shaking, his mind now racing to find explanations for Sabiha Bano's presence in the academy. Also thinking of secret signals that he could send her to make her say that she is a long-lost cousin. He thinks he should probably warn Malang that he has a visitor.

But you can't do that when the door is already open, you are already inside, and there is no guest in sight. Maybe she is hiding in the kitchen, the bathroom. Wise girl. Maybe he can get rid of this police party quickly without being found out. His eyes scan the bookshelf which she had commandeered for her clothes and little pouches – all gone. Has she left? What should have been a relief brings with it a new panic: where did she go, how did she leave, what was he going to tell Molly? He had one opportunity to take care of a widow and book himself a place in paradise and he had lost it.

Malang orders his constable to take the food to the kitchen and decant it onto a plate. He looks around. Baghi's eyes follow his. Sabiha's dupatta, white and yellow embroidered nargis flowers on white cotton, is lying on a pile of books on the floor. Malang sighs like an old man returning to his village after half a century of exile. 'Such fond memories. Even now when I think of those days I get tears in my eyes.' He had graduated only three years ago and had visited almost every month. 'I am what I am all because of you.'

'Your life has just begun, young man,' Baghi says, indulging his streak of self-glorification. 'With some hard work you'll go far.'

A smile breaks out under Malang's lush, black, neatly trimmed moustache. 'But still imagine, janab, just imagine. A potter's son becomes a police officer, tops his course and gets posted here, in the place where you made it all possible.' The constable puts a plate of meat and lentils between them and unrolls the newspaper with rotis. The newspaper is all black with a full-page red tear and screaming headline: He Lives?

'Please go ahead,' Baghi says. 'I am not hungry yet.'

Malang shakes his head. 'How can I dare to eat before my ustad? It's my duty to serve you. Even if I were to serve you till my dying day, I would still not be able to pay you back. Imagine my father the potter losing his livelihood when people started using steel pans. Now look at me.' He points to the two stainless-steel stars on his shoulder.

'Eat,' Baghi says, trying to muster up his teacherly authority.

Malang refuses. 'How can I, a humble student, eat in front of his teacher? Please, you start.'

And suddenly Baghi feels that this humble request is an order he needs to obey if he needs to get rid of him. He breaks a piece of roti, dips it into the meat and lentils and takes it to Malang's mouth. Malang, taken aback, opens his mouth and takes it in. Then he sucks his moustache. 'Such an honour, sir, such an honour.' After they have wiped the plate clean, he gets up, brings Baghi a glass of water and offers it with a bow. And while Baghi is still sitting on the floor he stands above him. 'Sir, if you don't mind, may I ask you a work-related question?'

Baghi looks up and shrugs. 'Work?' The boy who used to talk without verbs is all purpose now.

'Sir, you taught us that life is continuous education, that a man is always learning. I am learning, sir. I want to continue to learn.'

Baghi has never said any such thing. He is known for condensing life's education into a six-month basic English course that actually frees you up from other education. And here's his star student, a potter's son who, on the strength of one hundred and fifty words, badly punctuated but correctly spelt, has become a feared police officer and is now using his cheap and cheerful education to interrogate his own teacher.

'You were at the Iron Syrup & Other Herbs the day it burnt down?'

'And?'

'And you told everybody it's no accident?'

'I said no such thing. People there were saying it.'

'So it's just a rumour? You heard anything else?'

From the corner of his eye Baghi can still see the dupatta, covering his books as if trying to shield his life's learning from this former student who has come to interrogate him.

'I was thinking maybe you knew something. And I could learn from you and pay my respects. I am sorry for taking this liberty. Also, remember once I brought the Iron Syrup for you and you spat it out after one sip. I remember because I learnt the word "foul" that day. Before that I used to think foul is what happens in football or hockey. I was wondering why you went to a shop where they sell foul syrup. But then people change, as you used to say. That's the beauty of life. There's this new military intelligence officer in the city. He is going around looking for Bhutto burners. And he has been mentioning the mosque a lot. He seems to think you started those Bhutto Lives rumours here and I told him how can Sir

Baghi support Bhutto – at least look at your own files. He is going to raid your friend Shahid's studio. I tried to tell him that he is an artist and this city needs artists more than ever but do these military men listen? Sir, imagine military and intelligence, what a joke. They don't even remember you challenged Bhutto when he was the boss of them all. But they are the bosses now. Maybe I should have a word with Molly sahib.'

Malang starts to leave and then turns towards the pile of books on the floor, runs his finger along them, as if deciding which one to choose, picks up the dupatta with a flourish, sniffs it and says, 'Female students?' And doesn't wait for an answer. 'I thought you stopped teaching girl students a long time ago.'

Baghi is caught off guard. 'I give the occasional tuition,' he says. 'Need to feed myself.'

'Sure, sir, sure. It's a good idea. Educated girls, they are our future.' Malang flings the dupatta back on the floor. Baghi notices that Sabiha's homework sheets are piled neatly on the floor too. 'If only they didn't leave their dupattas lying around carelessly like this.'

This, Baghi tells himself, this is what you have done, created a monster by teaching operative verbs of English.

HOMEWORK 6

A VIP Comes to Our Village

It's a commonly ignored certitude that when an event of historic nature unfolds people have no idea that they are witnessing a historic event. Those who boarded Noah's ark could not envision that their survival will lead to a world so populous that we'll need famines and wars to redress the balance. Those who witnessed Jesus of Nazareth on the cross could not have thought in their wildest dreams that one day the world will be full of crosses of many dimensions and people will sing songs of redemption around them. It's only retrospectively that people come to the conclusion that it was indeed a momentous occasion. When I follow the urchins who are running after the descending helicopter, we can't even imagine in our happiest dreams that the prime minister of the country and undisputed leader of the Ummah, Chairman Bhutto, is about to alight from the above-mentioned helicopter and churn the wheel of our family fortunes forever.

The police jeeps have trampled through the potato fields and made a cordon around the patch of evergreen where the helicopter is to land. Village folks rushing towards the helicopter are scared and delighted by the gusts of wind propelled by the propellers on the helicopter that greet them as well as repel them. A photographer has placed himself strategically to immortalize the moment on his camera film for posterity. He seems to be the only one determined to make it a historical moment.

A sizeable crowd has gathered by the time helicopter blades begin to slow down. A man hoisting a green and red flag, adorned with the image of a sword, the flag of the party of the man about to alight from the helicopter, is running, and as he comes into clear focus, I recognize him to be none other than my esteemed father. He appears to be shouting something but his voice appears and disappears because of the phenomenal but fading ruckus of the helicopter's propeller blades. The man who manifests himself out of the helicopter, nay, jumps out of the helicopter, is a familiar face indeed, adorning thousands of posters and banners we have imbibed with our adoring eyes all our life. He looks puny in real life, his face and bald head look bigger. He waves to the crowd, bends down and pulls out a potato plant, the crowd goes into a frenzy, he waves the potato plant, its leaves so lush as if it has sucked the nether of the earth, its fruit ready to travel the world. Bhutto waves the plant like a flag at the crowd. Esteemed father with his real flag comes running and crashes into the cordon, a burly police officer of medium but solid build restrains him, esteemed father pushes against the police officer with the ferocity of a wild beast. The Jiye Bhutto scream that comes out of his demure body stuns the crowd and catches the attention of potato-waving Bhutto, now bending in to but not listening to one of the army officers besides him. Bhutto shouts in his squeaky but authoritative voice and says don't come between me and my people to a police officer. The crowd goes into raptures of applause as esteemed father rushes to meet him, comes to a halt a few paces away and bends down to touch his feet as a gesture of adoration, but Bhutto in his own magnanimous gesture reaches down, grabs both his arms and gives him a hug. The crowd is stunned into silence then embarks on a rally of slogans, declaring Bhutto the pride of Asia, a brother of the peasants, a friend of the industrial workers, a sweet brother to poor sisters, a son of revolutionary mothers, a naked sword against the oppressors of working classes and a flower of the desert. My urchins raise their fists without understanding what is being rejoiced. As the crowd chants its litany of epithets, esteemed father is whispering something into Bhutto's ear who is nodding enthusiastically as if he has landed in these forlorn fields only to hear what esteemed father has to say. Bhutto waves to the crowd, signalling them to quiet down. Then he takes esteemed father's hand and raises his arm like referees do with the winning wrestler. Then he makes a short speech squeezing father's hand and hugging him and declares to the world that our labour leader Comrade Abid Ali Abid, this son of the soil, this worker of the mills, is my true brother. The mill that he works in belongs to all the labourers he represents. Labour to the Mills, Mill to the Labourers. Comrade Abid Ali Abid is Zulfikar Ali Bhutto. Zulfikar Ali Bhutto is Comrade Abid Ali Abid.

By the time Comrade Sadiq Ali Sadiq and his cabal of other union workers arrive at the scene with their welcoming garlands and banners, the helicopter has just taken off, it is still hovering over the potato fields, and the crowd have picked up esteemed father on their shoulders and are shouting Bhutto's friend is our friend. A visibly crestfallen Comrade Sadiq Ali Sadiq puts the garland that he had brought for Bhutto around father's neck and kisses his hand. The fortunes of the Satlaj Cotton Mills Labour Union are going to go through a seismic shift but not in the manner esteemed father and his new best friend Chairman Bhutto envisaged.

FIFTEEN

I Just Want to Go Home

THE FIRST MISSION THAT CAPTAIN GUL ASSIGNS himself is to save the life of a local artist and track down the protagonist of a smutty video, a mission that will spark his last carnal obsession and first true love and threaten to further derail his fledgling career.

You can't become a successful intelligence officer by merely carrying out the mission you are assigned to. You need to embed yourself in the treacherous civilian world that surrounds you and then work your way outwards.

As Field Intelligence Unit's white Corolla arrives at Shahid's Friendly Art Photo Studio, driven by Captain Gul, Laal Khan sits in the back seat, sulking at not having been briefed about where they were going and why. Captain Gul made a stop at a petrol pump and asked him to buy a gallon of Super. Captain Gul didn't offer to pay. Laal cursed the petrol-pump attendant when he asked for money, then gave him a twenty-rupee note and left as the attendant counted the change.

Climbing two steps at a time, Gul rushes up the narrow stairs that lead to Shahid's Friendly Art Photo Studio, giving a cursory glance to local legends immortalized by Shahid's Pentax, amongst them a young Baghi with a French beard holding up a poster, Asia Is Red, and Chairman Bhutto hugging a nameless mill worker. He finds Shahid staring at a strip of negatives with a magnifying glass. Captain Gul doesn't feel the need to introduce himself. He believes that if you have to tell someone your name and rank you have already lost some of your power. 'So are you the man who wants to kill himself, good sir?' To Captain Gul he doesn't seem like a man in a hurry to meet his maker. Shahid puts the strip of negatives aside and tries to speak but can't get a word in. 'Are you going to bring a bad name to your own good city? Front-page photo: OK town artist kills himself, or would you prefer "sets himself on fire in a blaze of glory"? Let's say that you go ahead and do it and it's painful, as you know it will be, but what if you are not able to get yourself photographed? Maybe your camera doesn't work? Yes, sir, I have some experience of working with professional photographers, and trust me, sometimes even the best of them can't get the results we want. Or let's say everything works but the newspaper editor decides that the picture is either not of good quality or is against editorial policy. Family paper, children shouldn't be exposed to images of burning men first thing in the morning. What will your protest amount to then? Will you still go ahead with your protest if the government decides to ban cameras that day?'

'I am a citizen, sir. It's my right,' Shahid mumbles, still recovering from this ambush. 'And who are you to come here and tell me what I can and can't do with my own body?'

'I am a fellow fucking citizen. I have rights too.' Captain Gul snatches the strip of negatives from Shahid's hand and flings it on the floor. 'I have duties too. It's my duty to protect the lives of citizens. Even useless lives like yours.'

'The government can tell me how to live but the government can't tell me how to die.' Shahid claws back at his confidence, a determined but methodical martyr.

'Fair point. I love artists myself. They speak the truth,' Captain Gul says. 'By all means, go ahead and just do it. Let me help you. You get your camera. I have got Super.'

By now Laal Khan has assessed the situation. In this moment he has also become a devotee of his new boss. He has worked with some very clever, some very cruel bosses but he has never seen such emotional intelligence in his officer. Obviously his new boss is an artist when it comes to instilling the fear of God in a civilian's heart. He didn't even need to mention any of Shahid's family members. Laal doesn't need instructions. He splashes Shahid with petrol from his jerry-can, carefully, as if he is watering a sapling. Shahid scrambles to protect a stack of negatives and prints from his table.

'Now tell me.' Captain Gul pulls up a chair and sits at a safe distance.

The weather is May warm but Shahid is soaked in high-grade petrol and shivering.

His pet poodle, Mao, so furry it's difficult to tell his face from his bottom, dashes towards him, sniffs him then yelps at him, runs back and hides behind the iconic portrait of Chairman Bhutto, in which he is hugging the local labour leader Comrade Abid Ali Abid. Shahid shivers some more.

'Turn the fan off,' Captain Gul tells his lackey. 'Why do you want to make a great artist uncomfortable?

'Have you contemplated any final wishes?' Captain Gul asks. 'People usually ask for a last cigarette but given your current situation that would be highly irresponsible of me.'

Shahid feels deflated. The red-haired man is flicking a matchbox from his left to right hand. Shahid signals towards the door. 'Maybe let me go home.'

'Out into the world? In this condition? You want your audience? Give me the names of your collaborators and I might think about letting you go home.'

'I am my only collaborator. I just want to go home and change out of these clothes,' says Shahid, now shivering uncontrollably.

'It's not a very original idea. What happened to originality in art? You are not the first one to burn for Bhutto. Who else is there? Come out with the names.'

'Those others were misguided. They were protesting to save Bhutto's life. Now that he is a martyr I was planning to mourn his death. Can I go home now?'

Captain Gul shakes his head as if Shahid is missing his point. 'Let's see. I let you out and fifteen, fifty, a hundred people come out to see you, a burning man. Maybe you have changed your mind by now, but a man in your condition could burn easily. You'll agree that it's plain and simple violence. They will be terrified. Do you think this will inspire anyone? That man is dead.' Captain Gul points towards the Bhutto portrait.

Mao is scratching the floor with his paws, whining, yelping with his mouth closed like those kids who get scared of dogs at the last moment and don't want to be photographed with Mao.

'Call Malang and ask him to take this hero away. I need him alive. Ask him to get a doctor to evaluate his mental health. This city is going crazy. Everyone keeps waiting for a dead man. Those who can't wait want to go and meet him. We need to take care of him before he sets himself on fire, before he sets this country on fire.'

Mao manages a single full-throated bark from behind Bhutto's portrait.

'Do you mind if I borrow some videos?' Captain Gul points to the stacks of VHS tapes. 'I mean no disrespect to this city but there is not much entertainment around here.'

'These are people's private videos, marriages and birthdays, a funeral or two.' Shahid is trying to sound professional, reasonably certain that the state has spared him for now.

'I appreciate your concern for privacy but the government is your family. Extended family. Maybe a bad family. The kind of family where cousins fuck each other and the father wants to beat up the mother but it's still a family. Can we really hide anything from our family? Should we really be hiding something from our family? It has now become my duty to have a look.'

Gul starts going through the VHS tapes, then he probes behind the front row – he knows that's where they hide the good stuff in video stores – and comes up with a stack and dumps them on the floor. 'Let him go.' Captain Gul changes his mind. Now that he has instilled the fear of God in Shahid, he can be Gul's informer. He'll lead him to other jiyalas. And if he wants to burn then Captain Gul will pick the time and the place. 'He has an artistic temperament. He is an asset to the city. This city needs artists. And if he wants to kill himself, I guess that is art too.'

SIXTEEN

This World Made of Muscular Verbs

BAGHI PICKS UP THE WHITE DUPATTA, SMELLS IT, fading smells of mustard oil and motia, marriage and murder.

It reminds him of his first wife. The first fumble. His dear departed father's attempt to make him into a man. She was eighteen and yet more experienced than he was at nineteen. After three days of singing and dancing, when they were finally locked up in their bridal bedroom she told him not to hurry. She was murmuring something about them having a lifetime ahead and how they should learn to love each other slowly. She tried to kiss him on the mouth but he squirmed and she found his cheek. She took his face in her hands and put her ruby-red lips on his lips. He trembled and came in his groom's silk shalwar, she didn't notice. She tried to kiss him again. That kiss felt like an assault. She took him to bed and made him lie down, she tried to spoon him. It felt like arrest warrants. He pushed her away with some force. She turned him around and said, 'What? Do you not like me? I was asked to marry you. Weren't you too? We can make it work if you want.' He started to cry. She held his sobbing, jerking body and asked him if he loved somebody else. He said yes, he loved someone. He made up a secret lover. He gave her the name of a girl from his study circle who had only ever loved Engels. 'Lucky girl,' she said and turned around and pretended to sleep. She went back to her parents the next day. Over breakfast Baghi's father didn't touch his tea or rusk and asked him what happened.

Baghi said what kind of question was that.

His father repeated, 'What happened?'

Baghi kept quiet as if he had gambled away all his inheritance and now wanted another father.

'I didn't like her,' Baghi said finally. 'I don't like girls.'

'I know,' Father said. 'I should have got you a simple girl. Like your mother. Education makes girls unhappy. They never know what they want.'

'I'll marry when I am ready.'

'A man is never ready.'

Baghi stared into the space above his father's head.

'Tell me, what am I going to tell her parents? They are old friends.'

His sense of honour perturbed Baghi. His concern for her parents drove him mad. His raised eyebrows and hands waving in the air drove Baghi mad. 'Where is Molly?' he wanted to shout. 'Why is he not here? Why did you shut the door on him?' Instead he kept looking down and whispered, 'Tell them that your son is a gaandu.' He was hoping that his father would call him back when he got up and walked towards the door. He didn't. That was the moment his rebel career began.

Baghi would see his father twelve years later when a telex arrived summoning him back home with the news that he was dead. Baghi turned up ready to shoulder his father's coffin, but he wasn't gone yet, rationing his remaining breaths, still there, looking at him, waiting for an answer, pleading, tell me you were lying to me. Tell me you are not what they say you are. Just say that you did not like that girl. Say she was too fat for you, or too fast. Baghi had sat at his feet, refusing to look up at his face, and touched his father's feet only after he had stopped breathing.

He is folding her dupatta carefully when he realizes the absurdity of his actions. He throws it on the chair and stares at the door. Where was that woman who came and left him with this incriminating evidence? Emptiness fills him, fills this room made of words, this world being run by muscular verbs and still empty. When he can't think of something he usually picks up the thesaurus and tries to learn a new word or a new meaning of an old word. On page 567 is 'redemption'… to be forgiven. People find solace in holy scriptures, in travel books or slow-cooked food, in plastic flower pots, or in seeing their picture in the inner pages of a magazine, in a girl not slapping them, or a boy not kneeing them in the groin, or brushing their teeth twice a day. or knowing more than three languages, or saying I love photography, or travel is my passion, or I am not that political, or I am all for immigrants, in Russian novels, in their poetically named pet dogs, or in remembering their time outside the delivery room, or their holidays in the hills, or the time they met Munir Niazi, or when the jailer says you have a visitor, or when the roti turns out round, or when that tune finally comes out of the harmonium. Baghi has nothing against small pleasures and the thesaurus is almost a masturbatory aide. As he is finishing reading all the synonyms of the word 'redemption' there's a knock on the door.

He is getting too many visitors. 'Who is there?' he shouts but there is no answer. Again there is that knock, sharp and clear. And there she is. The girl who almost had him arrested.

The girl who'll definitely have him arrested. He steps aside and she walks in, plonking her bag on the floor.

'You called the police on me? Are you that type of Baghi? Ratting on your own comrades? I know you revolutionary rats. Comrades like you made my father their leader and then sold him to the police. You promised me protection then tried to sell me to the police?'

Comrades were always accusing him of selling out the revolution. When did she become his comrade?

'Where did you go?'

He doesn't ask her how she knows when to leave and when to come back.

He definitely doesn't ask her why she came back.

'What did they ask you about me? What did you tell them?'

'Answer me. Where did you go? How did you know they were coming?'

'Concerned about your academy? For once think about things other than your glorious life.'

He stays quiet and thinks about his life.

'They knocked and called your name, "Assistant Sub-Inspector here to pay my respects, I am what I am, and you are the best teacher anyone ever had…" What was I supposed to do? Sit here and let them break the door? When they went away, I packed and left. And now you are looking at me and thinking why I came back. Because I have nowhere to go. I saw them leave and they looked happy. What did you tell them? What did they ask about me?'

He takes a deep breath. 'Please, sit down, please. Have some water.'

She waves her hand in the air.

'He is my student and he came to say salam. I'm not proud of him but he is my student, no denying that. I prepared him for the police entrance exam.'

She is trying to decide if she wants to believe him or spit in his face. She takes the latter option. 'My life is full of sweet coincidences. I am running from a man and he comes to the exact same place I am hiding? Has the world really become so small?'

She is running away from A.D. Malang? And carrying a pistol. Has he just averted a shootout?

'Why are you running away from him? What have you done?'

'Everybody runs. You know what Malang does? He tells his prisoners that they are free to go then shoots them in the back and then says I shot him because he was trying to escape. If you are innocent, you run faster.'

'I never interfere in police matters but if there is anything maybe I can clarify the misunderstanding?'

'Everybody's done something. You taught him everything. Did you teach him to tell prisoners to run and then shoot them in the back? He is famous for that, your student.'

Baghi doesn't want to remind her that he had only taught him the essentials of a language. 'He really was here to say salam but he did mention your husband's suicide. He seems to have doubts.'

'I only ran away from a house on fire. Why did he ask you? Are you his informer?'

Tell him something bad about his past and Baghi will laugh, accuse him of being a loser and he'll laugh with you, call him a fallen revolutionary and he'll agree enthusiastically, but call him a bad teacher and you have made an enemy for life. Tell him that he is a police informer and he'll go get that gun back from Molly's bodyguard and shoot you, and not in the knee this time.

'I am not responsible for people who shut their herb store, say goodbye to everyone and then set themselves on fire at night when their families are asleep in the next room. I am not responsible for government servants shooting people in the back. I am definitely not responsible for people who are carrying guns and running away, leaving behind a dead husband and telling me they haven't done anything.'

She smiles and nods as if this was the answer she wanted. 'You have never done anything, have you? Sir, have you?'

Baghi knows that Malang can make crimes disappear. He has never asked Malang for anything. He won't say no to him. He doesn't tell Sabiha Bano about this plan to save her. He has just conjured up his own redemption. It gives him the confidence of a saviour.

'Where did you go?'

'I went to Noor Nabi but she says she doesn't tell fortunes on Thursdays,' Sabiha says, stretching out her right palm then caressing it with her other hand's fingers.

'You went to that fraud? She is not even a lawyer let alone a palmist.' Noor Nabi is a lawyer, of course. She wears a black coat although she bought her law degree instead of attending classes. Small-time fixer for small-time judges and criminals, takes money with one hand, passes it on with the other hand. While doing this she came across a book about palmistry called *Your Future in Your Hands.* And now she isn't just a lawyer who never loses a case, a rent collector for Molly, but also a practising fortune teller. Noor Nabi doesn't like Baghi because there is no rent to collect from him but she is always courteous, calls him professor sahib. Baghi has always tried to stay out of her way. She had offered to read his palm and he had asked her, 'Do you know what's going to happen to you tomorrow?'

'What will be, will be,' she had shrugged. Baghi had said good for you if you can make a living telling people that.

'Your neighbour doesn't like you but she knows a lot about you.'

'What does she know about me? You went to show her your palm and she told you about me? She just says what you want to hear. Did she tell you about your future? Did she say you have leadership qualities and once when you were a child you were very ill? Because that's what happened to everyone and that's what she tells everyone.'

'She doesn't tell fortunes on Thursdays.' Sabiha Bano smiles a mischievous, almost murderous smile.

'So what does she know about me?' says Baghi.

'She says you and Maulvi are brothers. Why did Maulvi never tell me? I should have known.'

HOMEWORK 7

Our New Best Friend

From time immemorial men have endeavoured to entice women with the promise of sweets. They have historic and unshakeable faith that if a woman accepts a gift of sweetmeats from them, she is accepting their whole persona, even the parts that are most undesirable, persona that everyone knows is non grata.

When Comrade Sadiq Ali Sadiq arrives with the box of sweets, like the conniving, cunning man that he is, he makes his entrance at a time when esteemed father is not home. Like his evil intentions, he has camouflaged the box of sweets well, in a stack of posters made from the famous photograph where esteemed father and his excellency Chairman Bhutto are hugging each other like long-lost brothers. The photographer has done well to balance the picture: although they are in an embrace of the equals, it shows Bhutto as a benevolent father, stroking esteemed father's head as if consoling a troubled child.

Mother Bano tells Comrade Sadiq Ali Sadiq to sit on the sole chair in our little front room, but instead of abiding by mother's request, he opens the box of sweets and extends a ladoo towards mother, and when she extends her own hand to accept it, he takes it to her mouth and she takes a little bite. And they both cackle as if the cosmos has cracked a funny one that only these two can understand. He endeavours to put another ladoo in my mouth, but I turn my face, extend my hand, take it and put it aside without taking a bite.

Mother Bano tells him that esteemed father is not home. Comrade Sadiq Ali is praising mother sky high for making her esteemed husband Comrade Abid Ali Abid a leader of the people. 'All the union's demands have been met, overtime, paid leave, bonus, profit share.' Comrade Sadiq Ali gesticulates. 'He is sitting with the mill owners, in the director's office. He is a big man now and all credit goes to you.' Mother Bano demurs and protests that only Allah can bestow such honours, as only He can bestow opprobrium.

Comrade Sadiq Ali offers his services, anything that I can do around the house. Mother Bano is first visibly surprised. Around the house? Are you offering to sweep the house, wash our dirty clothes? Comrade Sadiq Ali reiterates, anything that Comrade Abid used to do – now that he is busy serving the proletariat, the least I can do is to serve the lady who made him what he has become today. Mother Bano giggles at this proverbial attempt at flattery and his unusual offer and utters that she doesn't trust men with household chores. 'And I'm definitely not allowing you anywhere near our cow.' Then they both giggle. I cringe with embarrassment at this uncalled for bonhomie.

Comrade Sadiq Ali starts putting posters on the wall. Suddenly our front room is full of images of esteemed father at the most glorious moment of his life, but at the same time there is no esteemed father in the house. Like it has been happening since time immemorial, a great man has been replaced with his image.

SEVENTEEN

Wedding Night

CAPTAIN GUL MIGHT HAVE MISUNDERSTOOD SOMEthing about his new station but he was right about one thing: the evenings were long, humid and dull. Another cable from the headquarters stamped URGENT. MORE REPORTS OF B LIVES FROM OK TOWN. ARE YOU OK? Another call from his pregnant girl in Pindi wanting to discuss the décor for their baby's room. There is also a red-ribboned box of sweets from his commanding officer and aspiring father-in-law. Captain Gul gives the box to Subedar Laal Khan without opening it. Captain Gul needs a distraction. Tonight is tombola night at the officers' mess but he has no interest in winning fifty rupees from fellow officers' wives. There is an invitation for a mujra for the deputy mayor's son's wedding. He has no interest in men double his age fixating over badly made-up girls, lip-syncing to vulgar songs. He decides to hunker down and acquaint himself with local culture by sampling the video stash that he has hauled from Shahid Friendly Art Photo Studio.

He pours himself half a glass of Murree gin, takes a sip, reprimands himself, pours some water and immediately feels better. He slips in a VHS and watches for a few minutes with amusement, the quivering lips of a very young bride, shots of an adequate buffet, biryani and mutton qorma and five types of creamy salads and desserts. He inserts another video titled *Animal Planet*, watches red-assed monkeys jumping from one tree to another with an English man speaking in a godlike voice. As the man is saying 'these creatures are more human than we'll ever know' the picture suddenly cuts to two hippies fornicating, in trees and under waterfalls. Gul takes a long gulp and stares in the bottom of his glass. He tells himself that there's definitely more to this photographer man than his hunger to be a martyr. He is a peddler of filth. Gul knows it's against the law and he could have him thrown in jail for a few years but it would distract him from his real mission of taming Bhutto burners and make for bad communication strategy between civilians and their defenders. In his heart he knows that he is meant for bigger things than chasing perverts in small towns.

Captain Gul inserts another video with the hand-scribbled label *Wedding Night*, expecting to see another bride and groom drowning in silk and red roses and mutton qorma but what he sees makes him put his drink aside and sit up. Although Captain Gul is early in his intelligence career, there are few things that shock him about human behaviour. Bleeding green patriots could be paedophiles, daring macho men could be wilting lilies in private, some fiery mullahs could be hopeless kitten lovers at home and some nice women from good families could be complete animals in bed, but what he sees on the screen is something new yet eerily familiar. A white cupboard in a corner, a plastic jug on the side table, a rolled-up set of blankets on the side anticipating a sudden change in weather, the fuchsia-coloured bed sheets, a girl in silhouette, sitting on the edge of the bed, giggling, lifting up her face, covering her face, then laughing again, probably drunk, probably drugged, probably in the first flush of love, probably unaware that her shirt buttons were open, most probably unaware that there was a camera in the room recording her in bad light, preserving her crazed cackle for posterity.

Captain Gul pauses the video and looks around his room carefully. The plastic water jug on his bedside table, the white Formica cupboard in the corner, the rolled-up blankets on the side, a watercolour painting of a galloping horse hanging on the wall behind and the empty edge of his bed. He sips his drink and now it tastes foul like it had on the first sip. The video has been recorded right here. He feels a mixture of anger and disgust, this sacred place, his personal love nest, has been violated. In panic, he scans the ceiling, the walls for a camera – is he being recorded too? He finds nothing suspicious. Satisfied, he feels an uncoiling desire, opposite to the desire invoked by a girl with an unbuttoned shirt. He has the urge to save the girl from what is about to happen, to button up her shirt, to cover her head with a dupatta. He decides to not watch the video. He paces the room with his glass in hand, his libido on a short leash.

He plays the video again. Just a few seconds, just to be sure, he tells himself. He is shocked at the grainy horror unfolding in front of him. The girl says NO when asked to take off her shirt then laughs some more and takes off her shirt and sticks her chest out, then sticks out her tongue like a child making fun of a grown-up doing something stupid. Then she gets up and disappears from the frame, some more out-of-frame giggles and now she falls on the bed, says NO again but then pulls down her track pants in one fluid motion and poses like a runner in their stride, as if she is in a fashion shoot. *Click click* of a camera shutter. She probably does believe that she is in a magazine shoot. Captain Gul pauses the video and paces the room again. He is terrified for a moment but can't stop himself; another gulp of his drink and the play button is pressed. A hairy man enters the frame, his face is blurred but his hairy belly can be seen clearly, she is surprised as if not expecting him to come near her. He twists her around and throws her on the bed. He gives her a forceful back rub; she lifts her head from the pillow and looks around, as if she doesn't know where she is, then seems to pass out. At 14:23, when Captain Gul believes he has seen everything, the hairy man with blurred face mounts the girl, who is limp now as if trying to dissociate herself from the act, a muffled, tired repetition of NO, NO, NO. The man with the blurred face is methodical as if ticking a checklist. Fondling her breasts, another NO; running his hands through her hair, the girl moves her head from side to side with some effort, a faint whisper of no escapes her lips and this seems to excite the man more; he starts to grunt, keeps on pumping, all the while turning his blurred face to the camera, panting. At 18:51 he turns the girl around, she is unstable on her knees, he mounts her from behind, the girl cannot take the pushing and collapses. Here she mutters something and Captain Gul has to rewind the tape to catch her words. 'Get off,' she says. This seems to irritate the man, and he turns her face towards the camera and mounts her again. There's no pain or pleasure in the girl's face, just exhaustion. She is either under the influence of a slow-acting drug or owes the man a favour, because she is neither resisting nor accepting the man's actions. She opens her eyes, then opens them some more, yawns and buries her face in the pillow. The man uses more force to elicit a response from her. He finds none. As the girl tries to pull away her mouth opens for a scream but no sound comes out and the screen goes blank.

Captain Gul feels horny and then rage at feeling horny. A righteous anger uncurls in his chest. His bed, his room. Such indignities, such filth, did our forefathers sacrifice their lives so that we could—? He stops his runaway train of a brain and asks himself what it is that he wants. He wants to save this girl, for sure. He wants to avenge her honour. He is going to find this man and hang him by his balls. He is going to find this girl. How many girls in this fucked-up town could speak English? He is going to find her. And then what? He doesn't know what he plans to do but he thinks he might be, after years of faking it, after pistoning his way through life, he might be truly, madly in love.

EIGHTEEN

Name a Boy

NAME A BOY WHO HAS NEVER BEEN CAUGHT.

Boys preparing for exams have needed distractions since exams were invented, and when it's too hot to step outside they find distractions inside their homes. Some of the worst things in life happen on summer afternoons, when crows hide in neem tree branches and stray dogs roam the street in search of shade. On one such afternoon Molly and Baghi were home by themselves. Amma and Abba were away at a distant cousin's wedding to an even more distant cousin. Aapa Bani had gone for her chemistry tuition and, like any fourteen-year-old, Molly had a perfect plan. He always did. He wheeled out a tea trolley from father's bedroom with a 16 mm projector mounted on it, one luxury father allowed himself in his hard-working and austere existence. 'We are going to watch what they watch after we go to sleep.' Molly pointed to the reel under his arm. The handwritten label on the reel said *Love Lagoon*.

Baghi was studying for his ninth-grade English exam. The ceiling fan was in full flow and made threatening noises as if it was about to fly off with the ceiling. Baghi said he didn't have time to watch anything as he had to revise his notes on *Goodbye, Mr Chips*. There was always a thirty-mark question about Mr Chips in the exams. Mr Chips was going to give

Baghi a head start in his adult life. Molly had already failed once and was confident now because he believed that you only failed once. He had that look on his face which promised fun but always got them into trouble – stealing from orange orchards, pretending to be asleep and then turning on the torchlight and looking at his collection of three cut-outs from a lingerie catalogue.

Once he challenged Baghi to compare their penises. Baghi thought it was a dirty game but Molly could get Baghi to do things by appealing to the budding hero within him. 'What kind of man is afraid of having a small one? Do you have a small one? How small is it really? This small, this small…?' He raised his middle finger and then his little finger. Baghi hadn't really discovered his penis's relationship to the rest of his body or mind. He hadn't discovered the pleasures of self-abuse. He was at that stage in life where a boy thinks the thing between his legs is a symptom of a disease, only to realize later in life that it is actually a permanent ailment. Baghi was naïve but truthful and told Molly that he was not scared of the competition, but he didn't know how to make it stand up. Molly gave him a glossy page with the picture of a plump blonde woman wearing see-through flesh-coloured knickers and matching bra with neat little round holes around her nipples. Molly said stand in a corner and imagine your penis is inside her wrinkly armpit. Concentrate.

He left the room. Baghi glanced at the picture. He was scared and excited as if he had entered a grown-up person's bathroom and seen them soaping their privates. There was movement in his shorts and within a second he was poking the plump woman in the picture with his slim and hard penis. Molly returned, dropped his trousers and stood so close to Baghi that the tips of their penises touched. Baghi trembled and withdrew and said, 'No touching, you pervert. You can take your filthy stump and poke the wall but don't come near me.' Molly laughed. Before leaving, he said, 'You are not man enough. One day when you do become a man, come back and I'll show you who's got the bigger one.'

He was a year younger than Baghi but already had the beginning of a moustache above his lip and a few hairs on his chin that in time would bloom into a glorious jet-black, very famous beard. Molly was a poor and distant uncle's only surviving son. The rest of the family had been swept away in a flash flood, along with most of their cattle. Four-year-old Molly was found clinging to the branches of an old sturdy tree by a rescue team. After a few days of fame as the miracle survivor of the freak floods, he had been accepted into the family, half-brother, half-servant. 'Come, Molly, eat with us' and 'Why didn't you bring the water jug, Molly?' Molly played both roles with gusto.

This wretched afternoon Molly took a reel out of the projector, Father's favourite medley of black and white old songs in which men ran around flower beds and sang lovesick ballads while prim heroines in floral saris gave them that look which said what are you doing running around that tree, look at me. With a roll of Scotch tape clenched between his teeth, he mounted a white tablecloth with lacy borders on the wall. He inserted *Love Lagoon* in the projector, and as he fiddled with knobs, Baghi pretended to be buried in *Goodbye, Mr Chips*, looking at the blurry screen out of the corner of his eye. 'Movies are better than books,' Molly taunted him. 'Specially the ones grown-ups watch behind closed doors. Books are fake, full of fake words,' he said as a black stallion appeared from the right side of the tablecloth screen and started to gallop. 'When you see a horse in a movie, it's a real horse. In books, even the horses are made up of words. Mr Chips is fake, his goodbye is also fake – when will his goodbye end, when will he leave?' The horse ran in slow motion, its mane swooning in the wind, then they showed a bunch of words, names of English people emerging from a very still blue lagoon, and along with the last words emerged a head from the water. Golden hair, a very slim neck, perfect red lips, glistening cheeks and a face much lovelier than those on Molly's cut-outs. Thank God, they didn't show what was between her legs. Even then Baghi was scared of that thing between a woman's legs. The camera made a circle and went to her backside. 'She is probably my age,' said Molly, his voice full of longing. 'I could fuck her right now.'

'Shut up and let me watch.' Baghi cut him short. 'There has to be a story in it – if you keep talking, I'll miss the story.' Baghi pressed *Goodbye, Mr Chips* on his crotch; Molly's hand disappeared in his trousers. The horse stopped by the lagoon and did a little horse dance. The girl walked to it, kissed the horse's neck, patted it with both her hands and then, in one graceful leap, mounted it. The horse had no reins – how was she going to ride without reins? It was Molly's turn to ask Baghi to shut up and not spoil his viewing pleasure.

It was a miracle that she was able to ride the horse bareback, her hands holding on to the mane. As the horse gathered speed, she leaned forward and put her arms around the horse's neck as if giving him a hug. Then the picture froze. Molly cursed aloud, went to the projector, fiddled with it, slapped it on the side. A length of broken celluloid strip oozed out of it. The girl on the horse refused to move, still bent over the horse's neck. Molly pulled at the strip, took it very close to his eyes, spat on the hem of his shirt and rubbed it on it. He tried to insert the strip back in the projector – the screen flickered. Molly closed his eyes and said a prayer over the strip in his hand and then, worried that he was about to lose even this still image, decided to let it be. 'Why don't we ride our own horse?' he said, staring at the ceiling. Baghi had no idea what he was proposing. He went back to his book, the ache in his crotch spreading to his thighs, his buttocks.

Molly stood up, drew the curtains, picked up a large round satin-covered pillow that Abba used for his bad back, put it between his thighs and started riding it shamelessly, mirroring the girl stuck on the tablecloth. The light was dim. Mr Chips was being visited by a former student. Baghi closed his eyes and moved to the other side of the pillow. In Baghi's head the horse was still galloping, its mane flying, the girl's hair flying, her arms around the horse's neck. Baghi could never remember at what point he started riding that pillow horse from the other side. He could hear Molly's heavy breathing. He didn't make any noise but Molly was making guttural sounds as if urging the horse to run faster.

They didn't know when the door opened; they didn't know why Aapa Bani, maths genius and parents' pet, came back early from her tuition; they didn't know what exactly she saw when she entered the room. She couldn't have missed the frozen image of a naked girl on a horse. Baghi didn't know then that Molly had his penis out; he was sure that his own trousers were on. They were just two boys, separated by a fat pillow, humping that fat pillow. What she saw were two monsters doing unspeakably filthy things. 'Dirty things,' she reported, after she stopped shouting and throwing her shoes at the tablecloth as if she had seen a cockroach. Molly had bolted, not forgetting to pick up his trousers. Baghi stood there covering his erection with *Mr Chips*, his back to the girl on the horse. Aapa Bani threw her other shoe and then her book bag at him. Baghi tried to say something in his defence, something like 'I had just dozed off while reading, it's so hot in here' or something like 'It was only Molly doing dirty things and it's not what you think it is', when she flung her last weapon at him, a Sanyo scientific calculator.

They were separated for the night. Baghi was confined to the room he shared with Molly. Molly was asked to take his bedding from the room and sleep in the veranda on the floor. Late in the night, Baghi heard the sound of nails scratching on his door. He heard Molly whispering his name, 'Saleem, Saleem, I am scared.' Baghi pulled a pillow over his head and pretended to sleep.

Baghi suspected that Aapa Bani reported to his parents that they were fucking. She probably also told their parents that they were watching a dirty movie in which a girl was fucking a horse. Baghi could never understand how a pious girl, who scoffed at her friends who read Mills & Boons, could have a mind so filthy. The charge sheet was never presented to them. They weren't asked about the pillow between them and the girl on the horse on the tablecloth screen.

Baghi could never imagine Aapa using words like fucking and penis – he couldn't even imagine her using these words with the electrical engineer she was married off to. He tried not to but he could imagine her saying that she had found them naked, doing filthy things to each other while watching a film in which a girl was doing dirty things with a horse. Baghi was also certain that the material evidence against them was never examined, or her accusations would have fallen apart. It was only a girl riding a horse, OK she was naked, but white people sometimes do normal things in the nude. She looked too innocent to do something dirty. Even the horse seemed noble. It didn't even occur to him to ask if the film was so filthy what was it doing in his father's bedroom cupboard.

Aapa was so traumatized that she failed her exams and never went to college – even her genius in maths dissipated.

She was married off to an electrical engineer who took her to Kuwait where she would have four children with three-year gaps. She would become plump and grumpy and what people call an excellent homemaker and a good mother. Despite her annual visits and gifts of Parker pens and Sony Walkmans, they would never be together by themselves in a room again and he would definitely never laugh at her lame jokes about Arab sheikhs and their big cars.

Reprisals were swift and final. Abba, who had never made any drastic decision in his life beyond refusing to give credit to some of his clients when they reached their credit limit, silently imposed his will on their world.

By the time Baghi woke up and came out of his room, Molly was gone. The ageing imam of the Gol Mosque was called and Molly was handed over to him and it was requested that he be sent to a seminary, any seminary where they would exorcise the devil in him and from where he couldn't escape. Father also instructed the imam, life-long beneficiary of Father's credit and discount for people who matter, that he didn't want to know where Molly would be sent. Later, much later, Baghi would find out that he was sent to a seminary in South Punjab, one of the better ones in the sense that it wasn't really a jail but it was no picnic either.

Baghi's father broke another one of his life rules and borrowed money. He always pronounced with visible pride that any businessman who doesn't pay off his creditors before closing his shop for the day and fails to collects his dues every first day of the month should know that he is running a charity and not a business. He used Destiny Retails as collateral to get a loan and, with that money, Baghi was sent off to Superior Cadet College, a boys' boarding school where they studied and played, but mostly played at being soldiers. Khaki uniforms, black Oxford shoes, green berets during the day and white shirts, grey trousers and striped blue ties for evening meals. The first few days Baghi cried at night and then realized that the induction process was meant to make you cry. He was doing exactly what they wanted him to do. He didn't miss home much – the idea of home reminded him of someone scratching his door and whimpering 'Saleem, Saleem, I am scared…' He did miss Molly with a mixture of longing and terror for a while but then got distracted by friendships and hostilities at the mock military academy.

Baghi's Cadet College was supposed to be a prep school for middle-class boys who wanted to join the armed forces, but very few actually joined. The aim was to turn them into the kind of civilians who observe military discipline, civilians who could go into partnership with military men in real estate, stock exchange, movie making, civilians who would have shiny shoes all their lives. They were made to run, with their mock wooden G3s above their heads, to do front rolls on concrete floors, to jump hurdles and shout Allah Akbar at the top of their voices. Baghi was an average cadet by most standards but the classroom was his domain. He soon established himself as Saleem Angrezi wala. Anyone who needed help with English came to him. Sometimes, in the class, even the teacher asked him to help out with the spellings.

Every Friday, in their afternoon study hour they were given their mail and asked to write and post a letter to their parents. Baghi started writing his letters in English, showing off his linguistic skills but also taking a perverse pleasure in the fact that his father couldn't read English and would have to ask someone to translate them for him. His father wrote back in his shopkeeper's hurried handwriting, listing the family affairs like the receipts for all the groceries that he diligently scribbled for every customer. One Friday, instead of one letter, Baghi received two. The other letter had his name written in calligraphic scrawls, Saleem Ahmed Saleem; he could tell that it was Molly's handwriting. Molly had addressed him formally, Dear Saleem Ahmed Saleem…

From his letters, Baghi discovered that Molly had accepted his fate with characteristic enthusiasm, as if it wasn't a punishment but a reward, and thrown himself into becoming a man of God. Seven prayers a day, five compulsory, two voluntary, twelve hours of learning the Quran by heart, another six on Hadiths, five hours of sleep, three simple meals designed to keep the hormones of young men in check, mostly comprising daal, yogurt and stale bread. He excelled at his studies. His fervour and devotion to godly acts, his habit of sitting in the front row watching his teachers with loving concentration, his offers of helping other students, slower students, with lessons earned him the reputation of a leader of God's men, a God's man who could lead his lost men. After the first year they were occasionally taken out to participate in the funeral rites of the rich, who would feed forty students in the hope that their dead would have an easier time in the afterlife. They would sit in a circle, in their white shalwar qameez and embroidered caps, and recite the Quran while rocking back and forth, their mouths watering at the smells emanating from the mutton pulao being prepared for them. Here also Molly took the lead, dealing with the senior members of the household, coming in and out of the women's section, coordinating the distribution of food, making sure that there was an equal amount of meat on every plate, serving his teachers first, reminding his fellow students not to forget their prayers before taking their first morsel. He served himself last and always finished his food, but without appearing to be greedy, clearing his stainless-steel plate, not leaving a single grain of rice on it, then thanked Allah with a flourish.

He was a man of God who was at ease in His world, a trainee who was being prepared to run His world.

In his letters, Molly never showed any resentment at having been summarily dismissed from the role of a family member. Father never mentioned his name but Mother would get new clothes ready for him at the time of Eid when Baghi visited home. She would get his favourite food made, but Molly never came. Mother would make a parcel of his new clothes and ask Father to mail it.

Baghi kept listening quietly to his father's blatant lies about Molly. Whenever his mother asked him if they could visit him, he told her visits were not allowed. 'It's a madrassah, not a jail,' Mother would mutter. And Father reassured her that every week he called his seminary and spoke to the head teacher. 'Can we talk to him over the phone?' Direct calls to students were not allowed either. He became a ghost, fading from the family's life, a slightly embarrassing absence. Much later Baghi realized that the family had made a choice. Molly was banished. First he was saved from God's fury in a flood and now abandoned to His cruel world for his own good. And, as it would turn out, it really was for his own good.

Baghi's Cadet College was drowning in the testosterone of more than six hundred teenagers. After lights out it became a different place. Senior students sneaked into the beds of juniors and there were proper battles under the red blankets. It was difficult to tell if it was boy love or boredom.

Baghi managed to stay away from their after-hours shenanigans by being teacher's favourite and, in this teenage gangster culture, the one most likely to rat on them. And that suspicion kept them away from him. They still wanted to test him. They circled him in the library where sometimes he sat, often with a dictionary in his lap learning new words. They taunted him for being a book-fucker. One day he found himself cornered in the bathroom, towel in one hand, toothbrush in the other. Two boys, his seniors, blocked his path, one lunged towards his shorts and pulled them down to his knees, the other one grabbed his ass. Time slowed down. Baghi bit one senior's nose and saw his arms flailing in the air. He thrust his toothbrush in the other boy's eye. It didn't quite puncture his eyeball but the boy lost his balance and fell. Baghi threw his towel over the first boy's head and, holding onto his shorts with one hand, ran straight to the second headmaster's office. Baghi had never been in a serious fight before and dealing with two older boys gave him the confidence that would come handy later in life. It would also become a bit of a habit. Baghi told the second headmaster that these boys had tried to kill him in the bathroom. Semi-consensual encounters happened in the bathroom, which meant that usually one person was willing, but the boys' code of silence meant that the teachers had to pretend that nothing ever happened. But when something was reported it broke the code of silence and they were forced to act.

They hadn't made up their minds what was worse: future leaders of the nation buggering each other or future leaders ratting on each other after threats of buggery. The boys were called in front of the morning assembly, charges were read out, and they were told to explain themselves. Their laughable plea: it was a joke. They were given the standard punishment: go down on their hands and knees and crawl to the classroom. Baghi was asked to accompany them, marching behind them like a slave master. The incident earned Baghi the reputation of a militant homosexual, someone who was willing to chew off your nose, a take-your-eye-out boy, someone who ratted on fellow homosexuals. Someone who needed the help of the authorities to save his oh-so-precious ass. Baghi would earn this reputation without doing anything militant or homosexual. That would come later. He also earned the reputation for being violent without actually inflicting any serious damage, just a cornered boy trying to take an eye out with the help of a toothbrush and drawing blood with his teeth.

This became the blueprint of Baghi's life. First you get accused of something you haven't done. Then you do it.

They called him faggot when he didn't know what it meant.

He was declared a thug when he was just defending himself so he became a thug.

He was called a rebel and then he rebelled.

He never mentioned any of this in his letters to Molly.

Molly's letters to him started to sound like intimate little sermons. They always started with his gratitude to Allah and described his daily routine, the names and lovely qualities of his various teachers. Then a little bit about himself, about what part of the Quran he had learnt by heart, what a blessing it was to retain a big book, a holy book, in your chest. That when he recited it every day his heart was filled with light. He also did some off-hand preaching. Hope you are praying five times a day, hope they are teaching you Islamiat, I am happy for you that you are getting knowledge about worldly things but remember that this world is our temporary abode and one day we'll have to go to our maker, an eternal life awaits us and we should repent every day of our lives because Allah has made us in His own image. Sometimes there were hopes for Baghi's character-building: hope you respect your teachers, hope they are not corrupting you with Christianity because in lots of English-medium schools the main aim is not to teach you English but to soften your brain for secular and sacrilegious thoughts, and then, without any hint of irony, hope they are not corrupting your young and intelligent mind with TV and films.

Really? Baghi wanted to say. I used to know someone who was hell-bent on corrupting my mind with movies. But he felt obliged to write short, bland replies. We are eating chicken twice a week, I have started liking breakfast cereals, I topped my class in English but am struggling with maths, I am the full back in the field hockey team and a reserve player in basketball. Baghi avoided talking about family or his biannual visits home. The only sign of estrangement was when Molly wrote towards the end of his letters 'Please say my salam to your parents'.

My parents, Baghi thought.

They were your parents too?

Baghi sometimes still dreamed of someone scratching at his door and whispering his name.

Baghi once asked him if he would like to come home for Eid. He got an elaborate reply from Molly. Although this was an occasion for family and celebration, he said he enjoyed the empty madrassah when everyone was away and he could reflect on what Allah wanted him to do with his life. He could concentrate more on his prayers then, that he was taking all these extra courses in Islamic jurisprudence and it was fascinating how the modern secular law systems were all inspired by the Shariah which began 1,400 years ago, how we were unlucky that while the world had adopted Shariah and made so much progress we were aping crude western ways and had remained backward. Baghi wrote back saying that he understood. Molly wanted to become the 'top mullah'.

He wrote back curtly: 'There is no competition in the love of Allah. I am my only competition.'

There was no competition.

When Baghi was picked up and tortured in a dungeon for writing his open letter to Ummah, his comrades abandoned him. Mazdoor Militia put out a statement that he had been expelled as a member months ago, and now he was the only member of his one-man faction. Mazdoor Militia condemned his provocative letter and welcomed the presence of all the kings and presidents and asked for the harshest possible punishment for the culprit who had brought a bad name to the country's and labourers' struggle. Molly came to rescue him from the police dungeon, had him transferred to Home of Hope, a charity rehab clinic where addicts pretended to be schizophrenics and schizophrenics played at being crazy and made fun of junkies. Not once did he admonish him. Never asked him why he wrote that letter, never once said you were from a good family, didn't your parents teach you any manners?

NINETEEN

The Girl Speaks English

'I AM LOOKING FOR A GIRL,' CAPTAIN GUL SAYS, checking the label on the smuggled Scotch bottle Assistant Sub-Inspector A.D. Malang has brought him. 'I don't have a name or an address for her but that shouldn't be a problem for a professional like you, a son of the soil.'

Inspector Malang can tell when a man wants a woman and he knows that a man wants a woman badly when the man doesn't even know the woman's name or address.

'McDowell? Isn't this Indian?'

Malang nods. 'Yes, sir, made in India. Someone who does business on the border brought it and I thought there is only one person of fine taste who will appreciate it. So, this woman, sir, this girl, what age, any identification marks on the girl?' A.D. Malang is professional enough not to ask why is he looking for a woman whose name he either doesn't know or is reluctant to utter.

Captain Gul pours himself a finger and a half and tries to remember an identification mark on the girl in the video. He can hardly tell Malang that the girl he was looking for was last seen in his own bachelor officer's quarters making no-hearted love after saying NO thirteen times with a man who had a blurred face and hairy belly. Captain Gul takes a sip and makes a face.

'Or any family connections?' Malang presses on. Captain Gul realizes that, although he can see her clearly in his head, he can't describe her. 'A mole on the right cheek,' he says and Malang scribbles in his notebook. 'Long black hair, but not too long.' Captain Gul feels irritated with himself. For a moment he considers if he can share the VHS tape with the inspector, maybe a few seconds of it, but rejects this thought because nowhere in the twenty-one-minute-long video is she decent. It makes him angry that there isn't a clean mugshot somewhere in the video that he can share with the police to track her down, get her tormentor's name from her and hang him by his balls.

He had thought of calling in Laal Khan and asking him. Surely the pillar of Field Intelligence Unit would know who visited this room, brought a camera, got the girl through the security at the guard room. But he remembers the lesson from his Field Intelligence 101 course: always assume that the man who is spying for you is also spying on you. He makes a mental note to check in with Shahid the photographer. He takes a large gulp and says, 'This smuggler friend of yours who brings you this whisky, what kind of a man is he?'

Malang puts his notebook and pen aside. 'He is not really a smuggler, sir, just our informer who knows some smugglers, keeps an eye on them.'

Captain Gul opens the bottle and shoves it under Inspector Malang's nose, who recoils, having smelled this alcohol smell on the most debauched members of society, murderers and rapists and pimps. He himself has never tasted a drop. 'That sister-fucker is making a fool of you. This is moonshine and food colour. Cheap food colour.'

Inspector Malang is thrown by this allegation. 'Sir, I checked the seal myself but I'll beat the hell out of him if he has given me a tampered bottle.'

Captain Gul pours half a glass and takes two large sips. 'She speaks English,' he says.

Malang nods enthusiastically as if this was the key to finding the girl. 'Good English or bad English?'

Captain Gul takes another sip. 'How many girls do you know in this buggered-out city who speak good English?'

A.D. Malang shakes his head enthusiastically because he is already ahead of the game. He remembers the dupatta at the academy. He knows how to find the kind of girl Captain Gul is looking for.

A.D. Malang picks the bottle up and says, 'Sir, if this is not to your standard, I can go and get something else.'

Captain Gul takes another tiny sip, tastes petrol in the back of his palate. 'No, leave the bottle here. Go find the girl.'

HOMEWORK 8

Our Running Coach

Antithetical to the prevailing presupposition, corpulent men are not always lazy or slow, they just appear to be so in popular imagination. Our PT teacher at the ripe young age of forty-five has a paunch that precedes him and heralds his arrival into a room but he still has the agility of a youthful feline on the track. An early onset of diabetes of the blood has caused him to balloon up around his midriff, but his nylon green tracksuit with white stripes, and the colour of the province embossed on his chest, and a stainless-steel whistle around his neck bestows on him the aura of the champion runner that he was in the times of yore. He picked me out of a team of ten girls and announced to the school headmistress that standing in front of your eyes is the future district champion and he is so emphatic in his proclamations about my impending glory that he gets a special grant budget for my diet of milk and seasonal fruit to make my bones stronger. Furthermore, he wants to work on my stance. The race starts before the starting gun is fired, he thunders at me. It doesn't start here, he grabs my leg just above the ankle, it doesn't start here, he tickles my ribs gently, it starts here, and he pats my head, his pudgy fingers doing a little dance on my scalp and the posterior of my neck.

Stance, he tells me, is everything. How you position yourself at the start will arbitrate how and when you cross the finish line, arms aloft like a champion or your whole persona crumpled like someone who endures the sight of three fellow runners ahead of them. He moulds my body with his hands into a champion's perfect stance. He stands behind me, his paunch touching my posterior, and endeavours to correct my balance. His hands are touching me on body parts that are not part of the stance, but he insists that all body parts need to work together. When I have perfected my stance, he blows the start whistle, but as I take my first leap, I stumble and fall – the coach has flicked his foot into my perfectly stanced legs. I am shocked but then I see him laughing like a maniac as if I have told him a funny one. He tells me you can't become a champion runner if you don't know how to recover from a fall. I stumbled in the heats for the All Punjab Track Championship but still went on to win a silver.

After I win the gold medal at the All District Athletic Championship he is beaming with pride and joy and asks me to accompany him to his office to receive my special prize. I am also beaming with pride and joy as finally I have a shiny gold medal around my neck to show the world for all my endeavours. In his office after giving me my special diet of school-sanctioned milk and apples, he breaks me. I am stupefied, my body still perspiring from my winning run is immobilized, my fists clench but can't throw a punch, my mouth opens but no sound comes out, my legs go limp, I don't even recognize the exact moment he breaks me. I only know that I have been broken into when I feel thick liquefied materials running down my legs. He heaves himself from on top of me and starts pulling up his track pants. First I lie there in a state of complete and utter inertness, then life returns to my limbs and I begin to shiver uncontrollably, my legs are not obeying my mind's commands. He tries to hug me, I wriggle out of his grip and hobble to the bathroom on shaky legs. I clean myself with soap and cold water and by the grace of God there are no bloodstains on my shalwar, otherwise that would be impossible to expound to Mother Bano at this time of the month. When I come out of the bathroom, he is standing outside, waiting for me. He brings his face near mine as if he wants to expound on something about what just materialized. But he only kisses me on my right cheek and I let him. Then I run home hiding my shame, remembering that Mother Bano had warned me that a girl should not be broken before the night of her nuptials because if she is already broken what will her husband break on the above-mentioned night. I swear by the maker of all things beautiful and ugly that I'll never be betrothed.

TWENTY

Saima

SUBEDAR LAAL KHAN KNOWS THAT HALF THE INTELligence work is about in-house hygiene. He knows that Captain Gul has tasked the city police to look for a girl while he is receiving visits and boxes of sweet from the CO's daughter.

'Sir, CO sahib's daughter came looking for you.' It seems he wants to say more.

'And what did you tell her?' Captain Gul's lovesick heart is buoyed by the fact that a girl is looking for him. He is also scared that the girl has chosen him as the father of a baby she was carrying before she slithered into his bed.

Subedar Laal Khan knows that old army motto about doing or dying and never asking why. But he is not in the infantry and he is not under enemy fire. It's his duty to keep his superior officer aware of the impending threats. He is not pleased with Captain Gul's decision to let Shahid the photographer go. After a week of false starts they finally had a jiyala, a self-confessed one, who was going to set himself on fire and bring a bad name to his fine city, to his unit. Subedar Laal Khan is a local and had wrangled a posting to his hometown and then managed to get two extensions in the hope of retiring and living there. He has already built a modest house in OK town and wants to end his career on a high note. But his boss seems more interested in CO sahib's daughter than his day job of trapping anti-state elements. Laal Khan is a prudent man and knows better than to come between a young officer and his girl, even when the girl was also friendly with his last boss, the one who installed a camera in his own bachelor's quarters (a spy spying on himself, Subedar Laal Khan had wondered) and who, when transferred, vanished without a proper farewell, taking that 007 number plate with him.

Only the other day, Captain Gul had given him a box of sweets that had arrived from CO's house without even looking at it. The box had a note welcoming Captain Gul into the family. Subedar Laal Khan believes that his boss was walking into a trap.

Subedar Laal Khan treads cautiously. 'Sir, actually CO sahib's daughter came twice, she was asking about you.'

'Why didn't she come in?'

'Sir, I told her you were away, out in the field. I am not sure if you should be seeing her in your quarters. I dare not interfere in your personal life but I suspect CO sahib's men are watching you – I mean us.'

'We are supposed to be watching everyone, why would he watch us? Who dares spy on spies?'

'Sir, you know what fathers are like, specially when they have a daughter of marriageable age. Maybe you should not meet her at all. Sir, she is looking for a husband and she is in a hurry. I think our last boss left her compromised.'

Captain Gul groans. 'Why would she come to me?'

'Sir, when a girl is looking for a husband in a hurry, bachelors' quarters is the nearest place to go.'

Captain Gul first chuckles and then frowns and feels his subordinate is overstepping a line. Captain Gul doesn't want to tell him that he had said almost yes to an almost marriage proposal. Captain Gul thinks fast. His first instinct is to seek an appointment with his prospective father-in-law, give him all the facts, demand a proper pregnancy test and get it over with.

But then he has a better idea. He'll talk to her. He is better at talking to girls. If he could talk her into his bed after one phone conversation, he can definitely make her sit down, make her listen to reason and then walk her out of his life with his sweet, yet firm, words.

He doesn't want her coming to his bachelor's quarters. He's not worried about CO's men watching them. He is not sure if he can trust his own out-of-control libido. He remembers her slithering under his duvet at dawn.

He invites her for tea at the officers' mess. The waiters in white uniforms and turbans turn their faces away, suppress their giggles. They have seen this pantomime before. As Commanding Officer's only and pampered daughter she is respected, the service is prompt, they already know her order: a scoop of vanilla ice cream in a mug of cold coffee with extra jelly. Captain Gul is acutely aware of his surroundings. The mess walls adorned with paintings of white horses dancing in mustard fields and swordsmen twirling with the tips of their swords touching a very low sky. The stretching necks of officers' wives, admonishing their kids and avoiding eye contact, whispering to each other. 'Will you come with me to choose a wedding dress? Something not too flashy,' she says. Captain Gul almost chokes on his coffee and says he needs fresh air.

They both walk to the Martyrs' Park, which is empty this afternoon except for a very young maid with twin toddlers, trying to balance them on a rickety seesaw. Captain Gul guides CO's daughter to the furthest corner, where two metal-chained swings gently sway in the wind. They both sit on adjoining swings. They seem like an already married couple, taking an evening walk, full of anxiety about starting a family.

'I brought you something to drink.' She produces a quarter of brandy. 'My father keeps this for coughs and colds.'

Captain Gul uncorks the bottle, sniffs it, suppresses the urge to take a swig, puts it in his pocket and comes straight to the point or what he thinks the point is. He doesn't mention her pregnancy. He goes for the women's liberation angle. He hesitates, as he is still not sure what her name is, something starting with S. 'My love, I know your father loves you and so do I. But you don't need to be scared of him.'

'I am not scared of him, are you?' she says laughing. 'Don't be. He is a cuddly bear. He just acts stern because that's part of his job.'

'I could have told him then and there, but since you are an independent woman, I wanted to talk to you heart to heart. I mean, you should be able to make your own decisions.'

She looks at him, an encouraging smile.

'I don't think I am ready for this yet. We are not ready for this.'

'What? You are not ready to be a father? Do you think I am ready to be a mother? You brought it upon us. And maybe this is what we need at this time. Haven't you heard pairs are made in the heavens and every child that comes into this world comes with one mouth and two hands?'

Captain Gul reaches out for her hand, clasps it first tenderly, then firmly. 'Listen, Saima, I mean, you are an independent lady. You should make up your own mind. You are not the type to settle for an arranged marriage.'

She looks at him with wide, unbelieving eyes. 'Saima?' she blurts out. 'Who is Saima? Have you got another woman? You don't remember my name? Tell me who is Saima.'

She hiccups and clutches at her throat. Captain Gul is bewildered then remembers that he doesn't remember her name. He sees tears welling up in her eyes. Captain Gul has got this. He puts his arms around her. When a woman goes into convulsions and sheds tears, it means she has come around to accepting her fate. He strokes her back. He coos 'sweet baby' in her ear. She puts her arms around him, her head jerks backwards and, heaving and retching, she throws up a mixture of vanilla ice cream and cold coffee and bits of green jelly all over his chest.

The commanding officer driving leisurely on his evening rounds sees his daughter and her soon-to-be husband canoodling on the park swings, slows down his vehicle, thinks of greeting them and giving them a brief lecture about public displays of affection by telling them that this is not part of the Home of Braves culture, but he is satisfied at their dignified intimacy and drives on.

TWENTY-ONE

Your Fate, Your Hands

SURROUNDED BY DUSTY FILES CONTAINING PETITIONS filed by the Gol Mosque shopkeepers against the Mosque Trust for raising their rents and copies of eviction notices sent by the Mosque Trust in response, Noor Nabi is trying to light a beeri and simultaneously concentrate on the two palms spread on her table. There is a visible tremor in her hands and her eyes are watering with the effort of striking damp matches.

Noor Nabi seems brittle, her cheekbones protruding, her black lawyer's coat shiny after excessive pressing, her coat lapels speckled with fine dandruff. Her eyes are like little drill machines that bore straight through you. When she goes on her bazaar round, she doesn't walk so much as glide; shopkeepers see her coming and whisper, Here comes the cheel, followed by fake welcomes. 'Welcome, wakil sahib, what can we offer you, something hot or something cold?'

Beeri lit, she takes a deep puff and turns to Sabiha Bano's stretched palms on the table. Noor Nabi cares about her reputation and never touches her clients' hands, even when part of her art relies on feeling a hand's texture, its flexibility, the strength of its grip. She used to hold clients' hands when studying them but then started noticing that men always got too excited and some women became teary eyed.

Now she has hung a hand-scribbled note on the wall: No Touching, Your Fate Is in Your Own Hands.

'Touch your hand and tell me what it feels like,' she asks Sabiha, who is sitting very still. Noor believes that although her craft is a science it is an evolving science, not exactly organic chemistry. Maybe the lines in your hand can reveal the past, give a glimpse into the future, say something about your character, but ultimately fate is what you make it. You can change your fate by your actions. Your actions are your fate.

Noor also knows that sometimes people are just having a bad day. She advises them not to take their fate in their own hands on such days.

Sabiha runs her left fingers on the palm of her right hand and reports nothing.

'Is it a working man's hand, an artistic hand?' Noor asks. It's always insightful to hear how people describe themselves; that's usually half the fate.

'It's a hand hand – you are the fortune teller, you tell me. I am not looking for job advice. Tell me something about my future. I think I know my own past.'

Noor asks her to bend her right thumb backward and, as she had expected, it refuses to bend. It looks strong and stiff, the thumb of someone who would rather kick than concede an argument. Someone who would become a mayor of the city through their leadership qualities and then get killed or impeached for making too many enemies in the process.

'Long lifeline, very clear, very strong, goes up to eighty-five, but right now there's a crisis, health crisis most probably. I am not saying your bowels have stopped moving, or God forbid you have some actual illness, I am saying your emotional health is impacted. You find yourself at a point in your life where you don't know what to do.'

Sabiha Bano shifts her weight in the chair and clasps her hands together. 'I believe people come to you to get their palms read at a time when they don't know what to do in their life. If they knew what to do, they would do it. But they come to you. Why?'

'Many come to me when they have lost someone. Have you lost someone dear to you?'

'Lost someone? I have. I want to find out if I can get back what I have lost,' Sabiha Bano says, still wondering what kind of person runs a fortune-telling business in a mosque. The smell of agarbattis is overpowering but fails to conceal the strong aroma of Chitrali hashish. She is impressed by the gall of this woman, setting up a legal practice in Allah's house, then running a side business in palm reading and still finding time to consume copious amounts of hashish. 'The whole nation has also lost someone, you may have heard,' Sabiha says.

Noor Nabi points to another hand-scribbled note on the wall which admonishes her clients that all political discussions were strictly forbidden.

'This unbending thumb is willpower, or maybe just stubbornness. A lot of leadership potential, but remember, the branch that doesn't bend, breaks. There are some very strong winds in your life right now. Your heart and brain line, they have travelled together for a long time but now they have gone on separate paths, bye-bye, sister.'

Sabiha nods her head and lets her dupatta slip. Noor picks up her magnifying glass, flicks the light on it, spits on a corner of her dupatta and polishes it and then goes on a very slow voyage of Sabiha's palms. First left, then right, stopping to retrieve her beeri from the ashtray, finding it extinguished, cursing, putting it back, going back on her journey. She mutters Ya Ali under her breath, not sharing with Sabiha the discoveries that she is making. She flicks the light off, sits back with a sigh.

She is convinced that the person sitting in front of her with her hands stretched on the table is not a palmist's average troubled client but a bona fide Murder-with-Intent, Pakistan Criminal Code Clause 302 case. She has seen many hands in her life, child molesters, borderline schizophrenics, almost killers, hopeless lovers, but what she has seen in Sabiha's hands, a little star on the outer mount of Venus, a clubbed thumb, a very short forefinger, the signs are so clear, so definitive, that Noor is scared for a moment. Sometimes it's only a sign of mounting anger, where no options are left, sometimes just murderous thoughts, who doesn't have them, but here the combination of signs means that the murder is about to happen, that the person has made up their mind. Ya Ali madad – Noor Nabi invokes divine intervention as she realizes that her client doesn't even need to make up her mind. It's written in her hand.

Noor excuses herself, picks up her bible of palmistry, *Secrets of the Palm*, which includes a section on the handprints of famous murderers, turns to page 283, puts the book hurriedly aside and addresses Sabiha in a very solemn voice.

'You said you lost someone very close to you? You must be angry? Any thoughts of revenge?'

'My parents. Are they alive, when will they be released, when will I see them?'

Noor Nabi shrugs as if to say she is not interested in speculative futures.

She is all purpose now, transforming from a harsh fortune teller to a softspoken confidante.

'Your parents are not the only ones they took – there are many many more. When they decide their fate they'll let you know. I've tried filing petitions on some families' behalf, no judge will touch them even with their greased fingers. Meanwhile you have this other issue that you need to…' She opens a drawer and pulls out another incense stick and lights it with complete concentration.

Sabiha feels a sudden itch in her nose, an uncontrollable itch, and when she sneezes, she sneezes with such power that the chart of her destiny Noor Nabi has drawn flies off the table. 'Are you smoking charas? In Allah's house?'

Noor Nabi acts surprised and offended. 'I don't know what you are talking about, madam. I am smoking old-fashioned beeris. No paper, slows down cancer. And where does it say you can't smoke in Allah's house? Worse things have happened here. Don't believe me? Try it.' She extends her beeri towards Sabiha, who declines the offer. Noor puts it out in protest and looks into Sabiha's eyes. 'Grief can push one to madness. We can start blaming ourselves for what was our fate. We are only acting out our fate, sometimes just our suffering.'

Sabiha still hasn't made up her mind if she can trust this lawyer fortune teller who is telling her to be scared of her own fate. 'I need to get out of this place, does my hand have a line for that?'

Noor Nabi has no patience for clients who want her to draw a road map of their lives. 'Someone will come to take you out of here but he'll want your heart in return.' Sabiha Bano moves forward, attentive now. 'But you have to tell them that you have already given your heart to someone else.'

Sabiha Bano laughs a bitter laugh. 'Now you are making jokes with me. Good, I am laughing.'

Noor Nabi breaks her own no-touch rule, grabs both of Sabiha's hands and spreads them on the table, pinning them down with the tips of her forefingers. 'These lines are not funny. I already told you your heart said bye-bye to your brain line a while ago.'

'And where did my heart go?'

'I can't find missing things for you. I can only tell you what I see.'

'So if I tell this man, this man in my palm, that I've given my heart to someone else, why would he take me out of here?'

Noor Nabi sighs. She has had enough of these miserable women clients who only sit up straight and start paying attention when she says the word man. 'A man might want your heart but he is still pondering with his penis. And when you tell him that you have already given your heart to someone, the man will ponder about the other man and they will deal with each other and you might get a chance to bolt, to run for your life.'

That I can do, Sabiha Bano thinks, but she doesn't say it. She says thank you.

'Let's go and see your Sir Baghi. Sometimes it helps to read the hands of people around you.' Noor Nabi wants to get her out of her office. She can deal with devious shopkeepers and grieving parents but here is a homicide suspect accusing her of doing drugs in the mosque. The self-righteousness of it all. In her experience psychopaths turn on people who are trying to save them from their sordid destiny.

'There are guests,' Sabiha says, suddenly not sure why she is here wanting to know about her destiny from a bona fide fraud, a godless mosque lawyer, a fortune teller and a lackey of her saviour. 'They told me they'll call me when it's over.'

'Is there anybody else besides Maulvi sahib?' Noor Nabi needs an inside track on what's going on next door.

'They have some army officer, someone new. I didn't ask what it is about,' says Sabiha, wanting to leave but knowing that she doesn't have a place to go to.

Noor Nabi gets up from her chair, comes around and puts both her hands on Sabiha's shoulders. Sabiha squirms under her bony grip and is not sure if she should push her away or linger and listen. 'They never want us to meet anyone important. Let's go say our salam to the new officer. Who knows, he might help us sort out our fate. Just like they have sorted our country's fate.'

HOMEWORK 9

A Visit to Heaven Fair

It is a conjectural fallacy that the collective wisdom is an accumulation of centuries of human endeavours and conclusions drawn from it. It is often overlooked that the centuries' old wisdom that has arrived at our doorstep might be an ancient accumulation of lack of wisdom thereof or a litany of tomfooleries perpetuated through the ages. When happiness comes knocking at the door unbeckoned, look behind it where regrettably but inevitably the shadow of sadness lurks.

So it should not come as a surprise to anyone that a very happy day of my life turns out to be a catastrophic day of my life.

Mother Bano is in a gregarious mood. Esteemed father with his pocket full of new money from the Satlaj Cotton Mills and his status as the conqueror of capitalism and blood brother of Chairman Bhutto is in a very generous state of being too. They both take me to the fair in the village which transpires every year in the sprawling field next to the canal where my friendly urchins play their helter-skelter game of football. The fair is occasioned by the annual celebration of nine men buried in the same grave, holding a powwow until eternity about their ferocious battle against the giant who slayed them. There are makeshift tented shops everywhere and men selling sweets piled high and fortuitous shiny stone rings caged in glass boxes. There is a plastic sheet banner announcing in ornate calligraphy the battle between the most poisonous snake in the world with his child tamer, snake and child's eyes locked in eternal enmity. I see a charpoy covered with a quilt adorned with red and yellow flowers, over it a man with a woman's painted face and lower body of a fish. It's quite obvious to the observant eye that it's not really a woman, but a man with his face shaved rigorously and painted with rouge and lipstick. I go round and round, look at her fish tail. It doesn't make an iota of sense to me that here is a half man dressed as a woman with a fish tail – can it run, can it actually swim? Although I am well past the age of going on merry-go-rounds, my youthful urchin friends appear out of nowhere and make me sit on a wooden chair that goes round and round. It makes me so happy I get giggles in my stomach. A short man swallows a sword larger than his arm. A man makes fire from petrol with his farts. Mother Bano keeps looking furtively behind as if expecting someone for a rendezvous. Esteemed father goes into a tent and before leaving us outside he says that there are comrades from the mill inside the tents and he is going to have an impromptu study session with them about post-revolution strategies. The banner outside the tents says Double Your Money in the Blink of an Eye. Mother Bano sneers that esteemed father is going to gamble again. He is going to lose the money that he is supposed to be saving for your wedding. I blush. I never want to be betrothed to anybody but I feel anguished with shame and a forlorn longing deep inside me when Mother says the wedding word.

In the distance my wandering eye catches a glimpse of Comrade Sadiq Ali Sadiq, backslapping with a group of policemen in a state of bonhomie. He catches my eye watching him and he whispers something in a policeman's ear and starts walking towards us with purposeful steps. I drift off as I am loath to be part of his newly founded esprit de corps with Mother Bano.

I walk into a tent that's advertising a free puppet show. On any given day of my life I find dolls made of rags a ghoulish presence and that's why I am reluctant to make any friends with girls who dress up their dolls like brides in shimmering red. But these dolls are made of yellow flowery cloths and they dance and they indulge in a make-belief powwow. It's not so make-belief as I can see the strings that dictate their movement. It is the quintessential story of two lovers stranded on the opposite sides of a stormy river. They sing to each other ballads of love and encourage each other to jump into the river so that they can meet like true lovers in the middle. The man dictating their movements shakes a blue cloth in the background to make it look like a river in flood and he also expounds rain and thunder noise with his mouth. The love ballads play on tape recorder warning both dolls that they are doomed to a death by drowning in the above-mentioned tumultuous river water. The irresponsible and reckless love ballad is also urging the lovers to go ahead and jump anyway as it's better for lovers to drown together and live in eternal coupledom rather than waste their lives on the opposite sides of a river. I get scared and look around. There is no Mother, no Father, even my urchins have disappeared from the face of this earth. I stand and cry. The boy and girl dolls, made of rags, keep bobbing up and down in the middle of blue-cloth river. First I am happily distracted when they come together, then I get mortified because they hug each other and start drowning. Uncontrollably, inexplicably, I start bawling and hiccupping as if my nearest and dearest have been swept away in a flood.

A man comes to me and says, Are you lost my child? Through my hiccups I shout at him that I am not a child and it's not I who is lost, it's my esteemed father and Mother Bano who are lost. He asks me again with infinite patience and I explain to him that my father has gone into a gambling tent. He says there are too many tents to gamble. He says you are not safe. This place is full of wolves who will tear apart a youthful cub like you. My hiccups stop and he takes me to a stage where a young man is making announcements about lost people. He asks the boy to make an announcement that the child Sabiha Bano is lost, her parents, relatives, guardians should immediately report to the lost and found station. I am extremely annoyed at being dubbed a child but I am secretly blushing at hearing my full name for the first time on loudspeaker. Mother Bano comes running and crying and laughing and hugging me and beating me, all at the same time, and through her vale of tears demanding to know why did I leave her. I don't get an opportune moment to reply to her that it wasn't I who left her, it was she herself who wanted a stolen moment with Comrade Sadiq Ali Sadiq.

By the time we reach the gambling tent police has already handcuffed esteemed father, he is jumping and shouting Jiye Bhutto and trying to show them a poster to prove his close proximity to Chairman Bhutto. He is slapped in the face and told that his chairman is no more the prime minister of the country: he is in jail and that's where he is going. Esteemed father looks around in the forlorn hope of the approach of his comrades to show solidarity with him. Comrade Sadiq Ali Sadiq pretends to parlay with the police and tells them that father is a highly respected union leader and it's unacceptable for the proletariat to see their leader in handcuffs. The policeman, the same one who had been showing bonhomie to Comrade Sadiq earlier, waves a pair of handcuffs in front of him in an obvious, mocking, jocular fashion: Your union leader is running a gambling den – if you are part of his gang, we'll arrest you too.

Comrade Sadiq Ali Sadiq flinches and turns to Mother Bano like a wet cat, with the look that says *See, I fully endeavoured to stand by him in the hour of his need.*

I move forward to punch him in his face with the intention knocking off that wet-cat look but Mother holds me back.

Mother Bano whispers to me and expounds that maybe it's a good thing because with Chairman Bhutto no longer the prime minister, we are entering evil hours and maybe it's good because at least in jail Father will be safe and can't gamble away his fortunes. As the police lead esteemed father away, his handcuffed hands aloft, still holding a torn poster of him and Chairman Bhutto in a hug, Comrade Sadiq Ali Sadiq puts a comforting hand on Mother Bano's shoulder.

As it has been mentioned above, when happiness knocks at your door, look at the dark shadow lurking behind it.

TWENTY-TWO

Black Dog

MOLLY IS IN FULL-BLOWN HOSPITALITY MODE. HE has brought a bucket of ice, six crystal glasses and an assortment of savouries in little china bowls. 'It's our glorious custom, when somebody comes to our town, we put our best face forward.' He puts a package wrapped in a newspaper under the table. Baghi hates entertaining. What's the point of a bunch of men cackling over jokes about their wives and about corruption in public life? He himself might hang out with his students after a class, order samosas when he is feeling generous. Nothing more.

He hasn't ever seen Molly so enthusiastic about hosting a visitor. 'Best face forward,' Molly repeats. 'Even if we don't like the visitor, specially if we don't like them. Specially if they are going around asking questions. As the Book of Books says, invite the hunter into the cave before he sets a trap.' Baghi doesn't ask if this is what the holy book actually says or Molly just made it up.

Molly unwraps the package and Baghi knows Molly is on a mission: this bottle of Black Dog costs a small fortune, the kind of money that could marry off a poor man's daughter or the cost of digging a few wells in a desert.

Captain Gul arrives in a starched white kurta shalwar. He smells like he has just emerged from a small pool of

Midnight Mist perfume. He is effusive. 'I am such a lucky man to get this posting. What a fine city, full of poets and scholars, you don't get this kind of intellectual company in the officers' mess.' Baghi does want to ask him what he did to get posted here, must be a major fuck-up, but the captain is busy protesting that he is not sure if he should be having a drink with his hosts. 'My duties don't allow me to mix pleasure and business.' He picks up the bottle, brings it close to his face and checks its seal for any signs of tampering. 'It will be a sin to mess with a beverage as fine as this, but civilians, sometimes even our good-hearted civilian people, adulterate everything good in life, even Black Dog,' he says as he takes charge. He uncorks the bottle, sniffs it, grunts with approval and pours into three glasses, bringing them up to his eyes to make sure that he has poured an equal amount in every glass.

He is the kind of guest who wants his hosts to feel at home.

'So, what do people think of us?' Captain Gul asks, taking a first sip, a generous sip, and leans back in his chair which almost topples over. He recovers and leans forward. Baghi wonders if the captain is fishing for compliments for himself or for the institution he represents.

Molly gets in first. 'People couldn't be happier. The gutters are being cleaned, beggars have disappeared from the streets, liquor shops are shut. This country is too hot for democracy anyway.' He stutters for a moment. 'And now they have sent in their best. So things can only get happier.'

Captain Gul looks at Baghi and waits. 'Early days,' Baghi says. 'Times are changing definitely, but I am not sure if people are willing to change with the times. But with Bhutto swinging at the gallows...'

The awkward silence that follows is broken by a single shout from the road downstairs. Someone is screaming, Zinda Hai, Bhutto Zinda Hai. Molly looks at Baghi, Baghi looks at the ceiling. Captain Gul empties his glass in one long gulp, holds his breath as if trying to keep his drink down, then lets out a loud burp. Molly touches his glass to his lips, pretending to be a refined drinker, and says, 'May Allah protect you from all your enemies.'

Captain Gul is not here for his maker's blessings. He is here to collect on-the-ground intelligence. 'What do you think of this stupid slogan Bhutto Lives? Some people are saying this slogan started here, here in this mosque?'

Molly is quick on his feet. 'It's exactly that, a stupid slogan, and a stupid rumour.'

Captain Gul gets up, stumbles and lurches towards the balcony, peers down and turns around to look at both of them. 'There was someone who just shouted that, right under this balcony. You heard it, right? We all did, right, right?' He is looking at Baghi now, who stares at him and, in that moment of clarity brought about by two sips of Scotch, decides to tell Captain Gul the truth.

'The first phase of a tragedy is denial. People are in denial,' he says without looking up from his glass. 'At least some people are.'

'Are my friends one of those people?' Captain Gul pours himself a shot of Black Dog, looks around for the jug of water, then changes his mind and gulps it straight. 'Is he going to appear on this balcony? I am worried, are you hiding him somewhere in the mosque? Bring him out, let's drink with him. We may not like the man but he liked his drink. Royal salute.' Captain Gul comes to attention and offers a mock three-fingered salute. He knows that civilians like an officer with a sense of humour. But he has also entered his sentimental phase now, which his military colleagues know happens just before his fourth drink and is the most dangerous phase of his drinking evening. Once, in this phase, he tried to hug a three-star general at the annual Armoured Corps war games and almost got court-martialled.

This morning, another cable arrived from his headquarters with the simple question: Bhutto Lives? He decoded it thrice. First, he thought it was a joke. But what kind of joke comes with a question mark. Then, on his way here, he saw a poster on the wall saying the same thing without the question mark. And now someone is down there shouting it up at him. Bhutto Lives. He was sworn to secrecy, otherwise he could stand on this balcony and shout back some historical facts.

What the bloody hell, he thinks, bugger his oath of secrecy. He stumbles back to the balcony, surprised at how he got so sloshed so quickly, then remembers that for a change he is having good stuff, Black bloody Dog. In a mosque.

He stands on the balcony, raises his glass and shouts at the deserted road below. 'I saw the dead man with my own eyes. He was dead. He stays dead. Now go back to sleep. Bhutto Lives. In your damn dreams,' he slurs.

Having solved his Bhutto problem for now, Captain Gul remembers that he might be in slightly bigger trouble than a dead man's ghost haunting this city. He stumbles towards the bookshelf. 'Have you read all these books?' he asks with genuine curiosity. Then he notices women's clothes piled on a shelf. 'So you read all these books and get ladies to take their clothes off too? You are my brothers. True brothers.'

He decides to share his own love dilemma with his hosts, and since it was a personal matter and not a service secret, he is absolutely clear in his head that he is not violating any Field Intelligence protocols.

Captain Gul sits down, pours himself a glass of water, takes a chunk of ice from the bucket and rubs it on his eyes. He does this when he is dead serious. 'I know I am in the right place. This is a place of learning so can I ask you a religious question?' He leans forward, all concentration. 'Or maybe this is a question of science. But promise to give me your honest answer. And my question and your answer, honest answer, stays here, with us, the three of us. Us three brothers.'

Molly and Baghi look at each other, a look of whose-idea-was-this, a look of fear. What have they got themselves into? Molly thinks it may not have been such a great idea, this welcome drinks party. 'If we knew anything, you would be the first one to know. Those flyers, those posters, they are just stupid gossip, stupid rumours. Next Friday in my sermon I am planning to address the issue of falsehood in public life, the moral plague of our times.'

'Brothers, is it possible...?' Captain Gul hesitates. Years of intelligence training and a soldierly habit of not asking questions stands between his oath on the Official Secrets Act and his need for survival. He takes another tiny sip and decides to frame his question in theoretical terms. 'Is it possible that if you do the thing with a woman that you do after taking off her clothes, she becomes pregnant by the next afternoon? This, I want to insist, is a theoretical question, but in a way not so theoretical because at this very moment a very dear colleague of mine faces that question.'

Molly clears his throat but Baghi decides that it's a matter of science and not spiritualism. 'Someone is trying to mislead you,' Baghi looks him in the eye, almost patronizing now, 'or your friend. Or you are pulling a trick on us.' Baghi goes on to explain the biological mysteries. An egg takes forty-eight hours to fertilize. Pregnancy-test-level hormones will form in another ten days, so if his friend says he has made someone pregnant within twenty-four hours of doing it with them, one of them is lying. 'Maybe your friend is saying this to impress you. It's very common for men to exaggerate their sexual prowess to impress other men. Some men have claimed that they can impregnate a woman just by staring at them for a long time.'

Captain Gul is still trying to take the answer in when he hears a woman's voice and, with his bloodshot and blurred eyes, sees two female forms advancing on him. He shrinks in his chair.

'Only one person in this city who lies and lies…' Noor Nabi walks in, dragging Sabiha by her hand. 'And that's you.' Noor thinks she is addressing Molly, but she finds Captain Gul staring at her, as if trying to focus on her face through his dilated eyes. She walks up to him and extends her hand. 'I am the chief lawyer for the Gol Mosque Trust, and it's an honour to welcome you to our city.'

Captain Gul is too stunned to get up from his chair. He tries to make up for this by offering a very firm handshake. Beyond Noor Nabi's shiny blazer and straw-nest hair he sees that girl from the VHS and he is not sure if he can ever get up from this chair again.

'What a firm hand,' says Noor Nabi. 'May I have the privilege of reading your palm? I have never had the pleasure of reading a young officer's hand. Poets' hands I have seen, senior politicians, two famous actors, but never a young officer's hand, a hand that will one day shape our destiny, your hand.'

Captain Gul extends his right palm, steals a glance towards Sabiha Bano and thinks surely this woman is not the girl from that videotape. How could it be? He is hallucinating. Sometimes a quick intake of whisky makes him do things which are hard to explain the next morning. Once he had got into a Model T 3 tank thinking it was his car, and turned the key in the ignition to go to the cantonment canteen to buy cigarettes and condoms.

'Extraordinary leadership qualities,' Noor Nabi says. 'Some people work hard to become generals. Some are born with the hand, with a general's four stars drawn on the hand. A hand to shape not only this country's but the entire Ummah's destiny.'

The mole on her right cheek is unmistakable. But her face is filled out. He clearly remembers the way her limbs strained away, how her ass collapsed, but why can he not recognize her face? She is a montage of innocent laughter and disgust in his head, a victim of a predator, a symbol of heroic resistance, a vision of dimpled cheeks and thick pubic hair and breathy 'No no no' in slurred English. But how in God's name, how could he ever forget this face? Maybe I have had too much to drink. But surely if you have had too much, how do you know that you have had too much? Captain Gul decides that he needs another drink, a very small one, to clear his head. He doesn't want to stare at her.

He doesn't want her to know that he knows.

'Your name,' says Noor Nabi. Captain Gul is confused. Why is she asking his name when they have just been introduced? Noor Nabi leans forward and lowers her voice to a whisper. 'Your name will be spoken in Delhi, in Washington DC, in Moscow, in Germany, even in Belgium.'

At any other time, Captain Gul's interest would have been piqued and he would have asked searching questions about how his name would reach these distant cities, whether it would be uttered with fear or respect or would he be remembered as someone who bungled on the hanging-night duty, but now he just blushes and looks at Sabiha again. She is sitting on a chair now, helping herself to peanuts from a bowl. Her dupatta slips off her head, and Captain Gul is sure now; hair, this hair, how can he forget this hair, the way these locks framed her face when they fell around it, the way her face changed when they were pulled back, the way she growled.

Noor Nabi is slightly frustrated at the lack of response from Captain Gul. She raises her voice. 'One day the American president will salute you, and when he salutes you, you'll remember then that Noor Nabi, chief lawyer of the Gol Mosque, in this academy, in this city, told you that a living American president will salute you and will then mention you in his autobiography. Shah of Shahs will serenade you, kings will kiss your hand, the most famous man in the world will feel honoured to be your personal chauffeur.'

Captain Gul finds some residue of courage and after mumbling a thank you to Noor Nabi asks, 'You have not introduced me to your friend?'

'Sabiha,' she says, giving him a cursory glance. 'Sabiha Bano.'

Before Captain Gul can introduce himself and start a conversation, another cry from the road downstairs announces the imminent resurrection of Mr Bhutto.

Molly and Baghi go to the balcony and peer down. 'In God's name, let people sleep,' Molly says, more for Captain Gul's benefit than for the jiyala on the road.

Captain Gul has made up his mind. He is laughing at himself that he had any doubts a few moments ago. It's definitely the girl from the video but she has not said anything except giving her name. Now, she sits there mute, munching her peanuts. This makes Captain Gul first angry and then sad. Only if she says something in English will he know. Hell, he already knows, but he'll know for sure.

He looks at the bottle again. Did he actually drink three-quarters already? She suddenly seems scary to him, her tracksuit bottoms and dupatta over her head. She is not the girl he wanted to save, she is not the girl he was in love with.

But she was the girl in his bachelor officer's quarters telling someone in a tired voice to leave her alone. It's his duty, no, his fate, to love her, to save her. But first Captain Gul needs to use the loo, he needs a splash of water on his face. He needs a clear head. He lunges towards his drink, gets hold of the glass, looks for the bottle, can't find it. He saw it just a moment ago – it was on the table, right here. Bloody civilians, always thieving and conniving. They have stolen the bottle. Or hidden it. They probably think he is too drunk. He'll teach them, he is no ordinary fauji. There are no ordinary faujis anyway, but he is the commander of the elite Field Intelligence Unit. Even the faujis are scared of his unit, who do they think they are? He'll grab this girl by her wrist, drag her to his Toyota, drive to his bachelor officer's quarters. He must drive carefully, though, he reminds himself, because he has had a bit to drink. And then he'll play her that video, maybe not the entire video, only the beginning part, and ask her to reenact it for him, respectfully of course. He'll ask for the name of the man with the blurred face, track him down, hang him by his balls.

His glass is magically full again. Instead of bringing it to his lips, he bends over, tries to slurp from the glass and topples over. Molly holds his hand, the other hand on his back, he steadies him, a walk to the loo. Molly turns the light on and waits outside. Captain Gul stumbles towards the washbasin and retches, dark-brown fluid and half-chewed savouries all over the sink. He bends over the sink to keep himself steady and heaves some more. As his stomach empties, his head clears. This Molly seems like a smart man. He held his nerve. He held his hand and plucked him out of the party right at the moment when he was about to throw up. Captain Gul splashes water over his face, dries it with the sleeve of his qameez and looks in the mirror and smiles.

He feels he belongs here, that he is amongst his own people. And then in the mirror he sees the bathroom wall behind him, jerrycans full of kerosene and stacks of posters of that bald bastard Bhutto, his dead eyes mocking him.

Before his head hits the floor and he passes out, Captain Gul is thinking what kind of people hoard kerosene oil and Bhutto posters in these tumultuous times?

TWENTY-THREE

Snakes and Ladders

MOLLY IS SPRAWLED ON HIS BED, HIS BACK AGAINST a stack of pillows, his four children hunched over a board of Snakes and Ladders. It's an intense game, with the youngest one being initiated into the family's favourite pastime. Molly's wife sits on the floor, gently pressing Molly's feet and occasionally rebuking her children for giving their father a headache. Molly has a mild headache from the few sips of Black Dog he had last night but he is having a good day at the game, probably a sign that the time has come to make his move on the domestic front. His oldest reminds him that it's his turn. He rolls the dice and gets a five and asks his youngest one to move his token. The child hits the bottom of the ladder; the other three accuse him of cheating. You can't even count. No, you can count but only when it benefits you. You are always hitting ladders. Beginner's luck, says Molly.

Mrs Molly is working the toes now, takes one in her hand, rubs it then bends it. She caresses his calf, then cups it inch by inch onwards and upwards. Molly forgets to take his turn, looks down at her. She holds his gaze for a moment, then blushes and looks down. Molly knows that smile. Molly thinks of Sabiha Bano's tracksuit bottoms, forest green with two white stripes running on the sides. He mutters a verse that is supposed to ward off satanic thoughts and rolls his dice. He gets the number two, and his yellow token is swallowed by a curling anaconda. His wife's hands press on the backs of his knees and gently move up. 'You are very tense,' she says, moving on to the insides of his thighs, 'in all the wrong places.' Molly's leg jerks back from Mrs Molly's searching hands as if she has seen the image of another woman's legs in her husband's head. His youngest one is sobbing now: why can't they have just ladders to go up and down, snakes are scary. The boy starts playing with one hand covering his eyes.

'Allah has blessed you with insight. You can read my thoughts,' Molly says, taking her hand and pressing it gently. 'I have been thinking of widows, how to help them. Our attitude towards widows is the exact opposite of what our Prophet, may peace be upon him, taught us, what our Book of Books tells us.' Mrs Molly covers her head with her dupatta; she does it often when Molly goes from being a loving, attentive husband to a distracted man of God. 'Our Prophet himself set an example by marrying widows. But in our society we have made them pariahs. This is not true Islam. This is what we have learnt from Hindus who want to burn their widows along with their husbands. Now we don't burn them but we don't let them live happy lives – we burn them from the inside.' She goes back to pressing his feet again, her grip firm. 'Maybe because the widows in our Prophet's time were the mothers of the first Muslims. Allah himself chose them. But look at today's widows.'

Her hands on his feet are too forceful to provide relief. 'Today's widows are all whores,' she says. 'What kind of woman lets her husband die first? If they took care of them, their husbands would still be around and they would not be widows. They are practically murderers.'

Molly tries to retrieve his foot from her iron grip. 'But life is in Allah's hands. He gives and He takes. How can you blame some poor woman for her husband's death?'

'But taking care of a husband is a woman's work.' She looks him in the eye. 'Do you have a particular widow in mind? Did you hear about the one who put her house on fire, burnt her husband to death and then ran away? If I find her, I'll chop her nose off in front of the mosque.'

Molly had prepared himself for this moment. Shariah, history, Islamic history, secular history, gender imbalance, humanity, common sense were on his side. He had all the arguments and specific examples from the Prophet's life and gender statistics from the last census to explain how rescuing a woman from her widow-ship is the foremost duty of a man of his stature but now he is flustered. 'Many fathers come to me whose daughters have been widowed and I am trying to encourage them to get them remarried. Even if they are to become second wives.' He is relieved that he has found a thread back to his argument.

'Keep playing.' Mrs Molly admonishes her children, takes the dice from the youngest boy and rolls it. She gets a five and asks the youngest one to move his token. He hits neither the ladder nor the snake's mouth and declares that Snakes and Ladders is the most boring game in the world and he'll never play it again. Mrs Molly looks at her husband and grabs his foot again. 'You obviously know more about what Allah wants but Allah forbid, may Allah turn my tongue to ash, but if He was to take you away from me, would you like me to spread my legs in front of another man?'

Molly sits up in the bed, confused, then furious. 'What are you saying, woman? Do you have no shame? Children are listening.'

HOMEWORK 10

Our Summer Vacation

The people who congregate around you at a time of trouble are not always the people who want to alleviate your pain. Some of them are debt collectors. Comrade Sadiq Ali Sadiq sets up a solidarity camp outside our house, a tent and a few tattered rugs strewn on the street. Men from the mills sit around all day, passing around the newspaper and sharing cigarettes and talking revolution. Comrade Sadiq Ali Sadiq has convinced mother they need to be given tea every few hours if they are to be kept politically engaged. Our cow is milked thrice a day; Comrade Sadiq Ali makes the tea and serves himself. Mother Bano has never seen a man do household chores and looks at him with the kind of admiration as if it's God almighty himself pouring milk into a boiling cauldron of tea. After three days of this bonhomie and hospitality Mother Bano and Comrade Sadiq Ali go into a huddle, and after a spate of furious whispers I can start figuring out that they are arguing over money. Comrade Sadiq Ali is making a claim, and knowing his dubious nature a spurious claim, that Father owes money to the other comrades who have fallen on bad times because the mills' management has fired them all. And although he has started a fund to raise money for father's bail he has made no headway. First he looks at the cow and says that it will only bring enough money to cover the debts and then he looks at me, as if weighing me with his eyes, and says nothing.

Mother Bano decides to embark on a sojourn to our grandfather's village, who always lays the claim that he is ninety-nine years old. Mother Bano has envisaged a plan that since she was a wandering beauteous lass, ergo she was never able to ask anything from her esteemed father. Her husband is incarcerated, her cow can't provide sustenance for the cabal of men, so this might be an opportune time to lay her claim to her inheritance.

It's the monsoon months when monstrous black clouds make afternoons like the darkness of the ages and my urchins drag me to the canal to see if suddenly it'll start brimming with floods caused by rains. There are only puddles in the canal bed. My urchins make frog sounds, frogs come out of their hiding places, we catch them and dunk them in the puddles. They spread some grain on the roadside and set up bird traps. The birds of this region are too clever – they fly away and tell other birds about the traps. Mother Bano barges into our games, holds me by the wrist and drags me away, not respecting my dignity and honour in front of the urchins. My esteemed father is a political prisoner and here she is playing boy games with urchins, she expounds to none in particular.

The bus ride to esteemed grandfather's village has a soothing effect. I put my head on Mother Bano's shoulder, the wind is agreeable with my newly curlicious hair, Mother Bano whispers prayers and blows on my head.

Grandfather lives in a small hut with a commodious courtyard populated by his herd of sheep. He is a self-supported saviour of the old world and a shepherd who abhors the ways of the city. He prides himself on the fact that the only commerce he engages in with the city is salt slabs for his sheep. When mother tells him about her tale of woe and esteemed father's plight, Grandfather betrays no compassion. He berates the cotton mills, men who work there, women who marry them, men who get arrested, women who go begging on the street to arrange bail money for the above-mentioned men. But a father can't send away his daughter empty-handed, so he hands us a lamb. Mother Bano is crestfallen. A man is a shepherd and a woman is his sheep, without your shepherd you are lost, he expounds and he expounds. When mother goes out into the courtyard to camouflage her tears I barge into Grandfather's hut and point to the metal safe in a corner and challenge him to open it and prove that he has no hoarded wealth that he is so reluctant to part with in his most beauteous daughter's hour of grief and need. He sighs and opens it and asks me to take a peek. It's empty except for a revolver wrapped in an oil cloth. He narrates for a while the ways of Mother Bano when she was young. He proclaims that my mother is a very irresponsible woman and I should keep the revolver because the world is going to become an even more evil place.

The lesson that can be learnt from this sojourn is that sometimes normal humdrum life can be lived in tumultuous and uncertain times. Although we didn't accomplish our aim of raising money for esteemed father's bail, nay, we failed miserably, but on the return bus journey, I am hiding a revolver in my sports bag, and mother is cradling a baby lamb in her lap, and we speculate if the lamb will make friends with our youthful calf.

TWENTY-FOUR

The Mysteries of the Bermuda Triangle

CAPTAIN GUL MURMURS, YES, MRS GANDHI, AND inhales the fragrance of a little string of jasmine flowers that she is wearing around her wrist. The remnants of last night's Black Dog cruise through his blood, making his dream a very VIP affair.

They are riding in the back of her official Ambassador, the Indian flag fluttering on the wrong side of the car bonnet. Captain Gul is on a mission so secret that he can't even mention it in his dream. Mrs Indira Gandhi is looking outside the window, twirling the pallu of her sari like a miffed lover, the silvery bob of her hair gently swaying in the wind. He knows her type. When a woman is riding with you in the back seat of an official car and looking out of the window, she needs some attention, she wants to be asked things.

He would like to sleep a bit more, spend some more time in this dream, sort Mrs Indira Gandhi out for good.

Captain Gul has realized in this brief dream encounter that Mrs Gandhi is not the kind of woman to whom you can say thank you ma'am and walk off, so he is playing what some aggressively needy women might call difficult to get.

He also looks outside the car window on his side and can feel her sideways glance at the back of his neck.

The phone on his bedside rings incessantly. He grabs his pillow and presses it against his ear, wanting to smell that prime-ministerial fragrance a little longer. This is the smell of victory, when instead of annihilating your enemy, you steal their heart with stealth and charm and then convert their bodyguards to your cause and leave the annihilation business to them.

Through the corner of his eye he looks at Mrs Indira Gandhi's cotton blouse. A bit flat, he thinks and then looks ahead. The Indian flag is now limp on the car flagpole. Mrs Gandhi catches him glancing at her and he shuts his eyes and thinks about his plan. Soon, he is going to get out of bed, shower, get into his Corolla without Laal Khan, drive to Gol Mosque and request Sabiha Bano to accompany him to his bachelor's quarters. He wants to set the wheels of justice in motion by making tender, caring love to her, not like the brute in the video. He'll be respectful.

His sleepy hand reaches for the phone and he is relieved that it's not his boss barking questions about dead Bhutto but his pregnant girl from Pindi, surprisingly calm and formal. She doesn't even ask him what he did last night, although he could have told her, in some detail, that he went undercover in the field, infiltrated a gang of hardcore revolutionaries, got them drunk and made a major breakthrough in his search for elusive jiyalas, those bastards hoarding kerosene and preparing to burn for Bhutto.

'How's my baby?' Captain Gul coos into the phone, very smug at his double entendre. He decides not to tell her about his dream encounter with Mrs Gandhi, because although women like an ambitious man, they don't like it when a woman is involved, even when that woman is the prime minister of their number-one enemy country. He breathes his early morning slow kiss into the phone.

'Baby? What exactly have you done for the baby? Just calling to tell you there is no baby.' He can hear her yawn into the phone.

Captain Gul should feel relieved but he feels no joy; an old sadness rears its head, a sadness that he had felt on his first night away from home in the barracks where he had sobbed all night thinking of his mother.

'And congratulations. I heard you are getting married to your commanding officer's daughter. I hope you are doing it for the right reason. I hope you get your glory.'

Captain Gul feels a jolt and sits up in his bed, his hand searching for a bottle. He finds one, takes it to his mouth and sucks air. It's empty. 'How do you—?'

'Since you weren't answering your phone I got worried. I called up your commanding officer and he gave me the good news. And I gave him mine.'

'That's not what you think… It's classified but I am going to tell you in confidence.'

'No. No. It's not what *you* think. I got an abortion the day before. And don't get me wrong, I didn't call to ask for abortion money.'

Captain Gul looks around his room in confusion. He was about to broach the subject at some point but now he's been robbed of the opportunity to be generous and compassionate.

'It wasn't yours so don't feel too bad.'

'What do you mean? You are joking. I am on my way. I want my baby. I want it right now. Give me my baby, stop fucking with my head.'

'Your baby? Do you even know how babies are made?' He suspects she is suppressing another yawn.

'We made love. You said I was wonderful. We made love multiple times. No, actually I fucked the hell out of you.'

'What was I supposed to say? You gave me statistics about the Bengal famine to divert my attention from the fact that you couldn't get it up. You called my vagina the Bermuda Triangle and then spent all our time together lecturing me about the mysteries of the Bermuda Triangle. When you did finally get an erection in the morning, you couldn't find the Bermuda Triangle.'

He yelps, he moans, he gets fauji, he threatens to cut her balls off and shove them down her throat, and then he apologizes for being emotional. He tries his famous phone smooch, he threatens to quit the army and come back to Pindi and grab her by the nape of her neck and drag her back to his bachelor officer's quarters and take care of her and their baby. He tells her that he wasn't the kind of man to judge. Even if it was someone else's baby he would bring it up like his own child and even if there was no child he wanted another chance, another go at discovering, another way of loving her, a less talkative, a more caring, wholesome way of loving her and damn it who does she think she is, he'll fuck her like a bitch and give her so many babies that... He pauses and realizes that she has hung up on him and he has been pleading about finding another, more wholesome way of loving to a dead phone.

He doesn't want to go back to sleep. He doesn't know if he should laugh with relief or cry in despair. Captain Gul is furious. He twists and turns in the bed and is composing long messages about the sanctity of motherhood to her in his head, giving her statistics about how children from broken families turn to drugs and sexual perversions to scare her, to shame her, to make her reconsider her decision. It's quite obvious to him that she is bluffing, she hasn't had an abortion. She is testing his commitment. He is an intelligence officer.

He knows these things. She is jealous, she wants attention. What kind of woman would abort a serving captain's baby? He has almost made up his mind to jump out of bed, get into his Corolla, drive non-stop to Rawalpindi and drive back with the mother of his child, this time driving more carefully because of the baby, and bring them here, keep her under his own watchful eyes, because he knows that pregnant women go through a roller coaster of emotions, and while he is still making these plans, Laal Khan barges in without knocking at the door.

He rushes in like a demon, doesn't salute, lunges towards Captain Gul, tries to drag him out of bed, first towards the door, then makes wild gestures asking him to jump out of the window.

Scrambling for the empty bottles in the room, Laal Khan hides them under the bed, all the while begging him to leave the room, warning him of an imminent attack, making wild boxing gestures about an enemy at the door. Captain Gul doesn't like to be manhandled, doesn't like to manhandle, although it's an intrinsic part of his job, but whenever physical handling is required, he delegates and leaves the room. 'I don't want to know the gauge of your drill machine or the size of your pliers, I want answers.'

Laal Khan makes one last plea with his hands joined together, asking him to jump out of the window and disappear for a few hours. 'Why would I do that?' Captain Gul doesn't get an answer. Four tall men in matching navy blue tracksuits enter the room, salute him and stand silent.

'What?' Captain Gul asks, his authority already waning.

'Please come with us, sir, Commanding Officer has invited you for tea.'

'My balls,' says Captain Gul. 'My giant big balls to you and your commanding officer. Get out of my room. First knock, ask for my permission to enter, salute and maybe then you can have a tea party with my balls.'

They look at each other, then pile onto him. They don't hit him. Two of them hold his arms, the other two go for his legs, they pick up a flailing and cursing Captain Gul and head out. Laal Khan stands in a corner looking down as a thrashing Captain Gul is carried out of the room. Captain Gul looks back towards Laal Khan, who has started making his bed, pretending to be his batman, rather than the deputy head of the unit, who has nothing to do with this broad-daylight abduction of the head of his Field Intelligence Unit.

They throw him in the back of a waiting jeep. One sits on his legs, another one on his chest. Captain Gul has a coughing fit and feels his chest is about to give in; guttural sounds come out of his mouth. Something about making an example of them, his Field Intelligence Unit will find them. We'll find your children, your parents, your sister, we'll find out which school your children go to and who your whore sisters are married to.

When they present him to the CO, one man is still holding his hands behind his back, respectful now, but firm. CO looks at him with pity. He is also wearing a tracksuit, not the standard military issue but an Adidas one. Captain Gul remembers that at their first high-tea meeting CO had told him in very sombre tones that at heart he was a sportsman and had represented his regiment at the Inter-Regiment Welterweight Championship and won a silver.

'They didn't teach you to salute your senior officers?'

Captain Gul squirms in his tormentor's grip and his eyes make a gesture towards the goon's hands.

'You know that's a court-martial offence. You could go to jail for three years and get a solid red stripe in your file. For not saluting a senior officer.'

CO doesn't mention his crafty daughter. Surely he isn't going to bring up the subject of the marriage proposal in front of these lowly soldiers. But Captain Gul is no fool. If he is going to be humiliated in front of his troops for his personal life, for his one misstep in an intimate moment, he might as well bring it up himself. Captain Gul has rehearsed it in the jeep, while squirming under his abductors' asses. In fact, he has rehearsed two versions. That's just Field Intelligence 101. Always have two stories ready. He'll either be upfront and say that, although he did canoodle with CO's daughter, he never actually entered her and CO should look elsewhere to find the father of his grandchild. Or he'll say that he would be honoured to be accepted into the family but at the moment he is on a classified mission which he obviously can't divulge for operational reasons. He feels asking for some more time might be a practical as well as honourable way out of this humiliating grip on his hands.

Before he can decide which version of his case to present, CO asks him again if he would like to be court-martialled for not saluting a senior officer. Before Captain Gul can plead his case, CO comes forward. Gul doesn't see the right hook coming. Before the pain hits, Captain Gul remembers again his CO's silver medal in the welterweight championship. He feels a rattle of his teeth; his mouth is full of solids and fluids at the same time. His brain is a starburst. He sees CO's left hand coming towards him. He flinches in panic, but there's an envelope in the hand, which he slips in Captain Gul's pocket. 'Here are your marching orders. Go back to your whore and your little bastard in Pindi.' Captain Gul wants to explain that his Pindi girl wasn't his any more, the little bastard had been dealt with, it wasn't his anyway, but his tongue is an injured little squirrel, hobbling to its feet but falling again and again. 'I don't want to see this creep's face ever again within a mile of the cantonment's gates,' Commanding Officer barks at his men before turning away from him.

Travelling back to his bachelor officer's quarters, Captain Gul ponders his situation. This time no thug escorts, only a respectful driver who salutes him and helps him get in the back seat. His tongue seems to have disappeared. When he moves it, one bloody tooth falls out, then another. He tries to shift his position to see himself in the rear-view mirror but his right eye sees only a blurry shadow of a ballooned-up face. At arrival Laal Khan takes him into his arms and drags him to his bed, which he has made with a lot of care, as if he had been expecting Captain Gul to return wounded and in need of bed rest.

TWENTY-FIVE

English Lessons

BAGHI TELLS SABIHA BANO THAT HE HAS URGENT business in the bazaar and leaves the academy in a hurry. She is on her prayer mat, busy scribbling on her sheaf of paper, and barely acknowledges his rushed departure. He is surprised at her progress. The girl who couldn't string two sentences is now churning out page after page. When A.D. Malang sends a constable to pick you up and bring you to the police station, you don't keep him waiting because then he himself might turn up at the academy. Baghi is not scared of Malang, but he is sure there are people out there trying to hunt his new housemate down. This, he decides, is his chance to tell A.D. Malang that he should stay away from the academy. After all, he has made him what he is. It's time to call in his teacher's debt.

Pillion riding on the constable's Vespa, they break through red traffic lights, whizz around street hawkers. The constable raises his hand to accept salams, snatches a guava from a fruit seller's cart, curses anyone who tries to cross his path, then abruptly stops to throw a coin in front of a beggar woman sitting on the roadside, asking her to pray for him. The woman looks towards the sky, her eyes all white.

Baghi is received warmly at the police station. The constable gives him a knowing smile and ushers him into Malang's office. Founder of the nation Mohammed Ali Jinnah's official portrait, all cheekbones and a monocle, looks down at him from the wall. Under it a revolving chair, a large table covered with green felt. Across the table sits a woman in tight qameez and shalwar, blue and white stripes. She seems jumpy. Malang insists that Baghi sit in his revolving chair. How can a student occupy a chair of authority in front of his ustad? The woman sitting across the table gets up and offers him her hand to shake. Baghi is surprised again by this new plague of women wanting to shake his hand in this city. Baghi sees her face and realizes that she is a child made up to look like a woman, her bold red lipstick smudged where she has been drinking from a Fanta bottle with a straw.

Malang gets straight to business. 'Our friend in Field Intelligence Unit wants an English-speaking girl.'

Why, Baghi wants to ask but knows that he is not going to get a straight answer from Malang. He gives him his teacher's admonishing look.

'They are slightly shaken in the head.' Malang caresses his temple. 'During training we also parade all day long but these army men never recover from parade-ground pounding. They bang their boots on concrete all day long for five years and go soft in the head. Their reason barely survives. But let's not worry, Bubbly is here to help out.'

The girl-woman speaks up. 'I am telling Malang sahib, I speak English, I not know what kind of new English he wants me to speak. Speak to me in English. Say I love you and I answer in English.' She has a peasant girl's eyes; she sees humans as sheep, trying to decide if she should milk them, feed them or save them for a bad day when she might have to slaughter them. She is what they call in English full of life. Crossing and uncrossing her legs, throwing back her hair, flicking it sideways to show off her blonde streaks.

She is very aware of her young face and slight body; she has probably stuffed her chest to make it look bigger.

Baghi gets up from his chair in a huff and walks out. Malang follows. 'You know that I don't do private tuitions – it's against my principles. Just send her to the academy when it opens and she can learn with everybody else.'

Malang reaches for his shoulder. He does this when he wants something completely illegal done with the reassurance that if the protector of the law is requesting you to do it, it can't possibly be illegal. 'A personal favour for me.' He withdraws his hand. 'Actually, a personal favour for us, for our academy. If I don't send him a girl he'll come to the academy to look for one because you said you are giving girls tuitions now. We don't want one of your students falling into his hands. I mean, he looks normal but you can never tell how far these hot-headed young officers can go when they are going around looking for a girl without a name.'

'But she is almost a minor,' Baghi protests.

Malang shakes his head and tries to suppress a smile. 'Sir, let's say Bubbly is a working lady. She'll be happy for some business. He'll get whatever kink he wants to get from hearing her speak English. Probably where he comes from, girls say things in English in bed and he is just missing that. Just a few sentences and I'll be able to get him to stay away from our academy. You don't want him going after a girl student from a good family.' Baghi looks down and thinks of Sabiha Bano's dupatta that A.D. Malang saw in his academy. 'Half of law enforcement is that you let people take care of each other. I don't care if Hakim Wasif burnt himself or if someone else lit the match. I don't care if someone is giving his second wife protection. Do we want to drag women from good families to police stations? This girl here, you may not approve of what she does, but she has a family to feed. Look at me, I was a potter's son and you made something out of me. You can make her into something if you just spare a little bit of your time.'

Baghi had taught him how to spell the word intimidation. Now Malang has served it to him wrapped in a promise. Baghi doesn't want the law to come knocking at his academy's door and find Sabiha Bano.

Baghi returns to the table and speaks to her warily. 'Say something in English.' Malang has left them in his office so that 'you can focus on what you do best'.

The girl is coquettish now, as if she expects Baghi to teach her more than English. 'No, you say first. Say I love you.'

Baghi sighs, looks at the founder of the nation's portrait on the wall. He wonders if the Gujrati kid who first became an Englishman and then threw the English out of the country is laughing at his predicament. He couldn't have done it all if he didn't know English better than the English. 'I love you,' he says.

'I love you too,' she fires back, and then adds haltingly, 'but no kissing with tongue and no sucking and no backdoor entry.'

Baghi shudders in disgust. 'No, not that kind of English, child. Where did you learn such filth?'

She talks and talks fast as she explains that she was going to go to Dubai, where she had a job offer at an English-speaking bar. She was waiting for her visa and in her spare time she learnt English from her friend who had already worked in that bar. But then the friend got jealous thinking that she might steal her clients although she had no such plans but as a result her visa never came through and her friend was an insecure bitch because there is enough work for everyone in Dubai and sheikhs pay more for Pakistani girls because Indian randis have cornered the market but

God-fearing sheikhs like their whores to be Muslim and although I am in this dirty business but by the grace of Allah I am a Muslim and why should Hindu bitches get all the work anyway, don't our families need that money, but maybe it's not all my friend's fault, she has always been insecure about her thin lips, but you know there is something called destiny, you will get the money that's written in your destiny, and by the grace of God I have good clients here and Malang sahib has been very kind, never even tried to touch me, and if he calls you his guru then you must be a nice person too because you can tell a person from the company he keeps, no?

'Speak after me,' says Baghi. 'I want to go home. My mother is waiting for me.'

She looks at Baghi, puzzled, and asks him what he is going on about. Baghi explains patiently and breaks down the words for her, and she is suddenly relaxed and stops putting on her girl-woman act. 'I want to go home,' she repeats after him. 'My mother is waiting.' Baghi feels a surge of pride and then a wave of shame passes over him as he remembers the purpose of this lesson. 'And it's true,' she says. 'My mother always says she is waiting for me but I don't think she really wants me to come home, not yet, because I have a brother in class eight. I am not sure if he actually goes to school or just smokes ganja with his friends all day, and my mother always tells me that, although I am her daughter, she considers me her son and she loves me more than she loves my brother and all four sisters put together and I still have a few years left because in my line of work clock is always ticking ticking ticking.'

When A.D. Malang knocks at the captain's door in the bachelor officers' quarters to deliver the girl, Captain Gul half-opens the door. One side of his face is swollen and his right eye is a lump the size of a small hand grenade. He takes the girl by her wrist, pulls her in and shuts the door in Malang's face. Malang shifts his weight from one foot to another, wondering if he should go or stay and wait for feedback. The door opens and Captain Gul pushes the girl out and shouts at him before slamming shut the door in his face. 'It's because of sissy-ass people like you that this country is going to the dogs. I ask you for an English-speaking girl and you go and pick the first whore who walks into your police station. Are you a pimp or an officer of the law? Have some respect for your bloody uniform.'

Malang and the girl look at each other. 'He is a very unhappy person,' Bubbly says with the rectitude of a neutral observer of the human condition. 'And I think his tool doesn't work.' She mimes a bird-failing-to-fly type sign around her crotch with her hand. 'Thank God he didn't keep me – did you see his face? He seems like the type who like beating. We get many like this in my field, because a lot of them can't beat their wives at home, so they pay to fuck us but actually they want someone they can beat up because their wives at home wouldn't let them. Some of them even cry after beating us black and blue and ask for forgiveness.'

Malang is not new to failure. He has met thieves who took pleasure in his beatings and refused to confess even when he offered them tea and cigarettes and promised to send them home. Political types who raised slogans at every lash, and loving men who cried all night because they missed the lover they had just slaughtered. Malang walks back to the cantonment gate without looking at the girl. He has never failed at purposeful pimping before. Maybe he didn't understand Captain Gul's demand properly. Maybe he wasn't looking for a random girl who could ooh and aah in English but some specific girl that he had seen in his dreams. How is he supposed to get into an intelligence officer's dreams and figure out what he wants?

On the long walk back to the cantonment gate, Bubbly runs towards the swings as they pass the deserted Martyrs' Park. She rides the swing, going higher and higher and singing an Indian love song at the top of her voice. Malang has to cajole her off the swing by pointing to a passing military police jeep and reminding her of impending military action against her because she has just been rejected by a very important military officer. He drops her home and presses two hundred-rupee notes into her palm. She is reluctant to accept the money but takes it when Malang offers her a choice between two hundred rupees or two tight slaps.

'My mother says taking money from the police brings bad luck. I hope it's not true in your case because in my field we have to deal with police all the time but you are the nicest police officer in this district, and it doesn't matter to me what they say about you on the street, but you are a gentleman and it'll be a lucky girl who you decide to marry, and your teacher was very nice also and like you he didn't try to touch me when you left us alone in your office.'

'This money is your reward for taking an English lesson,' says Malang before driving off.

HOMEWORK 11

Our Mother Daughter Fight

It has often been said erroneously that you play with the deck of cards that fate deals you, that every coin has two sides and sometimes you find yourself impaled on the horns of a dilemma. People also use the word dilemma as a false quandary. Life's not a multiple choices exam, there's only your fate whipping you into a blind alley. Mother is cutting vegetables for supper and she is concentrating hard and she does it when she is thinking of something else and ergo she brings up the subject of marriage. There's a good man, a fine man, own house, own business, is married once before but he has enough means to take on a second wife.

I look at mother and reach the conclusion that if she is refusing to look me in the eye when she is talking about my betrothal then she is hiding something. I begin to be disrespectful. I expound, nay accuse, her of cuckolding with Comrade Sadiq Ali and not caring about esteemed father who rots in some unknown prison and what kind of wife abandons her progeny so that she can keep on philandering with a man who is traitor to our cause. The knife in her hand moves brisker and brisker and her eyes are welling up. I assume the tears are caused by onions she has just chopped and not by her progeny's harsh words. I am not getting betrothed ever, and then I change my mind and say that I'll only consider a marriage proposal when we have managed to secure clemency for esteemed father. And she abruptly starts chopping onions again and through her onion-tears-filled eyes says that the clemency for my father hinges upon me getting hitched so that she can secure enough bail or bribe money to get my father released. Are you planning to sell me to the highest bidder in the market? I demand to know in a voice that sounds shrill and mutinous even in my own ears. If you are doing it for esteemed father, my voice becomes a proverbial shriek, then why don't you get betrothed?

Mother Bano flicks the knife at me, my hands make an involuntary defence gesture and the knife grazes the back of my right hand followed by the sudden emergence of a gash and the gushing of blood. Mother Bano jumps from her perch. Now her tears are not onion tears but genuine misunderstood, anguished mother's tears. She hugs me, takes my hand in her hands, kisses it, and her face is crimson with my blood. Then she tears her dupatta, fashions a bandage for my hand. The bandage also turns crimson momentarily but the flow of blood stops. Mother Bano takes me in her arms and rocks me as if I was a proverbial hurt child and keeps whispering what am I to do, what are we to do. I kiss her forehead and whisper one singular word to her: protest.

TWENTY-SIX

Used

BAGHI DOESN'T LIKE BEING USED. REVOLUTIONARIES had used up his youth and then discarded him. Central Committee of the Mazdoor Militia had noted in its expulsion resolution, passed by a unanimous vote, that he was an individualist, a native informant, also an ordinary fifty-rupee police informer, a deviant, a cock-gobbling closet counter-revolutionary. He felt sometimes even his students, his pride and joy, were using him, sucking his time and his love for the language out of him to make their careers. Now A.D. Malang was asking him to teach his whores how to make bedroom noises in English. Men of all classes and tastes had used him for their sexual pleasures and then gone back to their wives and cuddly children. Now Molly is using his trust to hide a girl. She is a girl who might become a fellow comrade, but Molly wants her as his concubine.

This morning he still has a slight hangover from his two Black Dog drinks and a lingering metallic taste in his mouth, the taste of having been used. Again.

After their night of hospitality for Captain Gul, Molly has cleared up the academy, taken away all the pamphlets, thrown away the jerrycans of kerosene oil. Molly is sure that the captain was too drunk to notice anything but he isn't taking any chances. He has told Baghi to stop telling people that the slogan Bhutto Lives was first uttered in this mosque, and it was a prayer anyway, a metaphor, not a call to arms, not an invitation to douse yourself in petrol and then wait for someone to save you. The military regime wasn't so bad – after all, it was bringing in Islamic punishments and all this country needed was a few public hangings and lashings.

After leading his funeral prayers in absentia, Molly is looking to a new future, a future without Bhutto or his ghost. Now Baghi has to carry this burden, look after this girl who believes in God and spreads a prayer mat in this godless academy and keeps saying she didn't do anything, only ran from a house on fire. Sometimes she scribbles on paper, laughs, looks up and says that she likes doing her homework because she doesn't have a home. Baghi has to carry this burden like he has carried all the other heavy loads of this wretched city and at the end of it found himself always alone.

Molly is in the academy loitering, waiting for Baghi to leave on some pretext. He has reached the comfort level of a consummate abuser with Baghi, doesn't even give him an errand, doesn't even hint that Baghi leave them alone.

The worst exploiters are those who expect you to offer yourself up, as if it was your pleasure to bend over, get rammed and be grateful. Sabiha hasn't said it in so many words, but she has dropped enough hints that she doesn't want to be left alone with Molly. 'Sir, your friend talks a lot about Allah but when you are away he tries to give sermons with his hands.'

Baghi picks up *To the Lighthouse*. He wants to read it. He has promised himself that he is going to read it but now he starts turning pages idly.

Were they allies? Were they enemies? How long would they endure?

He gives up and starts randomly choosing the next five words he'll give his students to study.

Confound. Ramshackle. Musing. Gust. Lamentation.

Molly's attempts at small talk are gloriously ridiculous. 'Allah shows the way but He wants us to tread with our eyes open. Before I opened the mosque for women for daily prayers, I opened it for Friday prayers,' he tells Sabiha, who listens patiently but refuses to take part in his progressive religious-man-allows-women-to-be-led-by-him spiel. 'These things have to be done step by step.'

Baghi is infuriated at the idea that Molly is using his imam's authority to get into a distressed widow's shalwar. Baghi knows that religion is the opium of the masses but in this mosque it was being used as an aphrodisiac. Baghi wants to lecture Molly about uses and misuses of God but can't. Molly rescued him from a torture cell; Molly gave him a place to live, allowed him to set up his academy here. He turns some more pages, the words blur in front of him.

Gusts of lamentation.

'Islam has given women more rights than any religion in the world,' Molly says as he glances towards Baghi, who pretends to be lost in *To the Lighthouse*. 'Before Islam they used to bury their newborn daughters because they believed that those girls would grow up and bring shame to the tribe.'

'Bury all the girls? Why are there still so many?' Sabiha asks in a calm, mock-curious voice.

Molly is not used to being questioned on the subject of Islam or its history. 'Not all of them, of course, but many did. Islam forbade it. Islam said Jannah is at a mother's feet.'

'You must have met women who are not mothers? What's under their feet? Hell?'

Molly laughs a kind, indulgent laugh. 'Allah likes it when you make someone smile but He may not like it if you laugh at His expense.'

Molly keeps glancing towards Baghi, willing him to leave, but he just sits there, determined not to be used this time.

Molly gets up, walks over to Baghi, peers at his book from over his shoulder. Then a hand on Baghi's shoulder, a silent plea. Baghi refuses to budge. Molly looks at Sabiha, willing her to intervene, but in this silent moment sees that she has gone to the other side, Baghi's side. He is furious for a moment but realizes this is not the time.

He had tried to argue with his wife that marrying a widow is the righteous path. Molly remembers his wife's outburst and her cold grip on his calves. And he had spoken only in the most generic of terms. Maybe it's best for now to resist this living embodiment of satanic temptation.

He mutters something about getting late for prayers and leaves without looking at either of them.

Baghi keeps turning the pages; words swim in front of his eyes.

Gusts of lamentation.

'Good of you not to leave me alone with your friend.'

'I don't agree with his god but he's all right, he has given you protection,' Baghi says. 'If the police are looking for you, they won't come here.' Baghi doesn't know why he is defending Molly.

'If the police are looking for me does that mean I have done something? The police used to look for you all the time. What had you done? What did my father do? What about my mother?'

'I was fighting for a just cause,' says Baghi. He can't bring himself to speak the word revolution or about his open death-warrant letter to the leaders of the Ummah.

'I ran away from a burning building. That's a good cause, isn't it?'

Baghi puts *To the Lighthouse* aside. 'Molly says you were planning to set yourself on fire along with your husband.'

Sabiha gives him a withering look, takes the prayer mat, spreads it and sits on it. 'You know your Molly. He says there is holy light in his chest. But he is just pondering with his penis.'

'Whatever you say about him, he saved my life and now he is saving yours,' says Baghi.

'Yes, the police can't come in but can I go out? He has trapped me,' she says. 'I am a prisoner. I don't like to be anyone's prisoner. I was married, remember, sir.' Sabiha chews on the pen, stares at the page, crosses a line. 'When I want to be a prisoner again, I'll find out where they are keeping my parents. I'll walk straight into that prison.'

Baghi sees a glimpse of himself in her, questioning everything, breaking down doors instead of ringing the bell. He wants to hold her. He wants her arms around him. He is ashamed at this urge. He wants her close. He wants her out of here.

'He gets his penis hard by locking me up. It's the biggest aphrodisiac. I should know. I was married to someone who made them with herbs. But nothing makes a man harder than a woman on a chain, a woman in a cage, a woman on a chain in a cage. I was in that laboratory, sir. You are not so different.'

Baghi wanted a cuddle, he had got a kick in his balls.

'He is your friend. God knows how you became friends with him but it's none of my business. The door is there – I would love to have my solitude back. I have to get ready for my class. This,' he says, waving his hand around the room, 'may not mean anything to you but this is all I have. I might have failed you but this place has helped many poor children. This is all I have.'

Molly is using him to hide his concubine and the concubine is using him like his overnight truck drivers who sometimes stayed over in exchange for letting him tug at their cocks. Now she's accusing him of imprisoning her. Women, he thinks, you never win. Men, at least you can fondle and they leave in the morning.

She is not finished yet. 'You think you are better than him. He wants to fuck me. Did you not try to touch me when I was your student? But you didn't have the courage. You were scared then. And you are scared now. You say you don't believe in Allah because you think you are god. Scared little god. Oh my god, I am god.' She starts to laugh at her own joke and soon her laughter turns into a coughing fit and tears.

'I never touched you, I don't touch girls. I am not that way.'

'Maybe you did, maybe you didn't. I went to school and I believed that's what teachers do. They touch you, they break you.'

'Not me. Never. I don't touch girls. Any girls.'

Baghi gets up, walks over to his bookshelf, puts back *To the Lighthouse* and starts rearranging his books. *Wretched of the Earth* is moved to a lower shelf.

This is exactly where she stood, in front of the shelf, two books in hand, trying to choose.

He dusts a copy of Maxim Gorky's *Mother*.

He stood behind her telling himself to move away. He moved an inch closer.

What Is to Be Done needs another binding.

As he was willing himself to move away from her, she turned abruptly and his hand brushed against her shoulder. He didn't intend to. And then she was gone. He had cursed himself for that momentary lapse, then took solace in the fact that he had never touched a student; he had always sought his pleasure with random strangers at bus stops, cinema halls, in dark alleys. There were enough men in the city with hungry mouths and eager hands.

Now he hears her moving behind him, her arms snaking around his waist, her head on his shoulder and her gentle breathing in his ear. Baghi's first urge is to run away like she had done all those years ago. He hasn't been held like this in a long time, with tenderness and a beating heart caressing his back. Her hands run softly down his back and come to rest on his ass, casually, like asking him an intimate question and then waiting for an answer. A regretful shudder runs through his body; he wants to move back into her, abandon his ass, his whole being, to that girl-boy who has come back to hold him. She is grown-up now. He feels her chest against his back and knows that there's no desire left in him. For a moment he thinks of turning around and holding her in a tight embrace and telling her that, yes, once he had desired her, because to him she looked like a boy; he had wanted to bury his face in her sweaty, muscular shoulder. But not any more. He is scared of her ample chest pressed against his back.

He takes a deep breath and is about to turn around when she says something that brings Baghi back to his senses. 'I am tired of running. You are the only one here who understands me. Let's help each other. Let's run away together. There will be some school somewhere where you can teach English and I can become a PT teacher. Every school needs an English teacher, a PT teacher. I still have my medal. I would rather live with a man who doesn't want to sleep with me. You can do whatever you do with boys. But if you wanted to start a family, I'd be there for you. I'll wait for my parents to come out. I have heard that people sometimes go underground during such evil hours.'

Baghi breathes deep as if his lungs are running out of air.

'And promise you'll never send me to the cantonment and ask for a fauji's help for the release of my parents?'

'No. Never.'

'And you'll never leave me?'

'Never.'

Baghi knows that when you are falling for someone, to stop that fall, to slow it down, you must find another love, because one love will make you dependent and then redundant; it will make you sick and then kill you. 'I'll never leave you,' repeats Baghi, as he makes an escape plan.

Right now, what Baghi needs is a boy, someone to hold him, somebody who'll let him suckle and fondle, someone who'll be tender to him, or rough. He doesn't need someone who says they can't live without him, who wants to bring back into his life that worst curse of all capitalist curses: family.

Baghi is determined to break this fall; he needs to find some afternoon release. Baghi is hopeful of finding some boy love in Venus cinema where they are showing a film called *One Million Years B.C.* Or at least it should be educational.

TWENTY-SEVEN

Bhutto Lives, but Where?

Captain Gul is tucked in his bed, shivering under a maroon velvet duvet. Laal Khan has taken the gin bottle away with the pretence that his bachelor officer's quarters might be raided again at any time. After Captain Gul refused to go to the sick bay 'for security reasons', Laal Khan brought out his unit's first-aid kit, applied red tincture on his shattered gums and gave him a chilled bottle of Murree gin filled with plain water. A clever little deception for his tormentors should they return. They would think 'oh, we found booze on him' but it would turn out to be water. Field Intelligence Unit at its strategic best. Captain Gul presses the icy bottle against his swollen jaw. A cold wave of pain spreads across his face. His right eye has a life of its own, it twitches and pulsates. He buries his face in the pillow. He had avoided looking in the mirror and asked Laal Khan to describe how bad it was. 'I have seen worse,' he had said. 'I have done much worse.' Laal Khan at his reassuring best. Without thinking, Captain Gul uncaps the bottle and takes a swig, hoping for some relief with a sip of gin, but the water tastes of metal, stabbing at his innards. He dozes off. When he comes to, he thinks it's a new day, looks at the clock and realizes he was asleep only two hours. He also realizes that he has not had a drop for fourteen hours. This makes him feel like he is a man in control of his destiny.

With the clarity and determination of a newly sobered-up drunk soldier, he hobbles towards his cupboard, takes out all the cables he had received since taking the OK town command and goes through them one by one for any clues that he might have missed. Cypher messages, some of them not even coded. He had almost forgotten that he was on a punishment posting. Why is OK town going crazy about dead Bhutto? What do they mean when they shout Bhutto Lives? Maybe it is a metaphor? Maybe there are too many poets in the city? The idea lives? Or the man lives? And suddenly his sober might stumbles over a basic fact. Forget this rotten city, why are his headquarters going crazy about these bullshit rumours? They were very good at tackling rumours – hell, they were even better at starting them. Wasn't it the deputy head of internal security who had planted newspaper stories about Bhutto's uncircumcised penis and then sent Captain Gul on a mission to get photographic evidence of the same on the night of his hanging?

His sober mind takes another sharp turn and he thinks what if this is true? What if the bastard really does live?

He tries to retrace the night of the hanging. OK, he had knocked down a few before turning up at the jail. If you are required to be at a hanging at dawn with a top-secret but deeply unpleasant mission, wouldn't you need a few drinks? He remembers that when he was left with the dead man alone in the room, he had not actually seen his face – it was still covered with the black sack. The photographer had pulled the shalwar down and at that very moment Captain Gul had looked away. He was a soldier, yes, yes, yes, he was a soldier. He had taken his oath, he was willing to give his life for the country, but where did his oath say he had to stare at a dead man's privates? He remembered the stench of piss and faeces. He had let the photographer do his thing and asked him to report his findings. And then passed the negative report on to his bosses. At no point had he actually seen the hanged man's face or any part of his body. Just a no-face corpse with its head covered in a black sack and shalwar pulled down. What if these crazies of OK town were right? What if he had slipped through the noose? With his long neck and bald head it was not impossible. Then another thought occurs to him. What if they had hanged some random prisoner and passed him off as Bhutto?

It seems implausible at first, but then he remembers that as a second lieutenant his first interaction with civilians was when he had to deliver the coffins of two soldiers martyred in a landmine mishap and instruct the families – no, not just instruct but make sure that the coffins weren't opened, because seeing their martyred sons' faces wasn't such a good idea for the bereaved yet proud families. He had delivered the coffins, supervised the burials, but he had no idea what was in the caskets. Later, he had a sneaking suspicion that he had mixed up the coffins on his way to delivering them. If he, a young lieutenant, could replace one dead man with another, why couldn't his bosses and their genius intelligence?

He limps back to his bed. His hands shake, his legs curl up, he convulses as he remembers the CO's sneering face and his lackey soldiers trying not very hard to suppress their glee. Then he remembers that graceful fortune-telling chief lawyer in the mosque who had predicted his glorious future in Delhi, DC, Kabul. He was destined to be a prince of the Ummah but here he was being manhandled by a two-star general. He needs to take his destiny in his own hands.

Laal Khan brings him a hot, wet towel, gives him a sliver of black opium to calm his nerves and tucks him into the blanket. Bhutto is in Captain Gul's dream, his neck bruised, his tongue stretched out like a half-hanged man's tongue, and his eyes bulging out of their sockets. Gul can see his own reflection in them. He is trying to run away from the hanged man in his dream, another wet towel on his head, and this time Sabiha Bano comes to him with a noose in her hands. She sits astride his chest, fixes the noose around his neck with small child's hands. When, after twelve hours of opium-induced restful sleep, Captain Gul wakes up, he has an erection and a clear mission.

There was a Bhutto hanged that night, and there is another one haunting this city. He has to get rid of them both.

Captain Gul is impressed by his own recall of the hanging night. A sober mind, he is convinced now, is a superior mind. Captain Gul has always regarded himself a soldier of the mind. Yes, he understands you need tanks and missiles and men who can parachute behind enemy lines. But the biggest, the fiercest battlefield is in his head. He caresses his head and the pain returns.

And with pain, another insight. Why didn't they have a casket ready on the night of the hanging?

If you are going to hang an elected prime minister, a very popular chap, mobilize half the army to deal with the anticipated unrest, get planes to fly in the middle of the night, get someone to dig a grave, kick a bunch of random people in the ass to join his last rites, why would you not have a casket ready? Were they not sure until the very last moment that they could actually hang the condemned man?

He shudders at his own thought. Having unravelled the ultimate mystery of his time, he wants to share his discovery. He can't trust Laal Khan. He can't go back to his bosses and say I know my real mission now. Bhutto's not really hiding somewhere in OK town, not in Asia's largest vegetable market, not in the cornfields, not at OK Potato Cold Storage. He is hiding in the best hiding place of all. In people's heads. They hanged their man; they hoped that they wouldn't have to but they did.

Now his mission is to bury the idea. To smash its hideout, to raze it to the ground.

He realizes that he hasn't actually bashed any heads since he came here. Come to think of it, he hasn't even slapped anyone. He had let go of that photographer who was clearly a jiyala and those two in the Gol Mosque, drinking whisky in the House of Allah and mocking his sperm count. He had been softened up. He had become a civilian. He had forgotten his mission. What had that graceful woman in the black coat who had read his palm said? Hadn't she called it a general's hand? Hadn't she predicted his future on the world stage, in Washington DC, in Delhi?

At any other time, he would have pulled out his bottle of gin, taken a sip to celebrate the sharpness of his own mind, the promise of glory. But now he paces his room, stands in front of the mirror and shadow-boxes with the broken-jawed Captain Gul in the mirror.

Dance like a butterfly, sting like a bee, sting like a bee, where is he, where is she?

HOMEWORK 12

Our Protest for Esteemed Father

Since the time of the expulsion of Adam from Eden, homo sapiens have been standing up for their rights even if it means taking on the power and prestige of earthly and heavenly gods. We make numerous posters from the picture of esteemed father with Chairman Bhutto. Comrade Sadiq Ali Sadiq brings us markers and cardboard, I gather my urchins, and we spend entire day painting prison-cell bars over father's picture. We don't write anything about Bhutto, Chairman and his people can take care of him, we want our esteemed father back. Comrade Sadiq Ali Sadiq strategizes like a veteran campaigner and comes up with the idea that Mother Bano and I should be carrying the biggest banner and marching in front of the procession. 'The police are always scared of taking on women. They have standing orders that when they see ladies in a protest they must show restraint and not use force.' Mother Bano sports a big dupatta adorned with embroidered yellow flowers, she gives me a scarf to put on my head, she makes a big Thermos of tea as if we are not staging a protest but going for a picnic.

We are informed that the district administration has imposed sections 144 in the city and it bans a gathering of more than three people. Comrade Sadiq Ali has a solution: we'll march in twos, and we'll maintain a distance of three yards amongst protestors. I am surprised at the thoughtful endeavours of Comrade Sadiq Ali. He doesn't seem devious or double-crossing – he wants to make the protest successful. At the last minute he produces a plastic bucket full of onions and wet rags and demonstrates to everybody how to use these to ward off the harmful after-effects of tear-gas shelling that police are likely to resort to when faced with peaceful but determined protestors.

The bamboo cordons in front of the Satlaj Cotton Mills have been replaced with a metal sheet wall. Rolls of shiny silver barbed wire block the passage ways to the mills. Comrade Sadiq Ali Sadiq has strategized that first the protestors will raise slogans and appear to be at their most law-abiding behaviour. The police seeing a small protest led by two harmless ladies and a few urchins will be lax in its response. Then from behind this peaceful façade the members of the unions, many veterans of street battles, will surge ahead, tear down the barricades, barge into the mills and occupy them till the government comes to its senses, nay its knees, and agrees to release the esteemed father.

The police at the barricade are indeed lackadaisical in their policing endeavours, looking at mother and I holding our banner aloft, amused at the number of half-clothed, rowdy urchins following us. The policemen yawn, they scratch their backs with their batons, there is not a tear-gas gun or any other gun in sight. As we approach the barricades raising our rousing slogans for freedom for father, a truck pulls up, the police shuffle away, and they are replaced by ferocious men in starched khaki uniforms and menacing guns. Comrade Sadiq Ali Sadiq who is marching along with us but maintaining a law-abiding distance of few yards is visibly perturbed at this new dramatic development. The bored bonhomie of the yawning and guffawing policemen has been replaced by the stern-faced menace of army men. He raises his hand in the air giving us a signal to stop the march and then moves forward, ostensibly to initiate parlays with the military men and ensure them of our peaceful intentions. The spectacle of cocked guns, army men in camouflaged helmets, excites my urchins and they raise a ruckus, Comrade Sadiq Ali Sadiq turns around to placate the tempers of these youthful protestors, somebody from behind us starts pelting stones at the troops, one finds its target and hits the helmet of a soldier. And then the proverbial hell breaks loose.

The sound of bullets fired at close range does not ring like a blast – it's more like a tight slap that echoes through the cosmos. We erroneously come to the conclusion that the soldiers are resorting to aerial firing, which is a common tactic they use to scare the protestors, but Comrade Sadiq Ali Sadiq is down on the road, first on his knees and then on his knees and elbows, futilely attempting to crawl back, leaving a trail of blood in the middle of the road. Mother Bano abandons her side of the banner and rushes forward to aid a visibly wounded Comrade Sadiq Ali Sadiq, who is proven right in his dying moment as the army soldiers do show restraint and don't shoot at Mother Bano. Before she can reach Comrade Sadiq Ali Sadiq one soldier comes forward and assaults her with the butt of his rifle. Then another few soldiers drag her onto the road. I try to run to her rescue but suddenly there's another burst of gunfire. They pick her up and throw her in the back of a truck. In the scuffle her white dupatta adorned with white and yellow embroidered flowers is strewn on the road. I pick it up and run after the truck, which speeds away and takes away Mother Bano God only knows where.

TWENTY-EIGHT

Two and a Half Thousand Years of Civilization

SIX ASPIRINS AND TWO ATIVAN TABLETS IN AND Captain Gul is floating in the clouds. A single harp plays in the distance. He finds himself in a ballroom, in the presence of the Shah of Shahs, Raza Shah Pehlvi, his uniform a maze of gold braids, sashes, medals. So many medals. An attendant goes on his knees and offers the Shah a silver tray. Raza Shah Pehlvi picks his cap from the tray, puts it on his head and salutes Captain Gul, who is startled by his presence, by the elegance. Even the air in the ballroom is fragrant, purer somehow, and the Shah's skin looks like it is made of light. In his dream, Captain Gul is not wearing a cap and is slightly embarrassed that he can't return the Shah's salute. He comes to attention, arms locked at his sides; he clicks his heels together and bows his head ever so slightly.

Queen Farah Pehlvi stands one step behind the Shah of Shahs in a powder-pink dress, a tiger brooch made of emeralds on her chest, her hair coiffed. She is the epitome of royal grace. Shah gives him a benevolent royal smile and introduces him to the Queen. 'This is Captain Gul, the rising star of Islamic Ummah, soon you'll hear his name everywhere.' He winks at Gul as if they have a shared plan to bugger the

Ummah's future. Captain Gul doesn't know how to laugh at a king's joke and he has had no training in how to greet a queen either. 'Yes, of course I am aware,' Queen Farah says with a coy smile. She offers him her hand. Captain Gul bends down, holds it gently and air kisses it. She reaches for his right hand and, with a little tug, pulls him towards her. She clasps an arm around his stiff waist, a chorus of violins joins the harp somewhere in the ballroom, the lights go dim. Gul dances tentatively, glancing sideways to see if the Shah approves. Who cares, the Queen does. Captain Gul is hesitant in his movements but Queen Farah leads the dance. They find a rhythm, their bodies flowing in and out of each other's as if they have been doing this for centuries. Farah puts her chin on Captain Gul's shoulder; a slight shudder runs through him, maybe through both of them. At first Captain Gul inhales two and a half thousand years of civilization, then feels a tear on his cheek.

He turns his head slightly and finds Sabiha Bano's face on his shoulder, tears falling from her eyes, trickling down her cheeks. She is pleading, begging for him to rescue her. He tries to breathe, he can't. He wakes up, gasping for air.

He is disoriented for a while, then the pain in his broken jaw returns. Laal Khan comes into his vision and asks, 'Should I start packing, sir?'

'No,' Captain Gul mumbles. 'I have new orders, off the books.' He caresses his swollen jaw. 'This is just a showpiece to deceive the enemy. We still have some work to do in your city.'

TWENTY-NINE

Does Your God Kill Little Babies?

BAGHI TAKES A DETOUR TO VENUS CINEMA, WALKing on the potholed footpath along the Company Park, avoiding the bazaar. He doesn't want to run into another burning man or any of his students. A man pushes a cart hawking over-ripe, about-to-go-bad tomatoes, his voice full of despair. Baghi stops and buys half a kilo. The hawker, almost in tears with gratitude, offers to throw in another kilo for the same price but Baghi refuses. What's he going to do with a sack full of tomatoes in a cinema? A Municipal Corporation sweeper in his crimson uniform sits with his back to the park wall, broom in lap, a half-smoked cigarette in his lips, dozing. Baghi walks with his head down; he has pulled a scarf around his neck and chin in an attempted disguise. He doesn't want anyone to know where he is going. He cares about his reputation; he doesn't mind being known as a pervert, a failed revolutionary, but he doesn't want to be seen as someone who visits shabby cinema halls in the afternoon.

Sabiha Bano's embrace lingers. It had given him momentary warmth, as if he had been accepted by the world for who he was, a godless man in search of a boy with a warm mouth. Her offer to elope and start a new life, them teaching together in a far-off village school, replaced that warmth with a sliver of ice in his heart. One moment he was forgiven and in the very next sentenced for crimes he hadn't committed. He has no plans to marry, settle down or have children with Sabiha or anyone. Can't one hug a distressed comrade without being dragged to the marital bed?

In such moments of self-pity, Baghi feels he has been punished for things that he only dreamed of doing. He had no plans and no means to actually string up the despots of the Ummah in public squares. He was merely expressing his inner anguish. He wanted the world to know that he had ideas for a better tomorrow and he had words to express those ideas. Now he only expresses himself in the academy, where he feels safe, surrounded by his students.

He had learnt that the only way to go through life was with his head down and mouth shut, like he was doing now, walking on a sidewalk along the Company Park Road, occasionally glancing towards the park's boundary wall where citizens scribbled their dreams and discontent. The new military regime was on a whitewashing mission with soldierly passion; the slogans in red on the wall had been painted over. Where once it screamed something about Martyrs' Blood, the wall had been painted white and the new message read 'It's forbidden to urinate here, violators will be prosecuted'. Other slogans demanded total faith and promised rewards and retributions. An Arabic verse with Urdu translation read 'and clutch onto Allah's rope with firm hands'. Baghi smiles bitterly. Sure, hold on to that rope because you'll be hanged by it one day.

A bicycle hobbles past, takes a turn and blocks his way. Baghi looks up and sees Tanvir Anjum, a bodybuilder and district-level hockey player who has been taking Baghi's classes because he believes he'll one day play for the Pakistan national team and will need to speak English on his foreign tours. Baghi stops. He likes this student. He is not devious in his ambitions like many of the other students, who claim that they want to serve their nation but only want to become tax inspectors or judges or policemen. Any job with the scope of power and lucrative bribes. The best of them want to impress girls by copying love poems from obscure romantic poets and passing them on as their own.

After greeting him, Tanvir asks, 'When will the classes start again, sir?' Baghi resumes his walking. The boy walks with him, holding his bicycle and chatting away about how they are losing precious practice time because of what's happening in the city. 'Why should we stop playing hockey because of a hanging?' Baghi tells him not to worry, that the sweep of history is much bigger than a man dangling from a noose and a few other men burning themselves in protest.

'Sir, come, I can drop you – where are you going?'

Baghi can't tell the hockey player he is going to watch a matinee in the hope of finding a boy who is not his student. 'I am just taking a walk. Need to exercise my legs. Take these.' Baghi hands him his bag of tomatoes. The hockey player looks at him, uncertain. He can't understand why his teacher is walking when he can easily give him a lift on his bicycle. Baghi says farewell to the boy with a promise of reopening the academy soon.

'And, sir, you'll give us another book to read? I have finished mine. Maybe I didn't understand it but there is only one crime in the whole book. Not much punishment. The writer should have seen our city. By God, even God has gone AWOL.'

The last bit is aimed at pleasing Baghi.

He used to stir up students with opening his lecture with 'By god, there's no god, but yes, here's some grammar.'

Baghi smiles as he remembers his practised candour, a barrage of little blasphemies to drive inhibitions from young minds. 'Why are you even here? What language does your Allah speak? Why does he have so many names? Is he the creator or is he the destroyer? Is he the tender loving carer or is he all frothing-at-the-mouth wrath? You say he created us but does he even know what it's like to be human?' The stunned silence that follows satisfies him and he continues in a low theatrical whisper. 'Is he our creator or is he just a fart polluting this universe? Does he fart? Does he kill little babies? Does he unleash floods and earthquakes for a giggle?' That last bit is timed to address the suppressed little giggles that he has already got from his students with his god's fart. 'Look, if you need god you can find him in your own homes, under your parents' bed or in your cow's shed. Here, English first. Why, you might ask yourself. Why English? When you go to a court and ask for justice, what language do you ask in? Your lawbooks are not written in Arabic. When you apply for a job, you I-remain-your-humble-servant in English. If you get that job, your appointment letter, the terms of your employment are all in English. When you apply for that sick leave, you lie in English; when they throw you out, your termination letter will be in English. I didn't design this system. I am just preparing you for it. When you die, your death certificate will be in English. You think when you return to your Allah he'll welcome you in Arabic? If you believe that, go somewhere else. Go down to the mosque and bang your forehead on the prayer mat. Here we'll just learn some English.'

Baghi doesn't think he owes anyone an answer. He was often asked why, after spending his youth trying to liberate people from the twin yokes of capitalism and feudalism, he was now embarking on a mission to teach young minds the colonizers' language. What about mother tongues? Why was he abandoning the people's very own language and why was he intent on teaching the new generation the ways of their oppressors? The doubters thought Baghi was creating brown little sahibs, turning street-smart peasant boys and girls into the office clerks of the future, but Baghi believed he was creating the rebels of tomorrow, rebels armed with a language that would pretend to serve power but in the end would smash it. Because while teaching them English, who sowed that first seed of doubt in them? Who asked them where their Allah was? In their mothers' dried-up wombs, in their fathers' prematurely wrinkled faces? He taught them to question power in the language of power.

Yes, I am teaching you in the House of Allah but we are paying the electricity bill to the government. Unlike other revolutionaries, Baghi didn't hate religious people; he felt pity for them and he assumed their liberation was his responsibility.

If Allah did exist, he should come to the academy and learn to use some English words because he would need them.

On the day Sabiha Bano turns up in the class for the last time, Baghi is in his teacher-saviour mode. She sits in the front row, her worn-out sneakers tapping the floor, as if warming up at the start of a race.

He goes to the blackboard and writes Creator and Destroyer in a hurried scrawl.

'Your Allah is the creator and the destroyer. So he can do both? Let's learn some words that do both, that have double meaning, not just double meaning but opposite meaning.

'When you are using words with double meanings, be careful, learn the difference between creating and destroying.'

APPROPRIATE.

He prints on the blackboard in capital letters. He makes them write it in their notebooks, tells them that it means to be correct and proper and it also means to snatch something unfairly, to take something with force. He asks them to think of a sentence with two 'appropriates', then offers them one.

'Allah has made a world appropriate for human beings but then he appropriates it from his human beings.' He encourages students to come up with their own versions. They giggle, they struggle.

'Your mother's appropriate for me but your father has appropriated her from me.'

Baghi jabs the air with his chalk and demands appropriate behaviour from his students.

Sabiha looks confused. She keeps scribbling and her hand keeps going up and Baghi keeps ignoring it.

DUST.

He writes. 'It's dust. But it also means to clear the dust.' He takes his duster and rubs off the word dust from his blackboard. 'See, I dusted the dust with my duster.'

Sabiha looks enthusiastic, relieved, as if she was already internalizing the language. She has been dusting her house since she was six – she just didn't know what she had been doing. 'I dust the house every day because too much dust.'

She gets a nod of approval from Baghi who raises his voice now, trying to get his students into the spirit of the thing.

'Bound is tied up.

'And bound is also destined. You are bound. So you can't go somewhere.

'But you are bound to go somewhere.'

'Sir, if I am bound, how'll I go anywhere?' A boy raises his hand. He has shaved with such rigour that his face is covered with bits of newspaper, camouflaging his cuts.

'On the wings of the English language,' Baghi retorts. 'Play with it. Get it wrong. But play.

'Cleave is to stick together. And cleave is to take apart with force.

'This class cleaved here, but in a little while I'll cleave you apart and everybody will go home.

'Overlook. To neglect. Also to look after, to take care, to protect.'

Sabiha's hand goes up again. 'My mother overlook me because my father overlook me.'

'Yes but no,' Baghi says. 'Think what you are saying. Does your father not take care of you? He fights for the rights of workers. He fights for the dignity of labour. He sent you here, he wants to give you an education. How does he overlook you? Does your mother not overlook you sometimes? Am I overlooking you?'

Sabiha is embarrassed, she blushes and starts scribbling something in her notebook.

Baghi notices her reddening cheeks and changes the subject. 'If somebody overlooks you, you don't have to overlook them.'

He wraps up the class with the satisfaction of a teacher who has managed to inculcate in his students a sense of complexity. If they can hold the opposites in their head at the same time, within the same sentence, they are educated.

'Now go to the bookshelf, pick up a book and take it home. Choose what you like, read it if you like the cover. Read it if you like the title. Spend some time. Go one by one. You may not understand it. But stick to the page. One page a day. Maybe you will understand five per cent but your brains will expand.'

Baghi was feeling generous. He was finally doing something. He could not change the world, but if he could change one mind, his life was worth living, his vocation was revolutionary.

They made a beeline for the bookshelf. Some browsed, others picked the most colourful title, some the slimmest, said their goodbyes and walked away. Sabiha Bano was the last one in the queue and took the longest, picking up books, opening the first page, muttering, then reading haltingly, then putting the book back.

Baghi came up to look at what she was looking at. He stood too close. She turned around, bumped into Baghi, flung *Wretched of the Earth* in his face and ran away.

HOMEWORK 13

My Night of Betrothal

It's often stated that God works in mysterious ways. Oftentimes a prophet is born in a tyrant's house and sometimes a prophet's son becomes a tyrant. The maulvi sahib who performs my nikah ceremony is a gregarious fellow who dubs me his sister and says your husband's home is your home, but sometimes a new home can feel like prison. If that ever transpires in your blessed union always remember there's another house, Allah's house, now it's open for women also.

The match was arranged by Comrade Sadiq Ali Sadiq, now popularly designated the martyr of Satlaj Cotton Mills, who posthumously outshines esteemed father in popularity. With esteemed father and Mother Bano both incarcerated, nay, disappeared from the proverbial face of the earth, I am at strangers' mercy. My spouse-to-be is a famous herbalist in the city and maker of world-famous Iron Syrup. My urchins joke with me that I am going to be their Iron Syrup lady. On the eve of my nikah I harbour the mortal fear of someone who has failed to safeguard their purity for the night of her betrothal. It has been conveyed to me that, although Hakim Wasif Ali Wasif has another wife, he has good relationships with the army people and can help me find esteemed father and Mother Bano. I only get a first glimpse of him after the nikah ceremony when I am bundled up in a red suit, my heart in multiple tangles of fear and loathing.

It transpires that spouse Wasif Ali Wasif is a very corpulent man, and has an oily baby face, and speaks also in a childlike lilting voice, and looks into my eyes as if he wants to get inside my soul. He gives me flowers, roses so red they seem black, and expounds about his first wife that although she is a pious woman, a righteous woman, but she is also a troublesome woman, a cankerous woman, and what he was looking was for a true friend, because he says that, although through his hard work he has made a name for himself and for his country, but he has never had a true companion, only clients. All I can contemplate is that at some point he is going to do what people do in their marital bed and find out that I am already broken. But while delivering his mournful monologue about his lonely life he begins to hiccup and choke and tears start rolling down his chubby baby cheeks. He pleads with me to hold him in my arms. I don't think I have any choice so I hold his head to my bosom, his heaving stops, and he starts breathing deeply as if he wants to suck in all the air in the room. Then he delivers a long soliloquy about how he wants a friendly companion and a business partner, a union of the equals. He mumbles something that if I am sweet to him he'll share his secret Iron Syrup recipe with me. It sounds propitious and I want to tell him that I can be friend, I can be business associate and most assiduously be the best second wife if only he helps me reunite with my esteemed father and Mother Bano. But before I can make my declaration of allegiance and start parlays, he begins fumbling with the buttons on my red silk shirt and the double knots on my shalwar made of the above-mentioned material. It happens in a bleary fashion: for a few moments all his weight is upon me, there is heaving of a mound of flesh over me, a quickening of breathing for him, a humongous struggle to breathe for me, and then he rolls over and goes to sleep clutching my hand to his fleshy mountain of an abdomen. I stay awake all night thinking, my parents already incarnated in an unknown dungeon, am I now free or am I myself a prisoner for life?

THIRTY

What Kind of Death Do You Want?

DOCTOR PERVEZ ALAM PERVEZ INSPECTS CAPTAIN Gul's left cheek with light fingers, then compares it to the right, asks him to open his mouth, bigger, bigger. Captain Gul obliges despite the pain ripping through his jaw. He can't afford to show his suffering to a civilian, even if the civilian is a trusted doctor, an asset, an old-time ally, 'somebody we use when we can't trust our own military doctors', Laal Khan had told him. 'They ask too many questions. You want them to stitch someone up and they want you to fill out forms first. God forbid they end up in a real war. We'll all be martyrs before we can finish filling out three copies of their forms.'

Dr Pervez is taking little bottles out of his medicine cabinet, shaking them and putting them back in, mixing the right potion for Captain Gul's condition. 'There are doctors who want to document your wounds.' He pauses for effect, and builds anticipation like a poet saving his best for the next verse. 'There are those who want to heal them first. I am a humble healer.' He turns back to Captain Gul, with a cotton ball soaked in ethanol. Captain Gul inhales. 'Somebody must really love you,' Dr Pervez says, starting to stuff his mouth with cotton.

Captain Gul is irritated and speaks in a muffled voice. 'Hand-to-hand combat. You should have seen the enemy.' The pain is a dull thud now, fading. He focuses on Dr Pervez Alam. With his thick glasses, red ropes in the eyes and small but steady hands, the doctor has the demeanour of an insomniac intellectual.

'A few stitches on the inside of your cheeks, speech rest, liquid diet and within a week you'll be as handsome as you were,' he says, gently patting Captain Gul's good cheek. 'There will be no marks left.'

Captain Gul is reassured by his professionalism. Laal Khan had told him that his unit paid the clinic's rent and there is a room upstairs where he can stay as long as he wants to. 'We keep it off the books.'

With Captain Gul's mouth full of cotton and his communication restricted to nods and grunts, Laal Khan suddenly seems to have found his tongue. 'Dr Pervez is the finest post mortem artist in the entire district. Bring him a body and he'll give you the exact cause of death you want. Heart attack, drowning, suicide, electric shock, just name it and he'll give it to you. Not like our own doctors, sir.'

Captain Gul makes a vague gesture to ask Laal Khan to ask if he had heard from headquarters. Laal Khan can't decipher. Captain Gul shuts his eyes and tries to assess his situation. He hasn't relinquished his command and the CO has no powers to transfer him. Time might be running out but he is still the head of Field Intelligence Unit. He is in a safe house. It's an off-the-book safe house but bloody hell doesn't he know there is always a book for off-the-book safe houses as well. And if he knows it, then this red-haired bully knows it too.

'Dr sahib is a very fine poet as well.' Laal Khan's voice is distant now. Beware of a subordinate who wants to be a comrade. He wants to be you. Captain Gul dozes off to Dr Pervez reciting him a poem about the glory of the city, its canals full of frolicking buffaloes, its lush orchards, its hard-working people, and its women who would bring rustic but tasty snacks in the afternoon for their men as they plough the fields and who'd rather die than give themselves to another man.

Captain Gul yanks himself out of his stupor and finds himself propped up in a bed in a slightly shabby room. He looks up at the roof and gets a good look at his deformed jaw, which looks like there is a guava stuck in his right cheek. He shuts his eyes and curses the bastard who came up with the idea of mounting a cheap mirror on this dilapidated safe house's ceilings.

'You must get the burn cases?' he asks Dr Pervez, who has removed the cotton from one side of his mouth. Gul can do audible mumbles now. Dr Pervez stops humming and puts his hands together seeking Captain Gul's forgiveness as if he is about to say something that might offend Captain Gul. He is the kind of man who demands a guarantee of forgiveness before he can offend.

'Sir, the stink of burning flesh is stuck in my throat.' He looks down, not able to look Captain Gul in the eye. 'I am not the kind of person who imbibes before sunset, never on the job, but for these cases I have to drink half a bottle even before I can remove the sheet from their so-called face.'

Captain Gul contemplates a brown medicine bottle in Dr Pervez's hand but ignores it. 'You are a son of the soil. You sound so very sensible. So tell me, are they all crazy that they are setting themselves on fire to bring a dead man back to life?'

Dr Pervez has moved to his medicine cabinet now. He takes out a brown glass bottle, pours himself a drink in a plastic tumbler, downs it in one gulp and finds the courage to speak truth to the power. 'Sir, nobody loves our army more than I do but where is the iron rod that this nation needs? This is a very homeopathic kind of martial law. Wall-chalking against our uniformed martyrs, treacherous pamphlets and, may my tongue turn to ash, dirty jokes, many, many jokes about our beloved general. Stupid rumours about a dead man coming back to life? Sir, these things sound good in poetry if you know your rhymes. Why tolerate such nonsense? Sir, when will you bring out the rod?'

Captain Gul makes a mental note to include the phrase 'homeopathic martial law and where is the rod' in his field report but then decides that the time for filing reports is long gone.

From here on his actions will be his reports.

'Then where do they come from? What do you do with these burnt ones?' Captain Gul is all curiosity now; he is displaying the kind of professionalism that will take him to the conference rooms of Foggy Bottom in Washington DC. His name would be whispered with fear and reverence in Indian torture cells.

'Sir, call it my misfortune, because I have seen the frailty of human existence from very close quarters. I have been intimate with death in my working life and I have reflected upon it in my poetry but I have also kept documentary proof. This I must share with you. In my life, I have cut open all kinds. Old women, babies, even young men possessed by love. I have once had the singular honour of writing LOVE in the column for cause of death.' Dr Pervez notes that Captain Gul is not laughing at his career's high point. 'But these burnt ones, it's difficult to breathe around them. I have kept them all on my files, sir. And sir,' he lowers his voice to a whisper, 'they are being burnt, some by the police, some with the police's permission. Sir, even in poetry you wouldn't kill yourself to bring someone back from the dead. Why would anyone want to protest against such a soft martial law? I have worked with spies for so long that I have become a bit of a spy myself. I keep all the cases in a file – I have my personal filing system. As the poet says, you keep the company, and then the company keeps you, and then you become the company.'

Captain Gul fixes Laal Khan with a hard stare. A local civilian doctor with copies of intelligence files. Laal Khan flashes a silly smile as if proud of having cultivated this asset. Doctor Pervez continues. 'The last one I opened was so burnt that I was taking my scalpel to a chunk of coal. I found a bullet in his heart. The greatest herb master of our time, Hakim Wasif Ali Wasif. Sir, I saw him distributing free bottles of his Iron Syrup the day Bhutto was hanged. And the next day he sets himself on fire. Man celebrates Bhutto's hanging and the next day he sets himself on fire to bring Bhutto back? And before he sets himself on fire, he shoots himself in the heart? Sir, in this city you start a rumour with the man on your left, and before you can breathe, it'll go around the earth and the man on your right will be whispering in your ear and swearing on his children that it's God's truth.'

'So wait, if Hakim didn't burn himself for Bhutto, then who killed him?'

Dr Pervez lowers his eyes and goes coy. 'Sir, I am a doctor but I am a poet also, and I see things that a normal doctor can't see. Sir, keep an eye on the women – there you'll find the clues. Husband and wife are in the house. The house burns down, and there is only one body – where did the wife go? Sir, as the poet says …

The stars that you see today
Died a millennia ago
The stars that you see
Are not the stars you see…'

With his sober eyes, Captain Gul can now see what drunk people look like. Had he talked this gibberish when he used to drink? Is that why he has ended up here, in a filthy medical facility, with a drunk off-the-book butcher of the dead? But then, he thinks, drunk people also say things they can't say when sober. Has he said things that he wasn't supposed to say? Is this drunk doctor poet going around with his unit's top-secret files? Captain Gul remembers his duties, his future predicted by an honourable palmist. Fuck you, civilians, with your thick glasses, your hunched posture and so-so poetry.

'But a bullet in the heart would suggest murder. Your post mortem report said death by self-immolation. Motivation unknown.'

'Sir, I did what I was told to do. Police didn't want a murder investigation on their hands, so they said since it's the season of burning jiyalas, here's one more. As a poet said once, a poet much bigger than me, what the heart wants, only the heart knows.'

And now Dr Pervez Alam lurches forward, drunk on his own words. 'Sir, I don't blow my own toot but who came up with the words that have spread in all corners of the country? No, sir, not just the country, the world. London and Moscow also, sir.'

Captain Gul sits up in the bed. 'What words?'

Dr Pervez brings his voice down to a whisper, makes a fist, punches his chest and says in a hoarse voice, 'Zinda hai, Bhutto zinda hai. Sir, I work for your unit, so obviously I can't take the credit for glorifying a hanged man. And sir, I must clarify that I don't like the man. Not his ideology. But it's not the man, sir, it's his walk.' Dr Pervez stands up straight and tries to mime the funeral march, beating his chest. 'Sir, the way the man walked to the gallows. That walk is the poetry. Not his politics.' He starts to beat his chest again and goes on his endless bloody Bhutto refrain.

Captain Gul glances towards Laal Khan, demanding to know how they have a rabid jiyala in their ranks, and is startled to see that Laal Khan has also got his fist on his chest and is murmuring along with Dr Pervez. Laal Khan notices Captain Gul's glare and grabs Dr Pervez by his shoulder. 'Sir, Doctor sahib is an artist at heart, he gets carried away sometimes. Doctor, I know you wrote that beautiful poem about the city. I don't think Captain Gul has heard it…'

Dr Pervez is animated now, taking a little sip, forgetting his Bhutto walk to the gallows, and mesmerized by his own legend. 'Sir, this is not the time, but since you have brought it up, I'll recite a little.

Between heaven and hell,
Between the earth and the sky,
Perched very precariously
Purgatory, my home, my city
This beautiful, cursed city…
Giving life
Receiving its dead…
With a lover's open arms…'

Captain Gul jumps from the bed, grabs the bottle from Dr Pervez's hand, sniffs it, recoils, caps it and says, 'That's a very beautiful poem and we'll listen to it on a night when the moon is full over a bottle of something nice. But right now work needs to be done.' He pockets the brown medicine bottle. 'We need to dig up that body, do another post mortem, rewrite the report, write the truth. Let's nail that wife of his who put a bullet in his heart. If a poet like you can't tell the truth, who can? I think we should go dig up that Hakim. Let's dig up the truth. You and me. And then we'll show them our iron rod. And you, I promise, Doctor sahib, will be the first one to see.'

THIRTY-ONE

One Million Years B.C.

BAGHI CHOOSES A SEAT IN THE BACK ROW CLOSE TO a flickering Exit sign. On the screen Raquel Welch hides behind a steep cliff, wielding a spear. The ancient monsters can be heard snarling but they are not on screen yet. The film's title, *One Million Years B.C.*, has been translated as 'When Humans Were Naked'. The film has attracted a niche audience. A few men are dotted across the cinema hall, some looking at the screen then furtively looking left and right as if waiting for a companion who had promised to turn up for the film. A lone hawker walks the aisles, strumming his Pepsi and Mirinda bottles with a bottle opener, but finds no buyers. The lights go dim, and the Exit sign over Baghi's head flickers faster. Baghi doesn't look left or right. He pretends to be absorbed in the congress of fluffy monsters on the screen who have spotted Raquel Welch and are trying to scare her by making googly eyes. Her male companion, a bearded brute in sheepskin, is away arguing with another male companion, then beating his chest and yelping at the sky.

A boy, or at least he looks like a boy in the semi-dark, slides into the seat next to Baghi's, brushing his shoulder against his. Baghi knows the routine; he hopes to have a hand on his thigh soon. The men are absorbed in the movie now, some have got into pairs, others are helping themselves to Raquel Welch's thighs bursting out of a leopard-skin rag. Humans, after all, weren't completely naked even a million years ago. The boy, for a change, smells nice, the only nice-smelling thing in a cinema hall full of the rancid stink of oily popcorn and afternoon male desire. Baghi breathes into the boy's shoulder, inhales Capri soap and sighs. Before he knows it, the boy has put his arm around Baghi's shoulder and his hand in Baghi's shirt pocket. When Baghi tries to squirm and move away, the boy's other hand reaches for Baghi's crotch and pins him down. Baghi grabs the boy's hand in his pocket. He has kept some money in his pocket for specifically this eventuality but he doesn't like to be robbed. He puts his right hand on the boy's hand on his crotch, presses it gently, then caresses it in a reassuring way, as if to say we can get through this together. As a fallen Marxist he does see transitory sexual union as a transactional matter but he doesn't want to be exploited either. He wants to pay a fair price for the boy's labours but doesn't want to be treated like an old fool by this nice-smelling, smooth-chinned teenager. The monsters are angry now and, amidst their shrieks, Baghi hears a loud whisper from the boy who says, 'Money first. Let go.' Baghi lets go of his hand on the crotch but tightens his grip on his other hand in his pocket. Now the boy's touch is softer, his breathing heavy. Fake little sobs in his ear. Baghi knows they are fake because the boy has not taken his hand out of his pocket.

Baghi will never know if the police were there to arrest him or the military regime had ordered afternoon moral policing. Sometimes they showed dirty movies at Venus cinema but they made sure to pay off the police, frequently in free tickets, and locked the cinema-hall doors from inside. Here it was only Raquel Welch with her muscular, greasy thighs and ancient, jerky monsters battling it out for the supremacy of the planet over a barren, rocky terrain. When the three policemen with flashlights barge in, people in the cinema slink away, abruptly withdrawing their hands from their own or their neighbour's crotch. The police don't try to stop or arrest anyone. They shout abuses and loud curses at the degenerate faggots watching naked women and monsters in the middle of a Friday afternoon. Baghi and the boy are caught in the glare of one policeman's flashlight. They could have fled as easily as the others but they were locked in an existential struggle – Baghi trying to get love at a reasonable price and the boy attempting to get what he probably thought was Baghi's surplus capital.

The walk to the police station is humiliating. The boy walks as if he is taking an afternoon stroll, waving his handcuffed hands at acquaintances. Baghi is not handcuffed, maybe because they only had one pair of handcuffs or maybe one of the policemen recognized him. Baghi walks with his eyes down, pretending he is with a bunch of friends with whom he had an argument and has fallen out. When they pass by Shahid's Friendly Art Photo Studio Baghi notices the shutters are down. They have covered the burnt façade of Iron Syrup & Other Herbs with a dull green tarpaulin, patches of soot all over it.

Baghi is scared and a tiny bit disgusted with himself. Once upon a time he had been picked up by the police for threatening to bring down all the despots of Ummah. This afternoon he has been arrested while haggling over the price of a hand job in a sleazy cinema.

At the police station there is some confusion. Baghi and the boy are locked up in a crowded cell with the nauseating smell of ganja and piss. The boy keeps reminding him and other inhabitants of the cell that this uncle still owes him money for his services. After a few minutes the door of the lock-up is opened and Baghi is escorted to A.D. Malang's empty office. Profuse apologies, offers of tea and cold drinks and cigarettes. There has been some confusion because A.D. Malang had ordered his staff to take care of his guru if he ever ended up at the police station. Baghi can't figure out how A.D. Malang knew that he would end up at the police station.

He sits alone in A.D. Malang's office, not sure if he is still under arrest or being kept here out of a misplaced sense of hospitality. The door of the office opens and the boy comes in stumbling – somebody has kicked him in the back. He stands in a corner, confused for a moment, then looks around and is satisfied with his new circumstances. 'This is better. You are a freeloader but you are the only one here. There were a dozen in the cell waiting to take their turn.' He comes and stands close to Baghi, his crotch almost in his face. 'They all smelled as if they had crawled out of the gutter.' Baghi gestures to him to take a seat, but the boy goes to the door and locks it from the inside. 'You are the VIP here.' The boy bends over him and says in a hoarse voice, 'Do what you like but no mouth to mouth.'

Baghi gets up in panic, goes to the door and opens it. A constable comes running. 'Is the boy not behaving? Let me sort him out, sir,' he says, entering the office with a cane in his hand. 'No, no,' Baghi says. 'Where is A.D. Malang? I need to get back to Gol Mosque.'

'He should be coming any minute now, sir. They have got a big raid going on at the Gol Mosque. He asked us to request you to wait here.'

HOMEWORK 14

My Photo Session

In ancient times homo sapiens lived in caves and they endeavoured to etch images on the cave walls to identify things, to remember the names and numbers of their progenies, sometimes to make their progenies and their mates look more beauteous than they were in real life. My husband Hakim Wasif Ali Wasif has a hobby of making photographs with his polaroid camera. When he comes to commit his husband-sharing arrangement with me, he likes to take my photos. This is good American technology to ensure privacy and strengthen the husband–wife bond, he says. We don't need to take these pictures to Friendly Art Photo Studio and develop and print. I would not like anyone to see the bounty of beauty that God has bestowed upon me in the shape of my beautiful wife. He takes close pictures of my face, my hair, my neck and then blows air as the wet print rolls out of the camera. He insists on taking couple pictures, first putting our cheeks together, then with his lips on my cheek, it's ticklish but I let him do it. One day before bedtime he gives me a glass of milk with a few drops of his famous Iron Syrup and expounds that it will make my bones stronger. I feel light in my head; he takes my shirt off and instead of doing his corpulent spousal activities he starts to take my pictures. I am half asleep. Then he brings some magazines with pictures of pale naked women who have baby-smooth private parts without any hair. He suggests that I should also forego my hair to make better photos. I joke only little girls have no hair so maybe I am already too aged for him. He laughs and says I am a very funny girl. I say I am a funny girl with a serious problem.

He expounds that he knows that I am contemplating ways to trace my parents but this is a very precarious task given the military junta's heightened hostility towards anyone who had close relationships with Chairman Bhutto. He further elaborates that this task can only be undertaken with the help of the people who work for the military intelligence unit. He says that there is a unit chief who is new in the city but he knows him because they are part of a photography club. He is scouting for a model and if he takes my photographs I can appeal to his good nature. As a husband he should be taking care of our family matters himself but he states that army people are tender-hearted when it comes to women and I'll have a better chance if I plead my own case.

On the appointed day a man with henna-coloured hair and rude manners comes to pick me up in a white Toyota Corolla. The roads in the cantonment are wide, all the tree trunks and rubbish bins are whitewashed. The army officer I am introduced to is bulky for an army officer but has very courteous manners. I am offered tea and when I say I don't drink tea in the afternoon, he smiles and says it's the proud officers' mess tradition that no guest should be allowed to go back unless they have been served tea. I need to curry favour with him so I respect ancient hospitality traditions. I drink tea in one gulp and I pluck up the courage to bring up the subject of esteemed father's incarceration on trumped-up charges and subsequent arrest of Mother Bano. While I am still groping for correct words to plead my case, the officer brings out his camera and asks me to pose. I get up on my feet and stumble and wonder about the tea potion I have just imbibed. He takes me by the hand and makes me sit on the edge of the bed. His camera flashes, clicks, flashes, clicks, my brain goes through tumultuous waves of being alive and dead. He says smile and I endeavour to oblige but my mouth opens in a humongous yawn. He touches my face and adjusts my head and his fingers touch my shoulders. He says he is trying to capture my best face. I endeavour to say that I have only one face. But suddenly his hairy belly is in my face. I try to reason with him in my best English – I know army officers comprehend English as all the signboards in the cantonment are written in English. I say no but for some unknowable reason an incomprehensible sound comes out of my mouth, my words just get stuck in my throat. He is pummelling me in front and I go to sleep and when I wake up then he is pummelling me from the posterior, there's nausea stuck in my chest, I wake up and say no and go to sleep and then wake up and try to move my exhausted limbs and go to sleep. When I finally wake up I am in my own bed and Hakim Wasif is sprinkling water on my face. My mouth is dry and he gives me water. I want to cry but first I want to know what happened. He says that I got woman's monthly diseases and sometimes it can cause an upheaval in the body and mind. He says the army officer sent me back saying that I was sickly and the photo shoot was postponed indefinitely. He says that he has actually studied the shifting patterns of woman's monthly disease for a long time, and he has a special herb that will alleviate a woman's physical pain as well as mental confusion.

He is insinuating in his child's sing-song voice that it's my fault, that I was sent on a mission to rescue my parents and I came back dizzy and sick and sleepy. He gives me a glass of milk with his calming-down herb and I fall off to sleep and I never want to wake up in this world again.

THIRTY-TWO

American Dream

EVEN IN HIS DREAM CAPTAIN GUL CAN TELL THAT his American hosts have gone overboard with their hospitality. When he steps out of his humble Gulfstream G280 at Joint Base Andrews, a red carpet stretches from the aeroplane ladder far into the horizon. He sets foot on it and a twenty-one-gun salute rings out. For God's sake, he wants to tell them, have some self-respect. I am not the head of a state or a prince. I am just a silent soldier come to give a dressing-down to your nincompoops in Langley. He knows what they are doing, trying to impress him with the thunder of their gun salute, with the length and thickness of their red carpet. He walks and walks alone, ignoring the alert soldiers lined up on both sides of the carpet, in battle gear no less, and offering him salutes with every step he takes. At the end of the red carpet, the Beast awaits. He is impressed and not impressed. He knows the American president has replicas of the world's most indestructible vehicle. No missile can hit it, no aeroplane can bomb it, no radar can track it. In another life he had war-gamed some scenarios and found a way to blow it to smithereens, but now he slides in and sinks back in his seat. A silver ice bucket with Dom Perignon, his name engraved on the bottle in Urdu calligraphy, shaped like a flower, cold smoke still rising from its just uncorked mouth. He gets this too. A not very subtle hint that they have a file on him from his drinking days. They don't know him, they don't know he is a changed man, he feels no temptation from the bubbles gurgling in the bottle. This sad old whore of a superpower is badly falling behind the times.

He looks back, an old spy habit, to see if he is being followed. He is, by a convoy of marines on monocycles, his security detail. He checks out the Beast for its security features. He glances at the flickering lights of jammers on the dashboard and in a sideways glance catches a glimmer of the face of his chauffeur, a handsome man in a tuxedo, a black man. He knows that Americans are racist to the core and they have sent the presidential vehicle but they have tasked a black man to drive him to put him in his place. 'Brother, shall we…' Captain Gul sits up straight in his seat. The voice is familiar, very familiar, the thud thud thud of history. Captain Gul says, 'Are you by any chance…?'

Muhammad Ali turns back, the white collar under his black tuxedo shining like a dagger, his devilish smile, ancient mischief in his eyes. 'Yes, brother, I am honoured to be your personal chauffeur during your visit to the promised land.' As the Beast lurches forward, Captain Gul wakes up. He shuts his eyes again to force himself back into his dream but hears someone crying nearby. Laal Khan sails into his vision. 'Sir, that photographer will not stop crying. What shall we do with him?'

Captain Gul realizes that he is not going back to his American dream, no more infinite red carpets, no Beast, no Muhammad Ali. He jumps out of his bed, straight to the bathroom, does his ablutions with the speed and confidence of a blindfolded soldier assembling his G3 gun.

A quick glance in the mirror. He has started growing a beard to disguise his swollen cheek. He spreads a towel on the floor and offers his speedy version of prayers. It's a soldier's prayer, he has told himself, prayer of a warrior who has taken time off from a busy front, not a civilian who has time to linger during prayers because they want to prolong their break from work, or delay going home to a demanding wife or sulky children. Allah will understand that I am offering these prayers under enemy fire. Our land is being ravaged by conspirators and filth peddlers. Allah will accept my prayers because He knows that I have work to do, mysteries to solve.

Laal Khan has done some initial work on Shahid the photographer, a dribble of blood from his mouth, a bump on his head, his feet tied to a chair. His hands are still free, a nice gesture, an offer to negotiate: your feet might be tied but we are still open to ideas. Captain Gul doesn't want Laal Khan in the room when he springs the question so he sends him off. 'Get two gallons of Super. It's time for him to become the hero he was born to be. The hero that this city needs. Then you'll all be OK, OK.'

When Laal Khan is about to exit the door, he calls him back and asks him to bring the pliers. 'I might need to fix things while you are away.' Laal Khan looks back, a look that says Sir, you have never done this kind of menial work before, what am I here for?

Shahid looks around in panic. He has been here before to install the cameras. He fails to find any objects that might need fixing with the pliers. He starts to sob uncontrollably. 'He manhandled me, he hit me. There is no legal, no moral justification for this. I might not agree with the martial law government but I am a law-abiding citizen.'

Captain Gul takes out the *Wedding Night* VHS and waves it in front of him. 'This is the kind of law you abide? Recording and peddling filth? In military installations?'

A wave of relief passes over Shahid. He had thought they were after him for his planned protest. But they only had a smutty little video, shameful, ugly but definitely no threat to national security. He decides to come clean. 'I am guilty. You have all the right to ask me. I'll answer every question to the best of my knowledge.'

'Who let you into my bachelor's quarters, who asked you to make this?'

'Sir, I didn't make it.' Shahid clears his throat and is about to start his long-winded but accurate explanation when Captain Gul hits him on the head with the pliers. Shahid flinches, takes it with courage. This is all a little misunderstanding that he can clear.

'Sir, I only put in the camera. I swear on my mother, on your mother. I just did what I was ordered to do.'

'So what were your orders? Is this what your Karl Marx, your Bhutto has taught you?'

'Sir, you are right, I am a political activist, a committed Marxist but I am an artist too…'

This time the pliers are aimed at his face, Shahid tries to duck, his right eyebrow is split open. Shahid is hurt, a drop of blood finds its way into his right eye. But his sentiments are more hurt. He was about to fix it all for everyone with his truthful explanation. He feels pain but he is confident enough to make his final confession, a confession he is sure will absolve him. It's an admission of guilt but it's also the proof of his innocence.

'I did keep a copy for myself. It was government property and I shouldn't have. That's my only fault. I kept a copy and I didn't tell them but I swear I didn't show it to anyone.'

Captain Gul waves the pliers in front of his eyes. 'Slow down. Start from the beginning, and speak before I pull out your tongue with this.' He tries to shove the pliers in Shahid's mouth, but he throws back his head to avoid them.

'An army officer sent me his man to say I have to install a camera in the cantonment. At first I was scared. But the army man gave me the key to the bachelor officer's quarters, told me where to put the camera, asked me to show him how to turn it on and off. I did exactly what I was told. I thought they were spies doing what spies do. Film their enemies in compromising positions. When they brought it to me to blur his face, I made a copy for myself. I am sorry. I'll never do it again.' Shahid puts his hands together and wails. 'I'll shut my shop. Please take away my camera. I'll shut my shop. I am not a traitor. I am not an artist. I am just a masturbator.'

Captain Gul sits down, puts the pliers to the nail of Shahid's big right toe. What kind of man keeps his toenails so trimmed? He is tentative at first but then gets a grip. Shahid lurches forward, almost grabs Captain Gul's hair, Captain Gul jerks back and tugs at the pliers with both his hands, the pliers slip and he falls backwards. Captain Gul sits up with renewed intent and gets a steady grip and pulls. Shahid falls backwards and becomes what he never was, what he had never thought he would become, a blob of pain. He had put his hand on a candle to get the real feel of burning fire, to prepare himself for his protest, and he had managed to keep it there till a blister first formed and then popped. But now his body is a big heave, his nerve ends are stinging. For a moment his toenail is still there and yet not there. This captain is taking his time. It hurts but he doesn't know if it hurts in his foot, or his head, or if his innards are on fire. He is used to finding focus through his camera, so he tries to focus on a single point of pain, because then the rest of his body will be pain-free or at least will take him through this. It's coming off his skin, his whole skin is being flayed, and all he can think of is what a comfortable life he has had. He has never even been slapped in his life. He is pleading in all the grunts that pour out of his mouth. He tries to remember his favourite photographs, photographs that had moved him, brought him to tears, images that had made him a revolutionary artist. A man shielding his son from a soldier seconds before he is shot. A man on his knees with a gun to his head. Should the photographer have taken the photo or intervened to stop the shooting? A yellow skeletal child with a bloated body and face covered with ants. A man made to part his dhoti to prove his penis wasn't Muslim. It all seems decent to him now. Nothing like this has happened or been photographed. He feels as if somebody has taken a blade to his intestines and is twisting it slowly. He thinks fast. Anything, anything that he can say to stop this, and he remembers that he was asked for an answer. He lurches forward, grabs hold of Captain Gul's head. 'His name was Lieutenant Gul.'

For Captain Gul, who in training had marched fifteen miles with his 40 kg kit, pistoned through June nights without breaking a sweat, pulling out a nail was proving to be impossibly hard work. Perspiration on his forehead, his hands tremble with the effort. He is wondering if Laal Khan has finally defected. He bends down, uses his core to pull the nail and only half of it comes off.

'So what did you say his name was?'

'What?' Shahid wails.

'The officer's name?'

'Sir, you are a spy. He was a spy. I don't know what your real name is. I don't know if it was his real name. But I installed the camera in bachelor officers' quarters. I was told his name was Lieutenant Gul.'

Captain Gul thinks of his predecessor, the one who took the OK 007 number plate with him and is now doing tree-plantation campaigns in the north. That fat hairy bugger couldn't think of another name. 'What is wrong with you civilians? I am Gul.' He flings the pliers in Shahid's face before storming out of the room. 'I am the only Gul in this city. I am the only Captain Gul in this country.'

'I'm telling the truth, sir. If you don't believe me why don't you ask the girl in the video? She is Comrade Abid Ali Abid's daughter – you should know that. The Gul before you arrested him. I'll tell you where to find her,' Shahid wails before pretending to pass out.

THIRTY-THREE

Rose Water and Opium

NOOR NABI DRAGS SABIHA DOWN THE MOSQUE stairs, one hand clutching her wrist, the other buttoning up her own coat, then taking her dupatta, roping it around her head like a turban. She asks Sabiha to do the same with her dupatta. The police sirens around the mosque are wailing louder, closing in. As Noor Nabi approaches the landing, she asks Sabiha to wait. She clings to the wall, glances sideways and retreats when she sees two police jeeps coming to a halt just beyond the mosque door. She grabs Sabiha's hand and rushes towards the prayer hall, which is empty except for an old man with grey stubble, sitting against a wall, holding his shaved head in both hands. Noor and Sabiha look like two thieves on the prowl trying to sneak through the night undetected. They walk past the old man towards a corner where a moss-green Formica cupboard is full of copies of the Quran. Noor Nabi retrieves the largest one and puts it on a wooden tawla. They sit facing each other. Sabiha is agitated, not sure if Noor Nabi is going to sell her to the police or save her from them. Noor is quietly urging her to read, to pretend to read, her finger running back and forth on the page. She brings her face forward, their foreheads almost touching. 'This is one place they won't look for you,' Noor says, her forefinger pausing on the page, as if she is explaining a difficult verse to her.

A sob echoes through the empty prayer hall. The old man against the wall is crying hysterically and soundlessly. He has got his fist in his mouth, as if trying to push his own grief down his own throat. When she hears the sound of boots rushing upstairs followed by banging on doors, Sabiha bends forward and lets her forehead touch Noor Nabi's. Sometimes trust is not a choice.

'The girl has run away,' someone shouts from upstairs.

'Again,' another policeman chimes in.

Sabiha understands now why Noor has dragged her out of the academy without much explanation. She also wonders how she knew the police were going to come for her. She is determined to defend her innocence and the only way she knows is to go on the offensive. 'How do you know they are looking for me? How did you know they were coming?'

Noor Nabi keeps looking down, not interested in giving away her sources. 'There are rats in every government department,' she says. 'I feed them occasionally. I think they want to pull you in for your husband's…' Noor Nabi wants to say murder but changes her mind and mumbles 'death' instead.

'Do I look like a killer to you?' Sabiha whispers furiously to Noor Nabi. From a distance they look like two out-of-work pious men, locked in a theological discussion in the middle of the afternoon.

'Nobody looks like a killer. But you can't tell that to the police or a judge. They are going to dig up your husband's body. They think there is a bullet in his heart. He was apparently shot before he burnt himself. Or maybe after? Police will want to ask you.'

Sabiha hears footsteps approaching the prayer hall again and looks down at the Quran and starts to recite from the open page. Noor Nabi approves. Sabiha understands now why they are hiding in the open. She likes Noor Nabi's improvised disguise. It reminds her of school plays where the girl who got to dress up as a boy got flirty glances from the other girls for the rest of the year.

The old man's sobs have turned into hiccups now. 'I know you didn't do it,' says Noor Nabi. 'But why burn the whole place down?'

'I woke up when fire had already reached my bedroom and then I ran.' The police boots have retreated, the jeeps have driven off. Sabiha Bano begins to realize she is sitting in front of an open Quran, and although they opened it because they needed a prop, it's still open and she can't lie, also because the person asking the questions just saved her from imminent arrest.

Noor Nabi is trying to size her up as a potential client. Will she crack in a police lock-up? Will she melt under a judge's gaze? 'They are saying you were the second wife?'

'So? He has a big enough house. I lived upstairs, had my own bedroom. In my father's house I always slept in the same room with Father and Mother. Where was I supposed to go after both of them were arrested? Who wants a man all to themselves anyway, specially when the man makes and sells Iron Syrup.'

Noor Nabi suppresses her giggle; she can't believe that they are hiding in the mosque talking about Iron Syrup. 'Does it work? I've heard all kinds of miracle stories about it.'

'What miracle? It's rose water mixed with opium and some oil. It keeps men going all night and makes women drowsy. It keeps women smelling nice even when they are snoring in their sleep.'

'My clients swear by it.'

'Your clients probably get a good sleep, maybe that's why.'

'He didn't try it on you?'

Sabiha Bano looks down, closes the copy of the Quran and puts it back into its maroon velvet cover. 'I was his herbal lab mouse. It gave me migraines. But then he wanted to marry a third time. Someone younger. Maybe his lab needed a new mouse.'

The old man against the wall has stopped sobbing and is rhythmically beating his head against the wall and asking, Why Allah, why?

'And you got jealous? I have never met a woman who didn't want to put a bullet in her husband's heart in these situations. I have some clients who did. One got only seven years, I pleaded temporary insanity because of emotional distress, she was out in four.' Noor Nabi feels she can't help Sabiha if she doesn't trust her. She has managed to shield her from the police once but now that they have smelt blood they won't stop hounding. And with the military intelligence looking for her, the city will run out of hiding places for her. If you are not safe in Allah's own house, how far can you run?

Despite this Noor Nabi also feels scared of her. Sometimes saviours are scared of people they are trying to save. Noor Nabi knows that one murder line on a palm can multiply quickly.

Sabiha looks at her with complaining eyes. 'Why should I be jealous? Second wife, third wife, what difference does it make? Why don't you ask the first wife if she was jealous?'

Noor Nabi says that Sabiha needs to get a pre-arrest bail from the district court if she wants to avoid arrest. And after she is on bail she can volunteer to join the investigation. She offers to help her, no worry about fees. 'Judge is a friendly fellow.' Noor Nabi winks. 'He is specially friendly when he hears cases of young widows.'

'But I didn't do anything,' Sabiha insists.

'Precisely, because you didn't do anything I have to do something.'

'He was disrespectful to my esteemed father and Mother Bano.'

Noor Nabi sighs. 'They are military prisoners. No judge is going to accept my habeas corpus appeals.'

The silence between them is punctuated by subdued sobs coming from the old man, as if he has made his peace with Allah. Sabiha looks at Noor and is wondering if she should thank her, if she should tell her more or tell her less, when she feels a hand tapping her shoulder. Sabiha looks up and sees not the police but a man in white shalwar qameez with red hair, face severe, bored, strong. She remembers him. He had driven her to the cantonment before for her photo shoot. He had brought tea and then disappeared.

She has a moment where she thinks this fake lawyer has only saved her from the police to sell her to the army.

Noor Nabi jumps up, scuffs her lawyer's coat, says you can't take her, she hasn't done anything. 'Show me the arrest warrant. Show me your ID card. Don't you know who I am? Show me the arrest warrants. I have got pre-arrest bail for her. You'll be hearing from me.'

Sabiha looks back, spits at Noor Nabi and walks off.

When Sabiha gets into the white Corolla, she is surprised at how calm she is. Between the Gol Mosque compound and wherever she is headed, there is life to look at. Her streets, where she ran and ran as a child and then a teacher told her that she should join the school team. In the beginning she would keep glancing back to see who was coming after her, who was about to overtake, but then she learnt to look at the furthest object and run towards it, never even looking at fellow runners. Now she thinks that she should have run cross-country, or maybe never stopped running when she escaped that house on fire.

HOMEWORK 15

My Social Life/ How the Other Half Lives

The institution of marriage was invented, nay, it has evolved through human history in order to stabilize families, to protect the youthful progenies, to carry on this grinding circle of life. It's built on little compromises that one day take you to the grave. Time in my life slows down, there is no news of esteemed father, Mother Bano. Chairman Bhutto has been sentenced to death but nobody believes the military junta has the wherewithal to actually carry out the sentence. From whatever little information I get, the remaining comrades of esteemed father have been arrested. My husband assures me that he has sympathy for my family but he doesn't care for murderers even if they were prime ministers, even if they were best friends with my father who now technically is his father-in-law. One today grinds into another and Hakim Wasif Ali Wasif is too busy during the day. When at night I try to remind him about his duties as my husband he first gets perturbed and then starts to hiccup and cry. I refuse to hold his head when he starts to shed crocodile tears of loneliness. He offers to take me to his club but he doesn't want me to be shocked because in the above-mentioned club there are men and women who are modern and they do things differently.

A modern woman, he explains, should be able to laugh and sit with other men but always be modest in her modernity.

The club is the place where civilian officers and judges and businessmen come to frolic in the evening. There are always girls serving wine and giggling. I am offered a glass, I look towards Hakim Sahib for his approval, he nods, I have a sip, it tastes like bitter medicine of my childhood, but then I imbibe it in one gulp and start grinning at men clamouring for my attention.

I am shocked when one balding district magistrate loosens his tie and asks me to sit in his lap. I laugh at his jest and say that my legs are much stronger than him and he can sit in my lap. He doesn't laugh at my jest, instead takes a glass from a girl my age in tight clothes, imbibes it in one go then grabs the girl and makes her sit in his lap. After a few visits to the club I ask a district official about the fate of political prisoners. He puts his finger on my mouth and asks me never to utter that word again because there is no such thing as political prisoners, only murderers and criminals. I drink two drinks quickly and am giggling and crying at the same time. I admonish myself that this is a bad life and maybe Hakim Wasif Ali Wasif is not the honest hard-working man he asserts himself to be.

I go to the bathroom to wash my face and the girl who was giggling in the judge's lap approaches me and starts parlays by saying why are you polluting our marketplace? I say what market? She expounds that these girls gallivanting at the club get paid money to talk and laugh with the men and why am I going around giving everything for free and there are even rumours of you getting blue films made. I retort back that I don't know what she is talking about, that I am an honourable lady, married and here only to keep my husband company and in good humour. I try to plead with her that I am a working lady also, a business partner, but this girl, who really is a child dressed up in tight clothes to look like a girl-woman, tells me in the harshest possible tone that it's sisters like me who thrust a dagger in other sisters' back. Then she delivers a vengeful monologue about how she was supposed to go to Dubai but now can't go because a sister like me turned envious and got her work visa blocked. Furthermore she laments that now she is going to be stuck here for a few years and although there is work for everyone why should bitches like me undercut the market by giving everything for free. I suffer from the kind of nausea which rises up from your stomach but doesn't quite journey up to your throat.

In the forlorn days that follow I refuse to go to the club with Hakim Sahib. I tell him that I feel tired all the time. He gives me his soothing syrup and I go to sleep but when I wake up I feel tired again. I tell him to go to his first wife on Friday but he says no you are my first and last love. His words ring empty to me and I start going to the mosque to seek forgiveness for my sins and for the salvation of my incarcerated parents.

THIRTY-FOUR

A Time for Prayer Mat

HIS EXALTED HIGHNESS CROWN PRINCE SHAH Khalid Bin Saud escorts Captain Gul through the vast marble compound of Kaaba. They are surrounded by a small entourage of princes and governors in gold-braided keffiyehs. Captain Gul feels a certain awkwardness like you do when visiting a rich uncle's house. But the Crown Prince makes him feel at ease by squeezing his hand periodically. Alert commandos from the Prince's security detail clear the way for them. They go around the Kaaba seven times, sometimes mumbling, sometimes shouting Allah I come to you, O Allah I come to you. The door of the black cube that's the house of God within the house of God opens, and they are inside. Captain Gul can't see in the dark. He gropes in the air and finds himself touching the Crown Prince's goatee. 'I, the custodian of the Holy House, I shall be honoured if you lead us in prayer. We are in the House and you are the future of the Ummah. It's my wish that our useless princes and cousins pray behind you. I want you to be their role model.'

Captain Gul panics because he doesn't quite know how to pray, but then he is relieved because they are in the dark. Occasionally a shimmer of gold from the keffiyehs licks the darkness. He does know how to pray in a rudimentary kind of way. He can mime the whole thing but he doesn't know the verses, the exact sequences, he doesn't quite know how many times to prostrate, when to stand, when to sit. 'I am honoured, of course, but I don't feel that I am qualified, specially in the presence of Your Grace, to lead the prayers in this House of Houses.'

The Crown Prince caresses his cheek, then gives it a little fatherly slap. 'We have been led by useless clerics for too long. I want a warrior, someone whose name is whispered in the corridors of Washington DC and the prisons of Kashmir, to lead us in prayers, to guide us back to our lost glory. May Allah forgive our sins by way of your inspired leadership.'

Captain Gul frets, sweats, thinks of fainting, thinks of running away, but his feet are made of lead. Where do you escape to when you are already in the House of all Houses?

He is glad when he wakes up and realizes that he is not inside the House of Allah but in his bachelor officer's quarters, the cracked mirror on the cupboard reflecting his swollen jaw, which in this moment of relief looks less swollen.

He rubs his eyes and starts preparing in earnest for the life that awaits him, a life in which he will go from being a useless piston to a pious warrior, from someone who believed in nothing but his extreme thirst to someone who puts his earthly urges on hold because a much better afterlife awaits. 'Do we have a prayer mat?' Captain Gul asks in a humble tone, not his usual officer-like command.

Subedar Laal Khan can't believe it, doesn't want to believe his boss's transformation. An occasional prayer is fine by him but a prayer mat is a serious commitment. He has seen people turn to a prayer mat after they have survived a landmine where the person ahead of them had both his legs blown off, or when they lost someone close, specially a child, but he hasn't met an officer who gets his jaw broken by a pissed-off father of a loose-character girl who was clearly trying to pin someone else's baby on him and, instead of planning revenge, turns to God. Laal Khan has seen many commanders with unmanly habits. He knew one who wanted to start commercial rose farming, another was fond of young boys but could never bring himself to touch them, another secretly visited every third-rate saint's shrine in the hope of getting a promotion. Laal Khan believed Captain Gul was a real man, all about women and booze and kicking civilian ass but now here he was, jaw swollen, sedated by painkillers and asking him to find a prayer mat. Laal Khan himself has never tasted alcohol in his life but now he wishes that his boss and head of the Field Intelligence Unit would ask him to bring back his bottle instead of a little carpet to pray on. 'No, sir, but we'll arrange one.' Laal Khan knows when they start going to God, there is no turning back. He goes and buys a cheap prayer mat from the bazaar.

'And should I ask your guest to wait while you pray?'

'No, no, bring her in. Bring her in while I am praying.'

Laal Khan is relieved. His boss might have gone over to the other side where angels sing heavenly songs but he hasn't forgotten his earthly obligations. Maybe he is ready to use his rod. On a prayer mat.

Sabiha Bano is ushered into the room. She sees Captain Gul on the prayer mat, muttering something with his eyes shut, in deep connection with his god. She likes a man who prays. She doesn't know what to think of a man who prays and gets people kidnapped. She takes in the room, the blankets folded on a side table, the painting of a leaping horse over the bed. It reminds her of something. A man's hairy belly smothering her face. She doesn't remember much else. She doesn't want to remember. She is relieved that nobody offers her tea.

'Thank you for coming,' Captain Gul says after finishing his prayers and folding the prayer mat carefully. He is looking at her feet, trying to erase the rest of her being from his mind's screen.

'They picked me up and brought me here. What are you thanking me for?'

'I am sorry it had to be done this way but this is for your own safety, for your own good. The police were about to arrest you. And a police station is not a place for a lady like you.'

'Police. Army. What difference does it make to me? I didn't do anything.'

'That's not what my intelligence sources say. I know police were trying to save you and you have a crafty lawyer friend but a murder is a murder. Even in this city. A lifetime rotting in a jail cell. Not a place for a lady like you.' Captain Gul looks up and tries to hold her gaze, smiles to elicit a smile, an invitation to complicity, then looks down at her feet again. 'But I know in my heart that you are innocent. Sometimes we do what we have to do.'

'Some do. And some don't,' says Sabiha Bano. 'I didn't do anything. What did my father do? What did my mother do? I only ran away from a burning building. What would you do? What would anybody do? Arrest me, lock me up with them.'

'They are saying you set the building on fire. They say you started the rumour that your husband set himself on fire to protest Bhutto's hanging. My men are saying he was celebrating the hanging by giving out free bottles of his Iron Syrup. And then he shoots himself in the heart and sets himself on fire to bring Bhutto back from the dead? Police are talking about digging up the body and if they do...' Captain Gul trails off, expecting her to imagine a lifetime in jail, but she seems unfazed. 'But right now that's not my problem,' he continues.

'I am facing Kaaba, and I am in a place of worship. I have to tell you something and I hope you'll believe me.'

Sabiha prays, not five times a day but whenever she feels like it. Sometimes she finds solace in prayers, sometimes she feels sleepy, sometimes she feels like an estranged child seeking forgiveness for a minor mistake, like coming home late from school or climbing on to a neighbour's roof to trap a sparrow. Sometimes her burdens get lighter. She is not sure if it's because of the act of prayer or because during the time she is praying nobody bothers her. She can find a few moments of peace, but she is never sure if it comes from her communion with God or because for a brief period of time she can reject the world He has created around her. She does not have the prayer-mat conviction that this military man seems to have.

'Say it. Then we'll see.' She looks around the room once more and feels nauseous. She is relieved that she hasn't been offered the officers' mess's customary tea.

'I am in love with you. No, no, that sounds wrong,' he says shaking his head. 'God has planted your love in my heart. I go to sleep thinking of you, I wake up thinking of you. And then I meet you and I find out that you are running from the law, serious trouble, and I feel God has a plan for you and me. Who am I to contest God's plan? You might think my men have picked you up and brought you here. But it's Allah who has brought us together.'

She can detect a man's lust from a mile away, even if the man is a military man, but she has a hard time taking in this twisted, manipulative love that comes in the form of a saviour on a prayer mat. Someone who is trying to save himself by saving you. 'You don't know me. I only saw you once and you seemed in love with a Black Dog bottle. You didn't even look at me. How do you suddenly love me?'

'Yes, that was me but that was another person. I was a common sinner but then Allah showed me the way. He has big plans for me and you will be a part of this journey. Here is something that I need to tell you but I can't tell you. But let's say I saw you in a dream and since then I feel we have a shared destiny.'

Sabiha has heard men before who claim they were in love with her when all they wanted was to see her with her clothes off. There was a time when she liked that, dared them to be as ridiculous as they could be in their pursuit, but now she believes that love comes in many forms. The PT teacher who broke her claimed to love her, and then her husband claimed to be madly in love with her. She has been married and now she is a widow, suspected of being a self-made widow. She is still a widow and is being pursued by Molly, a man of God who wants to protect her from the world and keep her for himself.

And now there's this one in front of her, making his claim, making it through a dream that he had. She came here to seek help for her parents' release. Someone drugged her and took her by force in this very bed and now someone else wants to save her in this very room. Is he the saviour that Noor Nabi had seen in her hand? 'It's getting late. You've prayed. Now, may I?' She points to the prayer mat.

Captain Gul unrolls it for her, then sits and watches as she prays and tries to keep the images out of his mind where she is being taken from behind by a hairy man with a blurred face. She takes her time. She finishes, then she speaks to him from the prayer mat.

'I am engaged,' she says, not looking at him. 'I intend to marry again after my mourning period finishes.'

Captain Gul wants to shout that he'll have her fiancé hanged by his balls. 'May I know who the lucky man is?' he asks.

'I am in mourning. I can't take another man's name. But you can guess. He used to be my teacher,' she says, then gives him an encouraging smile. 'If you saw me in your dream why not keep loving me in your dream? Have family, make children, live happy forever in your dream,' she says. Then she lies down on the prayer mat and closes her eyes and stretches her legs slightly as if she suddenly needs a nap. 'Now, if you are going to tell me that you can help with my parents' release, do me a favour and don't.'

Captain Gul notices a spot of blood on her shalwar, blackish, dried up but unmistakably blood, and is horrified at the spectacle, a woman on a prayer mat, lying with her legs open with a bloodied shalwar. The daughter of traitor parents daring him. A wave of revulsion washes over Captain Gul. What heresy – not only she has no regard for his noble sentiments, she is openly insulting the prayer mat, defying the very maker she has just prayed to. Captain Gul feels the angels of hell descending over him. He mutters slut under his breath and walks out of the room in a huff and shouts at Subedar Laal Khan, making sure that Sabiha Bano hears it loud and clear. 'Take this whore away and do whatever you do with all your whores in this city.'

He calls Laal Khan back. 'Let's dig out her husband. Let's find the bullet in his chest. Get a judge to give her life. And then every jail guard in your city can do with her what you people do with your jailed whores.'

Laal Khan nods and goes out. Laal Khan knows where to take her.

THIRTY-FIVE

A Poem for OK Town

LAAL KHAN HOLDS A KEROSENE LANTERN ABOVE HIS head, his red hair a bloody dab in the dark night. The air is filled with the smell of kerosene oil and dried rose petals strewn on graves.

Dr Pervez Alam Pervez is working the shovel on the grave and is not liking the experience. The earth is soft and the grave mound is giving way steadily but Dr Pervez is panting. He is not used to manual labour. He is a man of scalpels and knives, an artist of the chewy innards. Sometimes he has had to take a saw to a skull or a disjointed bone but digging earth, he believes, is below his profession's dignity.

'I know you are a doctor and an artist and you shouldn't have to do this.' Captain Gul sits on a cemented grave, a military issue Night Searcher flashlight in his hand which he uses to spotlight Dr Pervez's face and then the work of his spade, steadily chugging away at the grave mound. He flicks his torch light off and on playfully, like somebody who has seen the lightning strike and, in that moment, has seen his entire future in blindingly clear, bold relief and now doesn't have a care in the world. 'Doctor sahib, you know that in our line of work we can't trust anybody. Sometimes not even ourselves.'

Dr Pervez Alam stops digging. 'Sir, I can write the post mortem report you want. You can tell me you want suicide,

I'll write suicide. If you want bullet in the heart, we can do bullet in the heart. Why do we need to dig up this dead man?'

Laal Khan lowers the lantern and chimes in with a suggestion. 'Should I bring the caretaker? I can wake him up. He is an opium addict but quite good at this work and he is a trusted man. It'll be quicker.' Laal Khan raises the lantern again; his shadow stretches over many graves.

'Your problem, Laal Khan, is that you trust people too easily.' Captain Gul fixes his Night Searcher on Laal Khan's face; two sources of light stare into each other. 'If everyone in this city is as trustworthy as you say they are, then why are we getting our asses buggered here? Even the whores of this city are taunting us.'

Laal Khan agrees with grunts of yes sir yes sir. He knows better than to argue with his superior officer in the dead of the night when exhuming a burnt body that may or may not have a bullet in the heart.

'Tell me one thing, Laal Khan.' Captain Gul focuses a circle of light on Laal Khan's head. 'What kind of spy goes around with red hair? Doesn't the whole city see you coming from afar? Look, here comes the spy with his red hooter. You are as subtle as an ambulance.'

Laal Khan feels a chill on the nape of his neck. None of his former field commanders have asked him anything this personal, so he weighs his answer before opening his mouth. 'Sir, my little son died of pneumonia, he was two years old. He was playing in my lap and went to sleep. He woke up shivering and his little body was on fire and by the time we got him to the Combined Military Hospital he breathed his last in my arms. Within a week my hair turned white. My wife insists that a man my age shouldn't have white hair and she puts henna in my hair every week. I think she believes that this will give us another son.'

Captain Gul is not listening to Laal Khan's tragic story. His flashlight is scanning the tombstones scattered around him. The little circle of light picks up dates of births and deaths and the Quranic verse *Every living being will taste death, Abbu we miss you* and *Oh mother who shall I tell? Now that you are gone*. On a small grave *Alas the little bud that wilted before it could bloom*.

'So why are the police protecting this dead man's wife?' Captain Gul asks Laal Khan. 'Or should I ask why are you protecting her?'

Laal Khan is startled. The memory of his two-year-old son, burning, shivering in his arms, then crying without making a sound, has made him melancholic. 'Sir, why should we care about the police matters? Why are we making him do this when he is willing to write whatever we want him to write in the post mortem report? We are an intelligence unit, not gravediggers.'

Captain Gul hears a note of defiance in Laal Khan's voice. He'll show him.

He turns towards Dr Pervez and addresses him distractedly. 'You do understand that absolute secrecy is the core of our business? That's why we can't get any help. I am sorry you have to do this menial work but your sacrifices will be remembered.' Dr Pervez, who had resumed digging, stops again, clears the sweat from his brow and listens intently. 'Come take a break. Have a drink. We have the whole night to do this.' Dr Pervez is visibly grateful at this offer, drops his spade and pats his clothes to shake off the dust. He furtively reaches for the brown bottle in his pocket, not sure if it's proper to have a drink in the graveyard in the middle of this national duty. 'Come on, bring it out, you deserve one. Recite me that famous poem of yours. Tonight is a good night for poetry.'

Dr Pervez walks over to Captain Gul and offers it to him. Captain Gul takes the bottle. Mustering his courage, he twists open the lid, brings it to his nose and sniffs, first a prickliness in his throat, then a convulsion in his stomach. He has to use all his willpower to suppress the bile churning in his guts, swirling up his throat. 'My stomach,' he says and gestures Dr Pervez to move away from him. 'You sit there and enjoy yourself and recite me that poem.'

Dr Pervez gasps for air, then takes a tiny sip and starts haltingly. He has been at many poetry recitals in his life, never the main act, but he rehearsed in front of a mirror before every recital and always won over the audience with his epic poem about his OK town. He has never recited in a graveyard, though, never at midnight, never in front of an audience of two men, three if he counts the half-exhumed dead Hakim in the grave. He feels the same anxiety that he has felt sometimes at the All District Mushaira, big stage, famous poets, district commissioner presiding and many in the crowd not familiar with his name or body of work.

Between the heaven
And the earth
Between hope
And despair…

When the shot rings out Laal Khan drops the lantern, the flame goes out and the air is suddenly thick with the smell of spilled kerosene oil. Dr Pervez is still clutching at his brown medicine bottle, his torso sticking out of the half-dug grave, eyes dead open as if still trying to take in the wonder that was his city or surprised at his audience's reaction to his harmless little poem.

Captain Gul's flashlight illuminates the dead lantern, a little puddle of oil around it. 'Do you think there is enough oil in it to burn him or should we just bury him with our friend?'

HOMEWORK 16

My God Saves Me

Man proposes and God disposes is a fallacious paradigm coined by men of slower imagination to explain away phenomenon they can't comprehend. I confine myself to my room and cut down on spousal services for Hakim Wasif Ali Wasif. He offers to buy me a necklace of gold and I inquire is he going to buy one for his first wife too because although our Allah allows a man to betroth more than once at the same time He also demands that he treat all his spouses equally. By now I know that Hakim Wasif Ali Wasif is piqued by the mention of his first wife's name who lives in the same house but I have never seen her.

He says that first he had a troublesome cankerous wife and now I am a cankerous wife too. I tell him in jest, nay, in all earnestness that he is still allowed to have two more wives – he should take them and see if they become cankerous too. He mumbles maybe he'll this time take a simple girl, a peasant girl of no education and definitely not one from a family steeped in treacherous jiyala politics.

I am very much perturbed by what the girl said about my character, my photos, what if esteemed father or, God forbid, Mother Bano sees them.

When I enter the main prayer hall in the mosque, suddenly everyone forgets about God and prayers and is gawking at me as if I am the angel of death who has just walked into the house of God uninvited. Maulvi sahib comes and leads me to a side room, a damp room which he expounds he has specially created where women can pray and observe purdah and not distract the righteous men from the righteous path. I sit in silence and listen to the verses being recited in the next room. I can't comprehend what is being said but my body feels sensations as if I am being reborn. Tears well up in my eyes, my legs begin to tremble. I rub my eyes, more tears come. I cover my face with my dupatta, in the process forgetting that when you are in the mosque dupatta should stay on your head. The prayers end. I hear the footsteps departing, men murmuring blessings and bazaar gossip to each other. I feel a presence at my side. Maulvi sahib is sitting beside me. Respectfully he pulls the dupatta over my head and says Allah likes it when you turn to Him in your hour of grief. This is His house and will always remain open for me even when the rest of the world closes its doors on me.

THIRTY-SIX

Property Prices

At Dr Pervez Alam Pervez's funeral, Molly is brisk and businesslike. He condemns the atrocity. The city's most revered doctor and people's poet found shot and half burnt in the city's graveyard was the devil's work. Allah, You are the most merciful and the harshest avenger, please bring an end to our evil hour. He prays for Dr Pervez's soul to find peace and a place in Jannah. He prays for the salvation of the city and wishes resilience and patience and grace for the bereaved family. He prays for the light to shine on the darkness that has engulfed the city. May Allah spread His mercy amongst us, specially the sinners amongst us, specially those who kill a human who brought to his community a healing touch and soothing verses. May these prayers be accepted and his journey become easier in the afterlife. He rubs his hands on his beard and turns around to greet his congregation and the first person he sees is Captain Gul, standing in the front row, just behind him, deep in meditation as if Molly's prayers were not enough and he needed extra time to seek salvation for the late doctor.

People come to Molly, absent-minded, sideways hugs, muttered words about death being the only certainty in life. May Allah give patience to the family. How will this city ever recover from this loss? May Allah lift this curse that has fallen on our city. Molly wants them to stay a little longer but they disperse quickly. Molly can't tell if it's Captain Gul's presence or if participating in Dr Pervez Alam's last rites has made them remember their own imminent end and they want to rush back home and tidy up their scattered lives. Soon it's just Molly and Captain Gul standing in the empty hall, holding hands, consoling each other, trying to circle each other in a dance of pieties.

'Huge loss for your fine city,' Captain Gul says, squeezing Molly's hand. 'He wrote that beautiful poem about this city. I was hoping you would mention it in your eulogy.'

Molly is scared of Captain Gul's scraggy beard, his warmth, his concern for the city's loss. 'I should have, I should have, but like everybody else I was in a state of shock. Mind just wanders.'

'Your prayer was straight from the heart, though.' Captain Gul looks around the hall, takes in the gold-leaf calligraphy on the arches, does a mental calculation of the price per square foot of white marble on the floor. He is buoyed by the morning telex he had received from headquarters in response to his 'mole met his maker' message. Buck up, boy, it had said, good to get some good news from OK town.

'Such a magnificent property,' he says. 'You are lucky to have it all, too bad that it's getting a reputation.'

Molly has never heard his mosque being described as a property. 'People of the city made it with their small donations. The rest is all His blessings.' Molly vaguely points towards the ceiling.

'How many shops around it? Forty-eight, I think? And offices too. Allah's house keeps giving.'

'Yes, it pays the mosque bills. We have electric fans in summer, hot water in winter and it pays my modest salary. Even imams need to feed their children.'

When people start invoking their children, Captain Gul knows they are already pleading for mercy. 'It's sad how all these rumours are reaching my bosses. Jiyalas coming and going, jerrycans of petrol, posters, leaflets urging people to set themselves on fire. They know about this place all the way in Pindi and for all the wrong reasons. You know what they asked me? Is Bhutto hiding in the mosque, they wanted to know.'

Molly gives a sheepish smile. 'Rumours. Exactly that. Stupid rumours.' And then a hint of defiance. 'We don't keep a register of who comes in and goes out of this place. It's never locked. Allah's house can't have entry permits.'

Captain Gul explains that rumours are his livelihood, his profession, his calling. 'There is not a single rumour in the world that doesn't have a twisted nugget of truth at its centre.' Molly waits for more. 'You led the funeral prayers in absentia for Bhutto? In this very hall? Rumour?'

'On that day,' Molly starts haltingly. 'Everyone was shocked. But there were no speeches. No slogans. Just a simple, silent prayer for the dead, it's our religious obligation – you can ask everyone who was there.' He looks at Captain Gul and realizes that he has probably already talked to them. 'Since I came here, Gol Mosque has been completely non-political. My only politics is Allah and the teachings of His last prophet. No other agenda here. I was the first imam to praise the general's Islamization efforts.'

'I know you and I believe you. But how do I convince my bosses that funeral prayers for a convicted, hanged murderer is not politics? On the one hand you offer funeral prayers, and from the same mosque, your friend Baghi is running the propaganda that Bhutto lives and he will return. That's the kind of confused politics I am worried about.'

Molly is sweating now, a little apprehensive, thinking forward. 'Nobody takes Baghi seriously. He even says that there is no Allah. He is slightly touched in the head. Your department must have his file.'

'I can take care of the file, I can take care of the man, that's not a problem. But my headquarters is suggesting that I should take over the mosque. These shops are mismanaged anyway. And it must be the only mosque in this land of the pure where you teach students English and tell them there is no God. Can't you see you are cutting the very branch that you are perched on, poisoning the very well your children drink from?'

When confronted with worldly powers bigger than him, Molly draws on history. He feels a part of something that precedes him, and as the silver-winged angels of ancient history descend, he feels a surge of power. 'You are right, it's Allah's house, but you have to remember that Allah is god of all, of birds and bees, of Muslims and Christians and Jews and sun worshippers and those who sleep with their own mothers. He is the god of all the galaxies. He is not only a god of those who love and worship Him. We can't push the heretics off the face of this earth. We give them love, and when they see our love and compassion towards them, they also come back to Allah…'

'So we should take over the mosque till your friend returns to Allah? He left his god a while ago. Isn't it a bit late?'

'Allah doesn't work on the government's clock,' says Molly, giving a benign but challenging smile. When he says that line in his sermons, his audience goes into rapture. Captain Gul looks a bit puzzled.

'We are standing where?' Captain Gul asks.

'In Allah's house. In Gol Mosque.'

What happens next would change the future course of OK town and leave a little void in Molly's soul. Molly doesn't see Captain Gul's hand reaching for his beard. He doesn't like it when his devotees try to touch it with reverence – even Mrs

Molly spreads her love on Molly's nose and forehead, her lips carefully avoiding touching his facial glory. Captain Gul grabs Molly's beard, twists it around and pulls him down. Molly's head hits his knees. Captain Gul punches him on his chin while still holding his beard, then shoves his head into his groin, jerks him back up, pats his beard and gives him a friendly slap on the shoulder.

'Where are we standing? On the property of Government of Pakistan?'

There are tears in Molly's eyes. Captain Gul puts his arm around Molly's shoulder; Molly tries to control a shiver that starts in his knees and moves up. 'I know you are a man of the times. Women in the mosque, in the academy. But between us, you want that whore, right? That traitor Comrade Abid's daughter you are hiding in your mosque? Are you planning to marry her or just keep her on the side? After every prayer, five times a day?'

'I swear I have nothing to do with her. She had left her home. She is Baghi's former student and he asked if he can keep her for a few days. I wish I had known.'

'So you want to keep her? Or keep this mosque? Or both? What are you going to do?' Captain Gul pauses for a moment. 'What are we going to do?'

Molly knows exactly what he is going to do. He is going to tell a story of forgiveness and redemption. 'You must have heard it but one of the most beautiful moments in the history of Islam is when our Prophet, peace be upon him, conquered Mecca and returned home a victorious hero after years of exile in Medina. What was the first thing he did? He forgave all his enemies. All the ones who called him an impostor prophet, those who wrote filthy poems about him, those who spat at him, those who threw garbage at him, those who plotted his assassination, even those who called him a heretic and an upstart. He came back to Mecca, cleared all the false idols from the house of God and said you are all forgiven.'

Molly pauses to breathe. 'That, my sir, is the true spirit of Islam. And you have brought it to this city. You have won our hearts. Our minds will follow. And that woman? She is bad news. A woman who leaves a husband in a burning house, how can she be trusted? She even tried to attack me once. But I forgave her. Our mosque will be a better place without her. Actually our city will be a better city without her.'

'You take care of your friend and his academy. When I leave this city, and trust me I plan to leave it soon, I want to leave it clean.'

'Sir.'

'What?'

'If you don't mind, I want to share something with you. The only thing that our prophet did with his own hands was that he cleansed the House of Allah. With his own hands. Broke every single idol with his own hands.'

'Molly sahib, you are too much, comparing a lowly sinning soldier to our last saviour.'

Molly is only warming up. 'Sir, just one last thing. Our own advocate Noor Nabi saw your hand and predicted some historical things for you, did she not? You may or may not believe her. Believe me, I have never shown my hand to Noor Nabi.' Molly pauses and looks him in the eye. 'I don't believe this fate in your palm nonsense but I am a student of Islamic history, specially the histories of early Muslim warriors. In your forehead I see the light that was seen on the foreheads of only two men. Khalid bin Walid, who rose from a desert peninsula and conquered Byzantium, and Omar bin Abi Waqas who, with his small band of believers, ran over Persia. That's what I see in you and I think you should start with this mosque. So that the people of this city will remember that a warrior was here. Clean it up with your own hands. We'll be waiting.' Molly holds both Captain Gul's hands, brings them to his lips and then touches them to his eyes. 'With these blessed hands.'

THIRTY-SEVEN

Two Answers for Every Question

'I THINK YOU LOOK YOUNGER WITH YOUR GREY HAIR.' Captain Gul is cleaning his service revolver with an oily rag. 'Red hair was against service rules anyway. Did nobody ever tell you?'

Since the night of the graveyard, Subedar Laal Khan had stopped dyeing his hair, or maybe his wife had. Captain Gul never bothered asking.

Laal Khan is not used to compliments from his officers. He blushes and grunts yes sir, sorry sir.

'Tell me something, if you don't mind.' Captain Gul rubs the barrel of his gun vigorously as if trying to erase the memory of Dr Pervez's astonished face. 'With your grey hair and your dead child does your soldier still turn up for duty?'

Laal Khan first looks incredulous but then grins. His officer is trying to be his buddy. 'Sir, my soldier is always on the march, ask my wife.'

'She never suspects you about playing away from home? I mean, you spend a lot of nights away from her.' Captain Gul is encouraging, gossipy, asking Laal Khan leading questions, a friendly interrogation technique that he picked up in a training module which they jokingly called 'play them before you slay them' module.

Laal Khan is willing to play. 'My wife knows my work,' he stumbles. 'I mean, she doesn't know my work at all. I swear I never talk to her about my actual work but she knows that I can be called for duty anytime.'

'You are lucky to have a woman like that. I mean, women are suspicious by nature. I am sure one day they'll make perfect spies.'

'Not mine, sir. I have one rule. If you are married to one woman then you are married to one woman. Sir, I have been around some beautiful ladies, sir, sometimes half clothed, sir, sometimes drunk and sometimes even half clothed and drunk and passed out, sir. There are some suspects we bring in who are ready to open their legs before they open their mouth but I have never touched another woman in my life.'

'What?' Captain Gul is aghast as if Laal Khan has casually waved a mutinous flag. 'What did you do with the whore who wanted to fuck me on the prayer mat?'

'I took her to a safe house, sir.'

'This is the safe house. We are in the safe house. Have you got another one?'

'No, sir, I took her home. No place safer than my home in this city.'

Captain Gul is furious that his grey-haired lackey is more loyal to his wife than to this Field Intelligence Unit or his commander but he can't really court martial him for not taking a traitor's whore of a daughter with force. A lesson will be taught. His loyalty will be put to test. 'So you never touched a woman except for your wife?'

'Yes, sir.' Subedar Laal Khan stands at attention.

'So have you fucked a man then?'

Laal Khan blushes and blurts out, 'God forbid, sir, what kind of question is that?'

Captain Gul has put the revolver back in its holster and is caressing it like a sleepy child. 'Come on, Laal, your smile tells me something. Just between us boys, we have all been in the trenches.'

Laal Khan wants to tell him that he is due to retire in four years and is not a boy any more but he knows he can't avoid his officer's question. He becomes philosophical. 'Sir, in field-work course we were taught that we should have two answers ready for every question. Even for basic questions like your name, your father's name, your school, which clan do you belong to, which village, both answers should be different but believable. I am sure in officers' course they probably want you to have more than two answers, many many many answers for the same question.'

Captain Gul is beginning to like this game. 'So, my question to you, Subedar Laal Khan, is have you ever buggered a man? Give me both answers, soldier.'

Laal Khan stands at attention, back in his basic intelligence course, observant and quick-witted. He can smash a skull as easily as he can crack a filthy joke.

'Sir, answer number one: who hasn't, in the barracks.

'Sir, answer number two: never, sir, never even thought about it.'

'And what if you have to do it because the commander of your Field Intelligence Unit orders you to do it?'

In his line of work Laal Khan has performed all kinds of duties, sat outside in the bazaar disguised as a beggar, played an opium addict, pulled many nails, broken some locks, made some close friends who never knew his real profession, but he has never been asked to do this. 'Sir?'

'Don't sir me. Give me a straight answer.'

'Duty is duty is duty, sir,' says Laal Khan hoping that he wouldn't have to go that far in the line of duty.

Captain Gul is effusive, greets Baghi with a bear hug, then half bends to touch his feet, mockingly of course. 'You have got some balls, sir, you have got unbelievably big ones for a civilian.' Baghi is offered a chair; Captain Gul plonks half a pint of gin on the table. 'I want to toast you. But I gave up. I swear I have been sober since I had that Black Dog with you. It went inside me and barked and barked and barked. You have to go it alone. But I want to toast your courage. Here's to your balls.'

Baghi tries to protest but Captain Gul has already poured him half a glass and is now making a big show of celebrating by clinking his glass with his own empty glass. Baghi takes a tiny sip and puts it back on the table.

'Sir, I just wanted to tell you that we are closing your file.' Captain Gul taps a worn-out pink file with a Government of Pakistan seal on the table.

Baghi can make out his own name and a faded stamp: SECRET. 'I feel honoured that a humble English tutor like myself has a file of his own in your esteemed establishment.' Baghi glances at the file on the table again. It's very thin.

As if they have nearly nothing on him.

Captain Gul pulls out a single sheet of paper from the file and starts to read: 'Kings, Prime Ministers, Princes. We'll get you in your palaces, we'll get you when you are pulling your cocks…' I salute you. Those big boys must have pissed in their pants. Rebels of tomorrow… what guts. Ahead of your time.'

For a moment Baghi is thrilled, feels a stirring in his loins, at his own words being read out to him. For a moment he forgets the painful memory of the aftermath and stinging stream of blood down his posterior.

His warning has come true. Bhutto, the man who hosted these despots, has been hanged. The man who led the prayers at this farce, the custodian of the two Holy Houses, Shah Faisal, has been shot by his own kin. History is on his side. He feels flattered, and although he can never condone military rule, he is beginning to like the man doing the flattery.

'But, sir, sir...' Captain Gul tears the sheet of paper, rolls it into a paper ball and throws it in the dustbin in the corner of the room. His aim is very good. 'You have got even bigger balls now. Come on, drink up to that.' Captain Gul gestures to his glass on the table. Baghi picks it up and takes a large sip.

'True story. In your city, I meet the woman of my dreams. I find out her father's a famous traitor, I still declare my love. Way beyond the call of my duty. I want to spend the rest of my life with her. No. Avenge her honour and then serve her for the rest of my life. Just like I serve this city, this country. And you know what she wants?'

He pulls out another single sheet of paper, tears it in two swift motions, and flings it on the table. 'Here, gone, Salim Ahmed Salim.'

Baghi knows it's his apology letter drafted by Molly and his powerful friends who wanted him out of that cell alive. Baghi appreciates the fact that Captain Gul has not read from it.

'You. She wants you. A traitor's daughter is being protected by a reformed traitor, who gave in writing that he'll never do politics. Or maybe, maybe you have a bigger cock. Let's see how big it is.'

Baghi chokes on his drink. He has a coughing fit. He pushes his glass away. 'Who are you talking about? I don't know any women.'

'Your student. The one you were hiding in your academy. Your file is closed, even your apology is in the dustbin. You can stop playing dare with me. I know old habits die hard but we are here, I am here. If two men with balls can't trust each other, who can?'

Baghi feels a creeping sense of camaraderie towards this young officer who is jealous because he heard a rumour about him and Sabiha living together. After all, he is the head of the intelligence unit.

Baghi bends forward. He has always been secretly proud of his letter to Ummah, and now that a member of the country's elite secret agency appreciates it, it makes him sentimental. His right eye wells up and he says something that he has never said to anyone before. 'There are men who don't like women, not in that way, you know – not that I have anything against women. In fact, I am all for women's liberation, it's just that they don't do anything for me.'

Captain Gul gives an appreciative smile, pours him some more gin. 'So you have no interest in marrying or fucking a woman named Sabiha Bano, the one you've been hiding in your academy?'

Baghi pauses for a moment, thrown at the harshness of the words marrying and fucking, then blurts out. 'No, she is Molly's friend. I am just a—'

'Good decision, she is a slut anyway, offered herself to me right here, in this room, and before that I don't know how many more.' Captain Gul is ringing his buzzer and shouting. 'Subedar Laal Khan, I have got a present for you.'

Laal Khan walks in, goes straight to where Baghi is still trying to think how to finish his sentence without losing all his dignity. Laal Khan holds him by his collar and jerks him out of the chair.

'Don't be rude,' Captain Gul says in a calm voice. 'Let him finish his drink.'

Laal Khan picks up the pint of gin from the table with one hand. With the other hand's forefinger and thumb, he squeezes Baghi's nose. As Baghi gasps for air, Laal Khan shoves the bottle into his mouth, the warm gin spills all over Baghi's face, he thrashes in his seat, Laal Khan lets his nose go and shakes the bottle vigorously into his mouth, making sure that there is not a single wasted drop. He drags the flailing Baghi towards the door.

Captain Gul is businesslike in his parting words. 'You did say you like men. Have you seen a more handsome man than Laal Khan? Don't be deceived by his grey hair. His soldier is always on the march.'

In the small adjoining room, Laal Khan is all bored courtesy and whispers. 'Boss wants you to make some noise, so let's oblige him. Bend down.' He gives him a full-handed slap on the face, which makes more noise than it hurts. 'You are an educated man. Why do you get yourself into such situations? The other day you were caught in the cinema fucking a boy and now you are here because you are fucking a woman who said no to our boss.' Baghi opens his mouth to protest his innocence, but Laal Khan cups his mouth with his one hand and twists his arm with the other. 'You think it's your punishment? You fuck pretty boys in Venus cinema and fresh widows in a mosque and I get your wrinkly ass.' Laal Khan knees him in the ass, spins him around, punches him in the chest, all the while encouraging him to make some noise. He sticks his right shin between Baghi's legs to tackle him to the ground when Baghi's semi-erect penis brushes against his thigh. Laal Khan lets loose a heartfelt cry of disgust. 'You faggot.' He punches him in the face and splits open his lower lip. Laal Khan goes at him with a professional torturer's measured punches, targeting his kidney, a knee in his groin, a hook on his right eye. Laal Khan knows the economy of causing pain. Baghi cries and a wooden rod strikes on the soles of his feet. Baghi whimpers and a jug of water is poured over his face and nose. He can't breathe. He covers his face, shields his groin with both his hands. He doesn't have enough hands to ward off the blows that keep coming. Baghi pretends to faint but finds no mercy and a boot smashes into his rib cage.

When Molly comes to collect a battered and bruised Baghi, his face is a network of cuts, his shirt a map of bloody patches. He is shivering uncontrollably but he flinches at Molly's touch, refuses to let him put his arm around his shoulder to help him walk and hobbles out of the door.

Captain Gul has left before Molly's arrival. Walking out he had given a satisfactory glance to Laal Khan. 'I told you to bugger him as a courtesy to this fine city, but you have really loved him up. Well done, soldier.'

HOMEWORK 17

The Morning After the Hanging

When the nations go into turmoil, oftentimes it's not reflected in the day-to-day humdrum of life. It only manifests itself in shutters coming down on shops and a general slacking and slowing down of the pace of existence. I find out about the hanging of Chairman Bhutto from newspaper hawkers shouting in the street. I feel a surge of panic and fear and I lock up the door. If they have hanged the pride of Asia, the undisputed leader of the Ummah, the brother of peasants and labourers, the flower of the desert, how will they spare his poor friend, my esteemed father? Will Mother Bano suffer the same fate? I cannot bear the terrible thought of a noose around her neck. My first urge is to run to the mosque and start praying. But then I remind myself that God exists everywhere even in a second wife's bedroom. I lock up the door from inside and start invoking His mercy.

I am in deep communion with God when Hakim Wasif Ali Wasif starts banging on the door.

I open the door assuming he wants to share the bad news and console me. He is furious and looks at me in an accusatory manner. I wait for him to utter something. When he stands there fuming, proverbial smoke coming out of his ears, I move toward him and put my hands on his shoulder in a gesture of bonhomie. 'What do you think will happen to esteemed father now?' He pulls a mouth as if he has imbibed a bitter medicine and mutters that I am more worried what will happen to you.

And ergo it occurs to me that maybe I am the next in the queue. Chairman Bhutto. Esteemed father. Mother Bano. Maybe they will come for Sabiha Bano now.

Hakim Wasif waves a videotape in my face and for a moment I'm frightened that maybe there is a video recording of the hanging of the chairman. Maybe it's that of esteemed father and Mother Bano. Hakim Wasif is frothing at the mouth now, little ripples of anger crashing and ebbing and coming back in his corpulent visage.

'You have been fornicating behind my back.' He wants to shout but it emanates as a hiss, half accusation, half lamentation.

I am first confused then furious at this unexpected and unfortunate turn of events. 'I have never asked you what you do with your first wife, who are you to ask me? On a day like this. What about my father? What about my mother?'

He expounds his wish that they be hanged too because of the progeny they gave him, already broken and still unfaithful to her husband who gave her everything that he has. I am confounded. I swing a blow at him, it hits his fleshy shoulder and he doesn't seem impacted.

'You are not just more troublesome, more cankerous than my first wife but also a shameless whore, my stars, my stars.' He holds me by the hair and makes me sit on the edge of the bed. He says look what you have done. He inserts the video in the VCR and what I see on the screen makes my skin crawl. My heart pumps faster but no blood is going anywhere. I catch a glimpse of my face and a hairy belly smothering it.

Hakim Wasif Ali Wasif is looking at me then looking at the TV screen, his face in a flush at my humiliation. I pick up a large glass bottle of his Iron Syrup and smash the TV screen in a million tiny bits. Sparks fly and a nylon curtain begins to smoulder. I pick up another bottle and aim for his wide-eyed visage. I miss and the bottle smashes against the wall, adding a little proverbial fuel to the fire. Hakim Wasif Ali Wasif runs towards the curtain, trying to douse the fire with his flailing hands and cursing my esteemed father, Mother Bano, expounding all the time that may my parents rot in jail for eternity, or be hanged and join Chairman Bhutto in hell. I move towards the cupboard assigned for my meagre belongings. In the cupboard is my sports bag, in the bag my medal, my revolver. By the time I retrieve the revolver the room is already full of smoke and flames are licking the ceiling.

THIRTY-EIGHT

The Little Coffin

A.D. MALANG'S JEEP COMES TO A HALT AS HE SPOTS Noor Nabi walking out of the City Court, cradling a stack of files, chewing on an unlit beeri. She walks without looking left or right as if it was up to the traffic to part for her. Mostly it does, except for a tanga-pulling horse who sneezes and air-licks as it brushes past her. A.D. Malang comes out of the jeep, opens the door and tries to take the files from her. She elbows him, gets into the front seat and plonks her files in her lap. 'Not letting you touch my case files. Everything you touch burns down.' She starts to rummage in her pockets for matches.

'My only friend, the finest legal mind in this city, is going up against me. Like you, I have been a humble servant of the law. We should learn to work together.' A.D. Malang is not in his uniform. He is wearing a neatly pressed sky-blue shalwar qameez. Without his uniform, he is relaxed and chatty around Noor Nabi. They could be an old couple who go on a drive and quibble over domestic chores.

'Flattery will get you everywhere. But it won't keep you out of jail. If you don't mend your ways...' she says, sucking on her beeri. A.D. Malang shifts into third gear; the police department sticker on his windscreen says NO FEAR in red lightning bolts.

'Are you telling me my fate, or are you talking about your feelings?' A.D. Malang gives her a flirty smile.

'Give me your hand,' Noor Nabi says. 'I have been studying hands of world-famous murderers. I want to do a proper count on your hand.'

A.D. Malang turns towards her, his moustache twitching under suppressed laughter. 'Sometimes I think you have started this whole palmistry business so you can hold my hand.'

Noor Nabi grabs Malang's hand, slams it on the dashboard then twists it around with her bony fingers.

'You have told half the city their fate. All I get is threats,' says A.D. Malang, feigning anguish. 'For now, I am taking your fate in my hands.' He swerves the steering wheel to avoid a child who has suddenly run onto the road, an irate father chasing after him.

'Assistant Sub-Inspector Allah Ditta Malang, you can fool the entire district administration, you can even fool your own fate, but you can't fool me,' she says as Malang gets off the road, parks near a fruit-juice stall and ignores the waiter boy who comes and stands next to his window.

'You know our pasts. You know our futures. You are the queen of the City Court. I always used to wonder why, in a city full of fat lawyers, Molly works with you. It's because you are scarier than a mad princess. Nobody can touch you. Not even the law that you practise.' He rolls down the window and raises two fingers to the boy, who rushes away. He already knows his order.

'Allah Ditta. Allah Ditta. Allah Ditta. I have this file, right here, eight burnt to death. OK, maybe you get some people to shout Jiye Bhutto, call them jiyalas and everybody forgets them. Eighth one was a child. Since when have children started burning themselves to bring back Bhutto? There is a judge who has a child the exact same age. You might think judges have no feelings but they get nightmares about burnt children in their jurisdiction.'

A.D. Malang looks away to avoid eye contact with Noor Nabi, in a half-hearted attempt at regret.

'Are they asking you to burn people now?' She hits the file on his chest, gently.

'No,' he says with a sly smile. 'The army people are asking for even more. To catch jiyalas before they go up in flames. So they can burn them themselves. They think they are not getting enough credit.'

'So this is your new hobby?' Noor Nabi taps the file in her lap.

'Old family dispute, I just encouraged them to sort it out amongst themselves. We are busy with matters of national importance. So I wrote it up as jiyalas doing what jiyalas do. They are not doing enough. I am just doing my job.'

Noor Nabi is staring at him, like a teacher nudging a child towards the correct answer.

'In my humble view, half of law enforcement is just letting people do what they want. Some people want to burn, others want to set them on fire. They take care of each other. If anyone is left, you take care of them in the court. I am just a vagabond, walking these streets to catch a glimpse of you, waiting for you to tell me that you are my destiny.'

'This is not going to go away with your honey tongue. It's in the papers. With pictures. There is a judge who wants me to file a writ petition, name you.'

A.D. Malang doesn't seem fazed. 'I know your motto. Screw the police, love the judges. I know some judges have strong feelings. For you. You know what they say about you? That when you hire Noor Nabi, the judge comes for free, wrapped around her finger.' He takes two glasses of pomegranate juice from the waiter and passes one to Noor Nabi with exaggerated reverence. 'Mine is the most thankless job in this city. There was only one jiyala who was going to set himself on fire and I saved his life. No medals for saving lives in this city.'

'Shahid, Friendly Art Photo Studio?'

'Yes, he is alive because of me. And doesn't your Molly sahib say that if you save one human life you save all of humanity?'

'You should see the humanity you have saved. He has shut his shop. Thinks photography is a sin. He says he wasn't very good at it anyway. Your friend in the FIU has reduced him to a skeleton. He can't stop shivering.'

'Still better than burnt flesh.'

Noor Nabi puts her glass on the dashboard, smacks her paper-thin lips that have turned crimson, lights her beeri and takes a deep puff. 'You are so cocky because you are running around with the Field Intelligence Unit. Your father went to his grave making flowerpots on his wheel so that you could become an officer of the law. Now Allah Ditta Malang has become a boy servant for Captain Gul, driving him around like his personal chauffeur. I want to see how this love story will end.'

'I'm driving around my civilian friends also, helping them. But do I get an additional star?' He puts his right hand on his chest and bows his head, like a movie star playing a slave in a queen's court.

'You want me to write you a thank you letter for letting me know that you were coming to pick up Sabiha Bano? Did you need all those men, those jeeps with sirens? You scared the hell out of that poor girl.'

'We did respect the sanctity of the mosque – actually we respected the sanctity of Noor Nabi Advocate & Palmist Associates. You think your turbans fooled my men?'

Noor Nabi finishes her glass of juice in one long gulp and gets to the point. 'This friend of yours, I told him his fate was in America and Kashmir and God knows where but definitely not here and now he is looking for love in this miserable town. He wants to marry her. Can you believe it? He gets her kidnapped so that he can propose to her? He has seen her once and he is begging her to marry him. Who does that after seeing someone once? Has this fauji got soft in the head or is this your bad company? I have seen her hand, you have seen her case. If she doesn't leave town, she might end up killing someone. You don't want a dead captain on your hands.'

A.D. Malang weighs his words before he speaks. 'To me it sounds like a match made in fauji heaven. Let's say she marries him, nobody will be able to touch her. She might even get some relief for her parents. It won't matter how many murders she has on her hand. Past or future. Haven't you heard that if you are in love, the first seven murders are forgiven? She has only begun. My hands are clean. You should read hers again.'

Noor Nabi doesn't have time for fate games. 'Nobody is getting any relief from these duffers running the country. If you can take a break from pimping for your captain, come with me and do what I tell you to do. Otherwise I'll make sure that this hand is chopped off. There's a new law for that, you might have heard.'

Malang drives in silence; Noor Nabi gives him directions. 'Take her and drive her straight to Sahiwal jail, women's wing. I have tracked down her mother. They are keeping her there.'

'The girl avoided jail after burning down her house with her husband in it and now you want to have her locked up?'

'It's the only place that's safe for her now.'

'And what are the charges?'

'I can trust you'll think up something. Only thing you are good at. Something light, bailable. Here's her judicial remand, signed and stamped. Just sign your name.'

They leave the main road, and drive through narrow lanes, Noor Nabi knocks at a door. The nameplate on the door simply says Laal Khan, no rank, no academic qualifications. Malang gives a welcome nod when Sabiha Bano comes out and slides into the back seat as if she has been expecting them.

'Take her where I told you to and if you are thinking of doing what you do when you want to bypass the judges, your run-and-shoot dramas, remember I am the last person who saw you with her. Anything happens to her, you won't be able to show your handsome face in this town.'

After Noor Nabi leaves, Sabiha moves to the front seat, looking straight ahead.

'This is not the first time I am driving a prime suspect out of my jurisdiction. Catching them, driving them, all my pleasure. You can relax. I am what I am today because of Baghi sahib and like me you have been his student?'

Sabiha looks at him as if she has no idea what he is talking about.

'Did you learn English?'

'He made me write essays. I am not very good. I failed once but I am trying. I need to get my things from the academy. All my things are there.'

Malang opens the glove compartment, takes out a pistol and puts it on the dashboard. 'This thing? You took it from your house.'

'People always take things from a house on fire.'

'This matched the bullet in your husband's chest. But anyone could have shot him.' He gets no response from her. 'It's your property. Keep it.'

Sabiha slips it into her bag without looking at it. 'Who gave it to you?'

'It doesn't matter who gave it to me, you should think who you gave it to.'

Sabiha shrugs. 'These are your fauji friend's orders?'

'I come from humble background like you. I don't know if you know but my father was a potter—'

She cuts him off in mid-sentence. 'Are you sure your fauji friend will not come after me in the academy?'

'They will not come after you today. They're busy burning someone else today.'

Sabiha slides her hand into her bag, feels the weight of the pistol on her wrist and remembers the silly thing Sir Baghi had said. If you shoot someone and kill them, you kill a bit of yourself too. But if you shoot someone in the knee, they remember you for the rest of their life.

'Please stop at the academy. I need to say my last salam to our Sir Baghi.'

HOMEWORK 18

My English Teacher

Allah is the teacher of all teachers but what do you do with a teacher who doesn't believe in Allah? Hiding in plain sight in Subedar Laal Khan's house, waiting for Noor Nabi to set her grand plan in motion, Mr Laal Khan's wife watches me with hawk eye but only asks me to eat with her and leaves me alone and I have time to think. When I reflect on my life and times I feel a righteous anger swelling up in my heart over my English teacher. I am supposed to be underground with Sir Baghi, in some no-name village, in a middle school, pretend living like husband and wife. But here I am hiding in the beast's belly. Although Subedar Laal Khan is not the beast that he appears to be outside the house, inside the house he is his wife's loyalist puppy. Maybe he is trying to make up for the time when he was given orders to serve me the tea that first almost killed me then corrupted my repute as a God-fearing second wife. There has been a cabal of men in my treatise from esteemed father who wanted to protect me, my PT coach who broke me and my late spouse who claimed to love me but who, let's say for the purpose of this treatise, met a tragic end because he didn't abide by the fire regulation in his work place.

Like the creator himself, Salim Ahmed Salim alias Sir Baghi is a bundle of contradictions. He expounds blasphemous claims about Almighty and lives and works in His house. He says he is a revolutionary and is imparting education to the children of the poor so that they can take on tyranny in their own idiom but he is best friends and blood brother with a dubious character, Molly Rafique, who expounds mercy and rights of widows but who has wandering hands and is most definitely in cahoots with the army and offers no assistance to a widow who needs to search for her parents. One day he even claimed that he was ready to take me on as a second wife if his first wife permitted him. For a man of learning he has learnt no lessons from the fate of the man whose second wife I once was.

My time in the academy was not much different than my time in Hakim's house – I was like a prisoner with a balcony view.

During my time there it became clear as daylight that Sir Baghi makes boy love, not with his students but he suddenly says he has urgent business in the bazaar and comes back smelling of other men's sweat. Maybe men loving men is better than men pledging to love women or the vice versa because someone either ends up crying or in jail or dead in their own house.

While staying with him, slowly I began to put my faith in this faithless man. He's a gentle soul around me; sometimes I feel he was a bit scared of me. When he took away my gun and expounded that killing was not a good idea I began to trust him with my life.

He is also a different man by day and a very different creature by night. In the day time he is defiant, he stands up to his best friend and saviour, he even spoke up to the army man who visited him and told him that people think differently outside the cantonments. In his sleep he is a terrified animal. Sometimes I observe him when he is sleeping. He shudders and screams, I gently slap him and he murmurs sorry and goes to sleep. He is not my husband but he is already behaving like one. We had some parlays, and although he doesn't speak much, I can feel what he means to say but is unable to utter. He promised me that we'll go away to a place where we can live, not like prisoners, and wait for esteemed father and Mother Bano's release. Sometimes I leave my treatise in his academy to check if he'll read it. When he doesn't read, I am disappointed, but he goes up in my esteem for keeping his word.

When I arrived at the academy after that fateful night of fire in my house, he didn't like me to be there. I don't know if he was scared of me because I was suspected of being a self-made widow or because of my famous esteemed father and his association with Chairman Bhutto. He had heard of my parents and kept claiming that although he doesn't agree with their politics he believed them to be on the right side of the history. He even called me a witness to the history. I wanted to correct him that I am not a witness, I don't want to witness anything – do I want to witness my esteemed father handcuffed and taken away in front of the entire village? I don't even want to see that vile man Comrade Sadiq Ali Sadiq on his knees, bleeding, still trying to parlay with the army soldiers on our behalf. I don't want to see Mother Bano dragged and hauled into an army truck. In concluding this treatise, I have to say that what led me to Sir Baghi was Allah's will. I didn't write my own destiny. And when Noor Nabi read my hand and predicted that a man is waiting for me to take me out of here, I couldn't believe that she couldn't see that the man was right there. When his friend Molly tried to use his hands on me, he was proven wrong in a short span of time because my arms were much stronger than his. And when Sir Baghi stands like a shield between that rascal

Molly who first called me his sister and now wants me to be his second arrangement, and when Sir Baghi stands between me and the police like a wall, I'm convinced that he is the man to pluck me from this vortex of history and give us a safe underground life.

But when the military man takes me Sir Baghi is nowhere to be seen. Has he given me up to the army? Why false promise of a life together, why holding me and telling me I am history's child and then abandoning me at the first sound of the boots approaching his abode?

I didn't object to his defiance of Allah, in fact I believed that by slowly getting to know me he'll become close to our maker. I didn't object to him disappearing and coming back smelling of other men's sweat. I leave my fate in Noor Nabi's hands and I leave Sir Baghi's punishment in Allah's hands. But before I embark on my journey into the unknown, I must gather my things from the academy, say a final farewell, collect my bag, my gun, all my homeworks.

THIRTY-NINE

A Tree Holds the Boy

MOLLY BRINGS HIM A GLASS OF WATER BUT BAGHI waves it away. Molly brings a handful of cotton wool to clean his wounds, Baghi snarls but lets him dab his bruises with Dettol, his face full of disdain, turning every shard of pain into a curse.

'Allah tests His best,' Molly says to cheer him up. There are distant shouts of Allah Hu Akbar filtering through the balcony. The city seems to have woken from its slumber and is trying to resurrect a god it had lost for a few days. 'Remember all the prophets who lost their siblings. Prophet Ayub went blind crying for his missing son who languished at the bottom of a well. Remember Hazrat Issa, the heavy wooden cross on his back, nails in his feet, nails in his palms, a big nail through his heart.'

'Why doesn't your Allah test you? I am being abused, beaten up by a fauji you brought into my academy, and you are sitting here getting fat, getting your feet massaged by your mrs and dreaming of sleeping with young widows. You have been circling her like a horny dog. Where is your test?'

Molly blushes in his beard. 'Allah has made me, He has made my lust, He has told me to fight it. That's my test. I failed that test once, I was punished for that. I was thrown out of my home, like Adam was expelled from paradise, and you were not even that tempting.'

Molly smiles. Baghi is angry to see him smile, then they both laugh. A childhood memory rears its head, is not acknowledged, but they keep on laughing for longer than they have in ages. Baghi's body goes through convulsions of laughter and then the pain returns.

'You have never forgiven me because my parents sent you away. You have kept me here because you want to feel like the better man, the forgiving man.' Baghi is hurting outside and inside. The brief bit of laughter has made his bitterness sharper.

Molly shakes his head. 'You were a child. I was a child. Your parents ran out of kindness. It was their test. They did what they thought was best for me. How can I ever blame you?'

'But I never came to look for you – you did come to save my ass. You saved my life when they were going to kill me. Twice.'

Molly holds his hand and gently caresses it in an attempt to comfort him. 'Remember there was the flood that took my parents away. In that flood, I thought I saved my life by holding on to a tree branch, but now I know it was the tree holding me. I got entangled in the branches. I shut my eyes but I could hear the gushing water running through my toes, trying to tug me along, but the tree held me like a mother would hold her child in a storm. The flood was whispering His name, it was unleashed by Him, or maybe the river was running away from His wrath, still whispering His name. Every drop of water was whispering Allah Hu Akbar. I didn't even know how to pray and He taught me. I promised myself that if I lived, I would pray every day, every night. But when I reached the safety of your home I forgot. I also became angry with my Allah. What kind of god leaves a four-year-old at the mercy of a flood that He himself caused and takes his parents away? The comfort of your home was the best thing that happened to me. But being thrown out of your home was even better. I knew I was still that child clinging onto tree branches with flood water running through my toes. I knew I had to make a home for myself in His home. I was forgiven so I had to forgive.'

'The only person you have forgiven is yourself,' says Baghi.

Molly smiles again and says one has to start somewhere.

'Who are you more scared of? Your wife? Or that intelligence officer? One day you say a prayer for Bhutto, the next day you lick the boots of his killers. Is this what your Allah has taught you?'

Molly shakes his head as if he has wasted all these years with Baghi. 'There is an order in the universe: rivers come down from the mountains and go into the sea, the sun and moon take their turns around the earth. Allah chooses a ruler and tells us to try to get along with our rulers, keep that order. Otherwise there will be anarchy – women will leave their homes, children will trample over their parents. Do small things, kind things, maybe even small acts of defiance, but never destroy the order that He has created.'

Baghi listens with his eyes closed, head tilted to one side.

'When Our Prophet, Peace Be Upon Him, couldn't stay in Mecca what did he do? He left the city, he left in the dead of the night, he stayed in a cave, and the whole night a spider spun a web at the mouth of the cave. And when his killers came looking for him, they couldn't find him. There is a whole chapter in the Holy Quran about that spider. We are blessed if we can be like that spider.'

'So you were sent away and now you want to send her away? Is that the order of your universe?'

'It's in her own best interest. For how long can she run from the law?'

'If she goes, I go,' says Baghi. He knows in his heart that it's an empty threat.

'I think it's best for everyone. For a while. I'll find you another place, and you can continue your teaching. But this is my only house now, where can I go?'

Baghi gets up, hobbles towards the bookshelf and starts packing her things in her sports bag. He'll leave this place before he is thrown out. 'I know her, she'll come to say goodbye, to take her things. She had a pistol. Can you bring it back? I don't want to keep any of her things.'

Molly says a prayer under his breath and leaves saying, 'I'll go and get it. I gave it to my guard. I hope he didn't sell it.'

Molly goes down the stairs, into his house, forgets all about Sabiha and her gun. He begins to look for some boxes to help pack Baghi's books. Sooner the better. He rushes out when he hears a single shot that echoes through the mosque hall. He rushes up the stairs towards the academy and hears Baghi scream. 'She shot me. The bitch shot me in the knees.'

FORTY

Starting Easy Fires

SHAHID CAN'T RUN BUT HE IS FORCED TO RUN. HE hobbles in the middle of the road as the white Toyota Corolla follows him. It drives slowly but not slow enough. His clothes are covered in splotches of sweat and petrol. He stumbles, falls, then crawls a few steps, but the Corolla is almost at his heels, growling. Half-dislodged toenails on his left foot are covered in a rag. His other foot, spared by Captain Gul's clumsy hands and pliers, doesn't want to move. He looks around, thinks of getting up. Subedar Laal Khan walks alongside him carrying a jerrycan of Super.

A crowd slowly gathers on both sides of the road, watching the spectacle, not wanting to watch but not able to look away.

The main road leading to Gol Mosque is paved with fear and confusion and speculation and faces covered by unbelieving hands and prayers for mercy.

From her first-floor office, Noor Nabi peers down, lights a beeri and draws the curtains. She knows how this is going to end but doesn't have the stomach to bear witness.

Captain Gul is behind the steering wheel. His foot presses down on the accelerator and then pulls back just as the vehicle is about to hit Shahid. He scans the crowd on both sides of the road and is satisfied with their defeated, mute faces.

Shahid tries to get up when he approaches the boarded-up Shahid's Friendly Art Photo Studio, shop sign still intact. Pictures of children with their pink cheeks next to Mao glare back at him. The owner of Hussaini Stylish Salon comes out, sees Shahid crawling, runs towards him, wants to help. Captain Gul presses on the horn and doesn't let go till Hussaini runs back to his barbershop and stays in for the rest of the day.

The man from the Himalayas watches for a moment and slinks away promising himself not to come down the mountains again.

Shahid wants to raise a fist, say something in defiance, give one last message to his hapless city fellows, but every time he stops to catch a breath, Laal Khan splashes him with some more Super. Captain Gul stops the car, gets out and puts his hand on Subedar Laal Khan's shoulder. 'That's enough. There are many books where we are taking him. Starting a fire won't be a problem.'

Laal Khan takes his jerrycan back to the Corolla and sits in the back seat. He has carried out his orders. He neither trusts the crowd, straining their necks to get a good look, nor his commander who walks in the middle of the road like a conquering hero. Laal Khan locks the door from inside.

A thin trickle of petrol runs in the middle of the road from Shahid's dripping clothes to the Toyota Corolla. 'Take me, show me your Bhutto. Show me where he lives. Take us there and we'll leave you alone. Bloody hell, I'll leave this city alone. Don't you want to be with your leader? Or do you still want your picture in the papers?'

Captain Gul is slightly dizzy with the smell of petrol in the air. His sobered-up brain takes a lazy spin as the fumes make their way to his lungs. Unsteady on his feet, he lights a cigarette, takes a deep puff without inhaling, blows smoke towards the crowd and, without thinking, throws the matchbox at Shahid, who stretches his right arm and catches it. He was the first-slip fielder in his high school cricket team, known for his diving catches. His hand trembles but he holds on to the matchbox. Captain Gul looks around at the crowd. Nobody dares to come between him and his quarry. This is the lesson this city needed to learn. His mission here finally accomplished. He is now done with OK town.

With his trembling hands Shahid strikes the match. First nothing, the match hisses and is about to say no, then a tiny flame leaps.

Captain Gul is furious at his defiance. The bugger doesn't even know if he is going to live or die, but he has found his audience. There's probably someone in the crowd with a camera, the treacherous photographer's treacherous comrade. Captain Gul surveys the crowd to spot the culprit. All he sees is eyes full of horror, mouths agape, some muttering prayers, others looking towards the sky, hoping to wake God from his slumber.

A child creeps up the stairs of Shahid's Friendly Art Photo Studio. He had been listening to Mao's whining and goes to check on him. He tries to take the dog in his arms, and when Mao yelps, he puts his hand gently on his mouth. Mao thrashes for a moment then starts licking his palm. The boy cradles him in one arm, patting his head with the other. Mao calms down and closes his eyes.

The cantonment gates open to receive the new head of Field Intelligence Unit. He presents his papers to the commanding officer, who accepts his salute, punches him in the chest, then looks at his appointment letter. 'Another Gul? You call yourself an intelligence unit, why can't you come up with new names?'

A lone donkey roams around the overgrown grass and rusting spinners at Satlaj Cotton Mills, chews at a tattered red banner promising a new dawn and gratuity fund for the workers of the Cotton Mills.

The owner of the Venus cinema makes a pile of his filthy prints collection and is surprised at how quickly reels turn to ashes.

'No photographs,' shouts Captain Gul, still searching for someone with a camera. And then he sees Shahid walking towards him, the flames from his clothes already dancing around his serene face.

His face is suddenly very hot. The fire from Shahid reaches him even before Shahid. As the first flame licks Captain Gul's face, two arms and a pair of mangled hands grab him in a shaky embrace as if he was a long-separated brother and refuse to let him go.

HOMEWORK 19

How I Run

Inspector A.D. Malang is a man in a hurry. He parks his jeep a few streets away from the Gol Mosque. He expounds in a professional manner to keep it quick, a couple of shots in the air. 'I have already booked you for aerial firing and causing damage to public property. Maximum two years if it ever goes to court as I have added emotional distress to the First Information Report, but for now I have got you remanded in judicial custody in Sahiwal jail. You'll not be spending a single minute in a police station. Trust me our police station is no place for a lady.' He is also a man who doesn't quite trust a woman to carry out her own obligations. He doesn't mention that Noor Nabi has arranged the remand and fixed the court. Before giving me the gun he makes a grand offer and volunteers to fire the shots himself, on my behalf, as a courtesy to a lady and a former fellow student.

By the time I collect my things from the academy, Sir Baghi is crumpled, bandaged and in a very apologetic mood. I inquire that what is he apologizing about, that hasn't he apologized enough in his life. 'You apologize with your pen, you apologize with your tongue but do you ever know what you are apologizing for? You should think about what you are apologizing for. Maybe apologize to Allah – He'll forgive you and wouldn't even make inquiries about what you are apologizing for.' What makes me angry is that he apologizes for losing my gun. He doesn't apologize about abandoning me to the army, not a word about the fake promise of underground marriage. I take out my gun and reassure him that he doesn't need to apologize – I have got my gun back from the people who he had given it to.

I'm destined for jail so I try to commit aerial firing, for which the police have already booked me and it obliges me to do the above-mentioned, but as is usually the case with aerial firing, a bullet goes astray.

Even in my wildest imaginations I don't think it went anywhere near his knee, but he makes a ruckus, a piercing shriek, a brouhaha about spilled blood even though there are only a few drops, gusts and gusts of lamentation, a pandemonium of pain, and in the end an anarchy of degrading, abusive adjectives. He actually believes that I have shot him in the knee. As the readers of the above-mentioned facts can testify I had no intention to do so as I don't care if he remembers me or not. The only thing I can never fathom is that when men are hurting, men both uncouth and those of high learning, they call you bad names, they call you misconstrued names, call you someone who gets paid in cash to provide bodily services, names that Sir Baghi wouldn't even want me to mention in this treatise.

On my return to the jeep Inspector Malang looks at me as if he has not seen me before. He takes my gun and says it's part of his evidence now. You don't want to come back to this city, he says under his breath. He hits the road that runs parallel to the canal, and suddenly, miraculously it is full of brackish red, rapid water. No miracles in this god's universe, Inspector Malang gives me the weather update. Heavy rains up in the mountains, resulting in flash muddy floods and much damage to upstream villages.

'How long?' I ask him, my eyes traversing the gushy waters.

'Fifteen miles, twenty minutes,' he says.

I ask him to stop his jeep and when he protests about his pledge to Noor Nabi I explain to him that I am a district champion runner and although I haven't done this long a run before I am in a reasonable state of fitness and I should make it before the jail shuts down for the night. Inspector Malang hands me my judicial custody remand notice and drives off without as much as wishing me bon voyage.

Mother Bano used to expound that if you walk on wet grass on the canal bank your eyesight will remain perfect forever. My eyesight is very good, maybe Sir Baghi did get a stray one in the knee.

I start walking and then jogging along the canal. The late-afternoon sun looks like a big ball of fire desirous of jumping into the canal to cool down, like my naughty urchins. I keep racing the water and then I see the wonderous objects that flood is bringing along. Mostly household things. A quilt, a metal trunk, chair and table and many pots from someone's kitchen, a big drawing of a leaping horse in a golden frame. Along come the things from that very happy day of my life. Much of the village fair comes floating on the canal's flood water. I see the wooden merry-go-round ride that made my stomach giggly and I see the charpoy covered with red-and-yellow flower quilt from where half-woman half-fish winked at me. Now I know the answer to my question about why she was dressed as a fish: she knew that flood water was coming.

I pick up speed, I am faster than flood water.

My shadow stretches along the canal water and my head appears on the other side of the canal where a single urchin stands waving to me, beckoning me to swim across the canal. I wave at him, asking him to turn back and go to his mother.

The shadow of my head on the other side of canal keeps bobbing up and down with every step.

I see two puppet dolls from the fair, one blue, one with tiny yellow flowers. They are in the middle floating, sometimes appear to be dancing on the water surface, not drowning. Cut from their strings they are floating free and seem lost. I run faster than water and catch up with the floating puppets. They come closer for one moment, go under water and then come up and do a little dance on water. Then they float side by side in middle of canal flood. I pick up speed and leave the dancing, drowning, floating dolls behind.

For a moment I'll sit down, preserve my breath, fling all my homeworks into the canal water and start running towards Sahiwal Central Jail. I'll be admitted to women's wing where Mother Bano will be surprised and then she will welcome me with hugs and tears and curses.

The milestone on the roadside says Sahiwal Central Jail: 9 miles.

THE END

ACKNOWLEDGEMENTS

Hasan Zaidi for that filmi idea. Changez for some excellent edits and always asking when are we finishing. Nimra and Channan for never asking when are you finishing.

Shukria to nice people who read and gave useful advice. Moizza Sarwar. Shami. Bajwa. Hasan Mujtaba. Amna Chaudhry and her writing workshop. Annie. Danielle Sharaf. Zani Syed. Harris Khaliq. Akber Notezai. Mirza Waheed. Joe Dunthorne. Shami. Arif. Houri. Mansi. Morgan Entrekin. Zoe Harris. Clare Drysdale and the best reader and cool Insta friend Clare Alexander.